FOR THE LOVE OF GRACE

A Novel by

JUDITH DeCHESERE-BOYLE

For The Love of Grace is dedicated to my friends, women and men, who have slipped past sixty faster than they ever could have imagined – onward and upward. In particular, I want to acknowledge a wonderful and memorable relationship that has lasted since high school with my pal, Louise Aaron Burke – nurse, artist, designer, confidant, and forever friend. The memories live on.

Time moves in one direction, memory in another.
– William Gibson

When grace is joined with wrinkles, it is adorable.
There is an unspeakable dawn in happy old age.
- Victor Hugo

It is the nature of grace to fill the places
that have been empty.
- Goethe

Chapter One

GRACE

If it had been up to Grace she might have thrown in the proverbial, damned towel years before, but she evidentially had not been afforded rights to final jurisdiction as to when the end might come, even though she possessed a very heady mind of her own; as a result, here she was, carrying on as if, indeed, there was a tomorrow. It's not that she hadn't considered the notion that the prerogative of ending it all, right then and there, was hers for the taking, but she had thought better of it. It would leave a mess. And, besides, she had never lusted for dubious attention. As a matter of fact, if the truth were known, the mere thought of such an impulse sent her mind reeling. For lost in a sea of memories, was a rather sordid chapter that she just as soon would have forgotten entirely if she could have. Unfortunately, with untimely, aggravating regularity recollection of the incident weaseled its way into her consciousness. That annoyance never had sat well, but what could she do? She could only visualize what had happened and then pack the memory away with all the others - and there was a litany of them - until next time.

And now, here she was, eighty-eight and counting; eighty-eight and reminiscing; eighty-eight and regretting, grieving, and often enough, rejoicing or savoring the many morsels of her life. A non-stop scramble of thoughts, reflections, and considerations swirled like a dervish around in her weary mind. And though at times she grew tired of remembering, it gave her something to do. She had to wonder though. *How in the devil did I come this far? And furthermore, for God's sake, what's apt to happen next?*

⌘ ⌘ ⌘

"Grace? Almost dinnertime. Are you ready?" Mildred queried as she poked her head around the doorjamb to peer into Grace's private apartment. "Were you dozing?"

Grace drew her eyes away from the bleak, winter landscape outside a large, partially draped window and gazed toward Mildred Watson . . . *Miss Millie.* Mildred, herself, already was nearing sixty, but she was strong, alert, and as dedicated as a lap dog in assuring that Grace was comfortable. She was not sure why she had taken so to the old woman, but she had, from the moment Grace had strolled into the lobby of *The Gardens* on the arm of her husband, Frank, four years prior. The couple had lived together at the plush retirement community for two years before Frank's quiet passing at the age of ninety. Neither Millie nor Grace would forget that day.

"No, not sleeping . . . just doing a bit of reflecting. Makes a long day more interesting sometimes," Grace chuckled. Her amber eyes, though not as wide and attentive as they once had been, still sparkled with light as though she was eager to tell a tale or two.

"Ah, now. Well, I hope you were thinking pretty thoughts," Mildred offered. Deep lines crinkled around her mouth and eyes as she spoke.

"I'll be damned if I can remember what was going on in this silly, old head of mine, Miss Millie. Sometimes I get so caught up in a memory I imagine I'm watching a picture show down at the Roxy just off the square in town. Then, again, thoughts flit through this feeble brain of mine like a swarm of lightning bugs. Can't seem to latch on to one for the life of me. Guess that's bound to happen when you're as old as the hills like I am."

Grace clasped her hands together and smiled. Though she was just two years short of ninety, she still had a pretty face – soft, almost wrinkle-free cheeks, a modest nose, and thinning lips that she still dabbed with red rose lipstick. It was her russet eyes, however, her dad's eyes, the color of copper, and lined with straight, jet-black eyelashes that drew folks' attention. She had been strikingly beautiful in her youth.

Millie listened to Grace's brief tirade and nodded in agreement. "Have to admit, Grace, I understand. Times alone, I'm likely the same way . . . but, enough about me. Meals are being served down in the dining room. We'd better hustle along so you don't lose your table."

Grace had made it a habit to commandeer a round table in the left, front corner of the dining hall where she sat with her back to the wall. From that vantage point she could observe the harmless carryings-on among a hundred or so other souls, men and women, who also called The Gardens home; sometimes she ventured into a conversation with a tablemate or two, or, she might ignore the others completely if the mood to interact didn't suit. Then, instead, she'd watch the sparrows, finches, jays, squirrels,

and other critters that flitted or scampered through the ev-
ergreens outside. Expansive windows on the exterior wall
of the dining room provided a view of cedars, fir, pines,
and junipers, a veritable forest that began just beyond a
wide sidewalk that bordered the building, and extended up
into the hills beyond. No matter the season, the outdoor
scene was bustling with activity, quite in contrast to the
much more subdued ambiance that was established when
the gray and silver-haired retirees, many of them aided by
canes, walkers, or the stiff arm of an attendant, ambled, at
painfully slow paces, into the room. Almost without exception, the residents plopped into their chairs and sat still
and obedient, waiting to be fed like eager, but well-trained
pups. Eventually chitchat or an occasional hoarse chuckle
dispelled the quiet, but the atmosphere generally was reserved as though the lives there simply were contemplating
their pasts and counting the days.

Perhaps that is why, more often than not, Grace chose
to gaze at the wildlife rather than to gawp at her retirement home mates. The animals' industry, energy, and fre-
netic activity made her feel alive, as though she were part
of something bigger than *The Gardens*, the walls of which,
sometimes seemed to close in on her, especially now that
Frank was gone. *Oh, how I miss that cranky, old bastard. Ah,
the times we had.* Simply thinking of her late husband, Frank
Ainsworth, caused a lump to thicken in Grace's throat and
wrenched her heart yet again. *Don't think I'll ever get you out
of my system, Frank Ainsworth. You were a pain in my backside
more times than I can count, but you were my honey. You always
were my honey, weren't you?* Though the din of the dining hall
slowly had grown shriller, Grace was mute. Her body suddenly had stiffened in the midst of the chatter, for she was
terrified . . . afraid that surely in the moment before someone had heard the crack of her heart, a veritable snap, one

more time, the fissure growing in a whole new direction. *Ah, Frank.*

After her husband's death, Grace had been forced to face an uncomfortable truth. Frank had been her protector, the buffer between her and the people who had come into and wandered out of their lives for years. She had depended on him for that. And now in the throes of his absence, she understood her new predicament. Simply smiling behind Frank's more gregarious demeanor was not going to work any more, if she were to have a friend in the world. Frank quite simply was *gone* and she was left to go it alone. So, as difficult as it was for her, Grace, on occasion, took her chances. She spoke first. She asked questions. She nodded and she grinned. When such exchanges were over, however, she often felt empty and a bit hollowed out, as though, like leaches, those with whom she had connected had sucked the very life out of her. *But so be it. Can't change the way you are, now, Grace, can you?* She knew it to be a fact. She was too damned old and too drained of energy to give *change* a go.

Nevertheless, in the two years since Frank's passing, Grace had suppressed her inhibitions and had made it a point to try to fit in as best she could, although doing so had been challenging. And it was annoying, for the truth was that Grace didn't care a great deal for humanity in general, certainly not the way Frank had. People had disappointed her. And though now she tolerated the *old* people around her, she knew not to let on for one second that even the tiniest bit of socializing took effort, that any attempt on her part to be affable was a farce, and that a furtive decision she was hiding was not to give a hoot in hell anyway. For goodness sake, her memories were much more entertaining. *Oh, Lordy, Grace, you can be sure those revelations let out from under wraps might stir up a hornet's nest in here.* She could imagine the residents' gossip. *"Who does that Grace woman think she is? Nose in the air. Thinks she's too good to give us the time? Why she's stuck in this place too. She's eighty-eight, I hear . . . years older than I am, and marking the calendar just like the rest of us, I would assume."*

"Are you a million miles away, dear?"

Grace started. Her eyes darted from an elegant, male Blue Jay that had been hopping in an arbitrary circle outside to the wrinkled face of a woman who had slipped in unnoticed to sit at Grace's table. She had towed with her a younger version of herself, a man - her son, Grace assumed, whose head bobbed in acknowledgement, but who said nothing. He bore an air of detached seriousness.

"Oh, I suppose I was," Grace admitted. "Lovely view out there, isn't it?"

"It's nice enough. Looks cold though." The woman's smirk revealed a line of large, straight, but discolored teeth. Her mouth had been daubed with a dark, maroon tint that hid in the crevices of her crinkled lips and her cheeks bore a smear of color as well - a deep red akin to mahogany. With cavernous, black eyes, she stared directly at Grace.

Grace found her appearance a bit daunting.

"I'm Maude Litzenburg," the woman said. "Moved into *The Gardens* this morning. My new home! This is my son, Henry. He finally got his way by shuffling his mother into a *home*, didn't you, dear?" She turned her eyes, riveting, on the man beside her. Henry sat rigid, a sneer rearranging his lips.

"Now, Mother." Henry shifted uncomfortably in his chair.

"Well, it's true, isn't it, Henry? At least now you won't have to worry about me losing my handbag in the refrigerator. Couldn't find the damned thing for two days. And with me out of the way you can concentrate on that career of yours, and on your family. Henry has a lovely wife and two kids, a boy and a girl - the perfect, little setup. So busy, though, aren't you, Henry? Surprised he could find time to haul his old mother over here to her new *home*. But I appreciate it, dear. Really. So here we are at *The Gardens*, once, for all, and forever, I'd imagine."

Grace was not certain if Maude Litzenburg was speaking to her, to Henry, or to both of them. She couldn't help but muse. *Maybe she's talking to herself . . . sorting out a garbage load of rage maybe.*

To ease the awkward moment, Grace took her chance. "I'm Grace Ainsworth. It's nice to meet you, Maude. And don't worry, *The Gardens* is not such a bad place to live."

"Well, we'll see about that," Maude retorted. "Is meal service always this slow?"

Grace looked from Maude to Henry whose face had blanched in the midst of his mother's rant. His lower lip appeared to jerk involuntarily to the left several times before Henry stopped it by biting down hard, his front teeth bearing into the soft tissue.

Oh, goodness. Grace's stomach tightened. "So, Henry, what do you do for a living?" she asked.

"I'm an attorney," Henry answered. "Estate planning."

"Sounds very important," Grace offered.

"And lucrative," Maude snapped.

"Mother, please."

"Well, it is, isn't it?" Maude continued, her hand clinched tightly around a cloth napkin. "Henry does very well for himself . . . Grace, did you say?"

"Yes, Grace. Grace Ainsworth. I've lived here four years."

"Oh my. Can't say I envy you. Henry, dear, will you stop fidgeting? Well, finally, our dinner's coming. Hope it's better than the service. Four years. My word, Grace, how have you managed that?"

Chapter Two

MILDRED

Mildred Watson had been a caretaker her entire life. That simply was the fact of the matter. It may not have been her choice, but any semblance of an option as to an alternative, very early on, seemed out of the question. She comprehended, and without wavering, accepted her calling in no uncertain terms by the time she was ten when she watched her mother bleed to death after childbirth, the image of the trauma indelibly etched in Mildred's memory.

Naked from the waist down and with legs spread awkwardly, her mama had gripped the metal railing of the box springs beneath her while her heels had dug into a soiled, lumpy mattress in response to each contraction. Mildred had been rapt, her eyes unmoving from the dark patch of hair between her mama's legs and to an ominous, bulbous opening that was pulsing, pulsing. In what seemed forever to little Mildred Watson, her mother's huffing and moaning - unsettling sounds that had filled the tiny room for hours - ended abruptly. A ghostly silence followed. Mama grew still her eyes slits; strands of her long, russet hair, tangled and moist, were pasted to the sides of her pallid cheeks. Her movements finally ceased save for her hands that fluttered momentarily and then dropped onto her stomach like dead birds. Mildred froze. And then she moved closer, seeing with her own eyes. In the midst of a dark, red, ever-growing bloom of liquid oozing from her mother's body lay a miniscule, purplish brown, stillborn baby.

The child had been delivered into an unwelcoming world in the middle of the night with no one to attest to it happening except for Mildred . . . little Millie Watson, and her eight-year-old sister, Caroline. The final whoosh had happened as quickly as a hiccup. But the steady flow of blood continued until the mattress was sodden and Millie's mama's breathing slowed before quickening again in a final rush until it stopped dead. Her skin had paled to the color of white smoke.

Mildred stood by, not touching, not wanting to look further, not knowing what to do. When Caroline began whimpering beside her, she grabbed her hand and dragged her away into a narrow hallway.

"Quit your crying, now, Caroline. You need to be still, for Mama . . . *for me.*"

Mildred glared sternly at her little sister's stricken face, but the harsh look was a counterfeit to what she felt inside - nauseous, numb, and oddly both empty and full at the same time. She adored Caroline. She did. But at an anomalous, base level she recognized that love was not going to be enough. Caroline would need her more than ever now that Mama was gone. *She is dead, isn't she?* A twinge of hope tugged at Mildred's senses. *She is, isn't she?*

She directed Caroline to the girls' bedroom and pushed her gently onto the bed. "Hush now. Sleep."

Caroline whined once more and then rolled to her side, her face buried in a tangled blanket. Mildred tiptoed back to the doorway of her mother's room. She leaned her cheek against the doorjamb and listened. Silence. A sickeningly sweet, metallic odor permeated the small space. She wanted to move to the bed to make sure . . . *to make sure,* but she instantly was gripped by such sorrow and fear she could not stand. She slid to the floor. Her head lolled to her chest and she sat still, her arms wrapped around her body, until she heard a dull thud against the apartment door. *Daddy. Daddy is home.* Her body trembled in anxious anticipation.

Though her mother had complained of minor, nagging, back pain earlier in the evening, her father had been unsympathetic, instead grumbling in response, "It's too early for any baby, woman. Stop your incessant carping. For Christ's sake, what's a man got to do for a little peace and quiet? If it's not the girls, it's you carrying on."

And he had left. He had left as he often did evenings, returning after midnight, later even, and entering the apartment with the stealth of a specter or conversely banging noisily into tables and chairs until the entire family was awake. Tonight, it was the latter.

Mildred jumped to her feet, scooted into the hallway, and waited, her lip quivering and her heart pounding. She watched the door swing wide open, the doorknob banging sharply into the wall. One of Mama's favorite decorative plates fell to the ground, shattering into pieces. A wooden crucifix careened on top of it.

"What the hell's going on here," he slurred. "Mildred, why aren't you in bed?"

"Mama," she began.

"Mama? Mama what?' He leered at his daughter, staggered a bit sideways, and caught himself from falling forward by grabbing the edge of a round, oak table.

Mildred did not move but managed to say, "You'd better check on Mama in the bedroom."

And he had.

⌘ ⌘ ⌘

From that unforgettable time forward, Mildred's father had stayed home evenings. Mildred and Caroline were with him night after night after night, but the words among the three were sparse. At first, a few orders were barked, but it took no time for the girls' daddy to realize any demands were unnecessary. His daughters were as compliant as little soldiers. It was Millie who took control of the household though. *Mama would have wanted it that way.* Millie was certain her mother would have wanted her to take care of little Caroline and, as for her father, her mother would have wanted that too. "He has his weaknesses," she had ventured, but she had shushed herself from saying more, as though speaking the truth was a betrayal.

For ten years Mildred, Caroline, and their father lived together in a mutual acceptance of their plight, each burdened differently with sadness that had nowhere to go. Not one of them was ever able to find words to express the feelings of grief though. Mama, not to mention the mummified baby, was never mentioned. The pall created was greater than Mama being dead; it was as though she had never existed. And so it was that the sorrow wrapped around them and settled in so profoundly that it oddly became a comfort to them all.

Chapter Three

MAUDE

Maude Litzenberg was livid. She sat perched on the edge of the wing-backed, parlor chair she had insisted her son, Henry, have delivered to *The Gardens* for no other reason than because she had said so.

"Damn it all to hell, Henry," she had whined earlier. "The least you can do is see that a few of my personal items are shipped over to that place. What's it called - that sanatorium you're trying to toss me into? *The Gardens*? Is that it?"

"It's not a sanatorium, Mother. You aren't going to a hospital. It's a community of older people, retirees. It's a retirement community . . . very safe, very nice with all the amenities you could want - a gym, hair salon, library, game room, common area, a garden, and a dining room. You're going to love it."

"I'll hate it. I abhor it already."

Henry had not replied. He knew it was useless. No matter how he addressed his mother now that the decision had been made to move her from her enormous, two-story Colonial to *The Gardens* several miles away, he was met with venom. He had tried to be kind and sympathetic, but that had only seemed to make her angrier. And when he had spoken with authority, explaining the facts regarding her failing health and periodic, mental lapses, she had closed him off, pulling her arms tight around her and looking off in an opposite direction. It was not uncommon for her to flip her fingers up into the air as though flinging Henry away like an invisible speck of dirt. He could almost read her mind. *Get on with you, Henry. You're a bad boy. How dare you and that awful doctor do this to me - shove me off to an institution with no hope of ever getting out. I detest you for it, Henry. And no matter what you say, I'll never forgive you. I won't give you the time of day ever again. You don't deserve it.*

Henry was as convinced as he was certain of his next breath that his conceived summation of his mother's thoughts was spot on.

⌘ ⌘ ⌘

Maude Litzenberg's intake at *The Gardens* had been every bit a nightmare as Henry had assumed it would be. She had been belligerent and rude, her face red with deep fury and her lips pursed tightly. She - quite atypically for Maude Litzenberg - had refused to utter a word to anyone. Instead, she had snarled at Henry and had glared at a kind and gentle assistant as though he were a monster. Now, from a distance, as Henry looked at his mother framed in the door of her new apartment and sitting as tense and irate as a coiled snake, he feared the worst was yet to come.

He had wanted his wife, Laura, to accompany Maude and him to *The Gardens* that morning, but she had refused, replying with a blunt, definitive tirade. "No way, Henry. Maude is your mother. You deal with her. I have no intention of going to that place to be abused by that woman . . . and you know that will happen, Henry. She takes her anger out on everyone, especially me. I'm not up for it. She may seem a bit *off* sometimes, but she's not senile. For the most part, she's right with the program and dishes out her rage any way she wants. I'll be damned if I want to be anywhere near old Maude when she finally steps a foot into *The Gardens.*"

Henry had bristled a bit when he had heard Laura's refusal, but he had understood. He had. Laura had never quite lived up to Maude's expectations as a daughter-in-law. *"She's quite simple, Henry . . . and common. Don't you think? My goodness, you are so intelligent. A lawyer. I'm not at all confident that poor Laura will enhance your practice . . . or your status in the community. You really could do so much better."* Henry recalled his mother's words spoken shortly after he had announced his engagement to Laura who, at the time, had seemed the girl of his dreams. He had been incensed, in fact. Yet in the years that had passed, from time to time, he secretly chewed on the fact that his mother may have been correct after all.

"You're right," he had acquiesced to Laura. "She's my mother." Pausing, he had added, "It's just that I had hoped for a little support. This won't be easy."

"Obviously, Henry. Your mother is *your* mother, however. Man up, honey. You can do this."

⌘　⌘　⌘

Without the director of *The Gardens* and a few assistants on hand, Henry quite possibly may have turned around and ushered Maude back home. She was as defiant and offensive as he had imagined she would be and he paid a price by being embarrassed and resentful of her behavior. He felt as though his choice in seeing that his mother would be living in a safe environment was correct, however. Allowing her to remain alone in a huge, five-bedroom, multi-storied, somewhat isolated home had become untenable. So, he had done what Maude considered the unimaginable and, furthermore, unforgiveable. Henry assumed, from the moment his mother learned of his decision, that she had damned him forever and to that point, he was probably correct. He possessed a law degree to back up his judgment about the situation though. *I know this is in her best interest.* With Power of Attorney documents in place, he had become the attorney-in-fact, with authorization to act on Maude's behalf in private and business affairs. And with a statement of fact from Maude's physician as to her health record and suspected deteriorating mental state, the initial surreptitious plans became a reality.

Maude had listened quietly to both Henry and her doctor as they presented their proposal. Her only movement had been an incessant twisting of her wedding ring around her thinning finger. She had tilted her head in consternation a time or two and rolled her eyes a bit, but, in the end, she simply sighed heavily and agreed. Smiling demurely, she had scrawled her signature on the Power of Attorney document in the presence of her doctor, but the moment he had departed, she had let Henry have it.

"You're a cutthroat, Henry, a despicable cutthroat," Maude had hissed. *He's throwing me into a godforsaken home.* She was certain this would be the end of her.

⌘　⌘　⌘

"Mother." Henry squared his shoulder and approached the doorway of his mother's apartment.

"Don't bother, Henry. Don't talk to me." Although her face was turned away from her son, Maude heard him quite clearly. *At least my blasted hearing hasn't disappeared on me.* Her voice quivered a bit, however. Henry was not sure the sound was genuine or conjured for affect. The latter was more apt to be true, he imagined. His mother, Maude, never had been easy for anyone who knew her well . . . her parents, her husband, or Henry, her only child. Henry often had wondered as a young boy why he had had no siblings, but as he grew older, he understood. His mother simply did not possess the capacity for nurturing, for giving, for thinking of anyone, even her little boy, before herself. The fact was that Maude was spoiled rotten. Even now. And it showed.

She had been coddled and protected as a baby, paraded about like a princess as a little girl, and envied by her peers as she grew older, for it appeared she had everything a young girl possibly could want. She attended only the best, private schools and prestigious Stanford University, an institution that garnered her a wealthy, career-oriented spouse, the only son of a well-heeled, fiscally established family, who continued where her parents had left off - yielding to her every whim or desire.

The result was not pretty.

Chapter Four

HENRY

Henry had been groomed to secure a place on the apparent fast track his entire life. Like his mother before him, he had been pampered and indulged as a child, but at the age of ten, he had been sent away, at his father's whim and with his mother's silent compliance, to a private, military school, miles from home. It had been his tenth birthday surprise.

"You're going to be taught to be a man now," his father, the Honorable David Litzenberg, had stated with such matter-of-fact authority, it was impossible not to believe. Henry still could envision the moment, watching his father, a giant man, groomed to perfection and dressed in his customary, dark suit with starched, white shirt and blue tie - the epitome of opulent superiority. His hands had been knotted and his face had been stern, as he had stared down at young Henry as though the boy were a deplorable speck.

"And a gentleman," his mother had added with equal conviction. She had not looked at her son though. Instead, her eyes had darted above him as if trying to settle on an illusive image or an imaginary presence that would not, for the life of her, take form. Henry had seen such a bearing many times - his mother seemingly searching beyond herself for an explanation as to why, just why, she was caught up in a situation she did not fully comprehend. On the day her son, Henry, departed for the remote, military school, Maude surely must have realized she had become a party, yet again, to another's impulsive decision - this one directed by a husband who, without fail, demanded control. And though she had agreed to *what was best*, she shuddered at the outcome; either a folly or shrewd judgment lay hidden, unknown.

As a result of the interchange with his parents that day, Henry had shrunken a bit for he had comprehended his place of importance perfectly well. *They want me out of the way. Father is too busy . . . and, well, mother is searching again for more important or interesting things to fill her time.* He had been only ten; but he understood at the deepest level. The pain of his parents' decision became a crucial influence in the years to come.

⌘ ⌘ ⌘

Henry would never forget his first nights trying to sleep in the drafty, would-be barracks on the bottom floor of the four-story, brick dormitory that was situated at the back of the sprawling military school campus. Afraid, homesick, and more than a little bit angry, he had buried his head under his pillow, trying as hard as he could to muffle out myriad night sounds from the beds around him - sniffles, stifled coughs, squeaky bed springs, the rustle of blankets, moans, farts, and yes, a sob or two. As alone as he felt those first days though, he strangely and very quickly began to feel a part of something - as though he were an indispensible component of a still-to-be constructed, fully operational machine. It caused him to be unsure, yet paradoxically certain that he would make it through this phase of his life stronger for the effort. And he did. He had purple-tinted keloid scars, provided at the hands of older boys, bullies, and braggarts, as well as from intense, physical training exercises, to prove it.

By the time he was twelve, he had moved to the second floor of the school's residential building; when he was fourteen, he was on floor three, and shortly after celebrating his sixteenth year, he had reached what he considered then as the pinnacle: fourth floor - top of the heap. Fortunately, the years had flown by. He graduated with honors. Academics had been easy for him and though he had struggled a bit at first to keep up with the physical regimen, in time he was strong and accomplished physically as well, his well-toned body rippling with muscle.

When his parents appeared, attired impeccably, at his graduation reception on a warm, spring day in May of 1972, he greeted them as the man - and as the gentleman - he had been instructed to be. He vigorously shook Judge Litzenberg's thick hand and stared directly into his father's eyes without wavering; then he turned politely to his mother, Maude.

"Mother," he said simply before placing a quick kiss on her soft cheek. She smelled like gardenias after a steamy, summer rain.

He thought he might puke.

⌘　⌘　⌘

Henry, despite his mother's contentious arguments over tradition and prestige, did not follow in her footsteps to

Stanford University. He opted instead for the University of California system, landing at Berkeley at the height of the protests against the Vietnam War. And that changed everything.

It took only two quarters at the university for him to set aside his affinity for the military and join new friends in the mounting movement to protest the seemingly never-ending Vietnam War. His hair grew long and shaggy, dusting his shoulders like a tangled mop, he sprouted a sparse, black beard, and for the first time, but not the last, he got so stoned he could do nothing but sit and stare. He had never felt so free . . . never, until, when he least expected it, he met someone.

Chapter Five

GRACE

By seven o'clock Grace Ainsworth was situated safely in her private living space, having removed herself rather hastily after dinner from the palpable conflict that simmered between Maude Litzenberg and her son, Henry. Maude had not let up on him, her muttering rebukes as to his character marked by sighs, smirks, and an odd moment of pointed silence. Henry had borne the abuse with restraint but Grace had noticed the tension of the man's jaw, a muscle high in his face pulsing, pulsing. She had caught his gaze briefly. Forlorn, glassy, brown eyes dominated his face . . . that, and the lower lip that still, from time to time pulled to the left, as if being tugged that way by a capricious, invisible puppet master. *Is Henry angry or sad?* Grace had wondered. *Why, it's probably both, by the looks of him.* While Grace may have held a remote interest in what lay behind the young man's tormented visage, she had pushed her curiosity aside. *It's none of your business, Grace.* She had tensed though, feeling snared in the moment, unable to extricate herself from an obvious, unresolved tussle of wills between a mother and son. Without a doubt, she had wanted no part of their wrangling; it was beyond her understanding but more to the point, quite simply, was of no relevant concern to her.

During the several minutes of unease she had endured while sharing a table with the Litzenbergs, her eyes had searched above the bobbling heads of the sea of residents, hoping to see Miss Millie who often flanked the dining area alongside other attendants. If Grace had caught Millie's eye perhaps she might have been rescued from the awkward situation. No luck. *Guess I'm on my own.* Finally at some point in the midst of Maude's ongoing, disconnected diatribe, Grace had managed to turn off the woman's blathering by focusing on the food in front of her. She had forced down the tepid dinner of under-baked, chicken thighs, brown rice, and buttered Brussels sprouts; the taste of the bitter vegetable had lingered like bile on her tongue long after she had swallowed. Instinctively, she had wanted to gag, but instead had coughed horrifically into a dinner napkin before escaping *her* front, corner table and the likes of Maude and Henry Litzenberg without a word of apology or justification.

⌘　⌘　⌘

Once in her small apartment, Grace unfurled the silk scarf from around her sagging, crepey-skinned neck, and pulled off her heavy sweater and soft, wool trousers. After slipping on a long, flannel gown and warm, fleece robe, she sat in Frank's recliner, her bare toes wrapped in an old afghan that had belonged to her own mother, Olivia Graci-Brown who though gone some thirty years prior, appeared at some point in Grace's thoughts every day. Perhaps next to Frank, she missed her mother the most . . . but, of course, there also was Percy. *Not now, Grace. Not now.* She silently rebuked herself for conjuring his image, for conflicted thoughts of Percy Rawling often would follow and fester for hours. Instinctively, to quash the memory, Grace reached for a golden-framed, sepia photograph positioned on her nightstand; she stared wistfully at the woman's face. Though the image was cast in tones of reddish-brown, Grace's mother had had thick, long, black hair, deep brown eyes, full lips, a classic nose, a chiseled jaw line, and olive skin . . . an Italian beauty. She had been stunning, smart, and strong both inside and out; Grace naturally had emulated her. It had been an innate, unmitigated, and loving choice. *Ah, Mother, sweet Olivia. You were a bundle of contradictions, but you did manage your life remarkably well. How did you do it? I know for a fact it was not trouble-free.*

⌘　⌘　⌘

Olivia Graci had immigrated with her parents through Ellis Island to the United States at the turn of the century, 1900. She had been thirteen. Her Italian parents, Giovanni and Sophia Graci, along with Olivia and her little brother, Carmine, only ten at the time, made their way to the heart of New York City's Little Italy in the borough of Manhattan where they found solace with others who spoke their native language and who shared their culture. With a little luck, hard work, and a small amount of money they had saved, Giovanni and Sophia opened an Italian restaurant, *Giovanni's*-named after Olivia's father although her mother, Sophia, was the chef, preparing every hors d'oeuvres, entrée, and dessert from treasured recipes stowed in her mind. Giovanni managed the wine selection and mingled with the patrons many of whom enjoyed the man's quick wit and gift for banter.

The Graci family's existence in New York was marked by abject poverty, even though the restaurant managed to stay afloat, buoyed by Sophia's superb culinary skills along with Giovanni's burgeoning eye for business and his personal aplomb. The family lived together in a tiny, drafty, four-room flat above the restaurant, but coped with the living arrangement because seldom were all four members there at the same time. Sophia and Giovanni constantly were busy running their restaurant, leaving Carmine and Olivia to manage time and activities on their own. They attended a parish school four blocks away, but when school was not in session, Carmine cavorted and played games with other children on the sidewalks of busy Mulberry Street that ran the length of Little Italy; Olivia, on the other hand, was tasked with doing the family's laundry and keeping the living quarters tidy. Though she resented her little brother's freedom, she did as she was told. Her father's anger could boil over with little warning, she had learned, and he demanded she do the chores he assigned; Olivia silently obeyed, but wondered, with unspoken consternation, why she alone bore the brunt of her father's ire. In time she would come to know.

⌘ ⌘ ⌘

Grace had listened raptly many times to her mother's stories of life in New York, re-creating in her imagination the scenes and scenarios as though she had been there firsthand. Now, alone in her room, she closed her eyes and envisioned once more the city scene her mother had described so vividly. Tenements stories high jutted straight up at the inner edge of the sidewalk, brick and mortar assuring the buildings' stability while at the same time, displaying their decay.

Cracks and crevices were noticeable adjacent to the frames of windows and doorways or traveled in random patterns down plastered seams between the bricks. Chinks of plaster and cement or chunks of masonry spiraled downward with indiscriminate regularity. The beaten sidewalks had shifted, the concrete filled with fissures, arbitrary veins that opened wide enough to capture hunks of debris that rotted in time and fouled the air. Olivia had identified myriad smells that filtered onto the streets as well: sweet, delectable odors from restaurant kitchens, garlic, liniment, leather, cigar smoke, alcohol, reefer, perspiration, feces, piss. But the smells were no match for the cacophony of sound: cries of infants, shrieks of children, moans of the infirm, barks of hungry hounds, thumps of brooms pounding dusty carpets, rumbles of horse carts . . . all, along with screeches, bangs, curses, and shouts - voices, voices, voices of every pitch and tenor. The resonance of noise jumbled altogether into a dull, monotonous, never-ending discord. Olivia had ascertained that the sights, smells, and sounds of her childhood life in Little Italy were etched indelibly in her mind forever. She clearly must have been correct, for Grace was sure the smells were with her now, at this very moment, as were the voices, distinguishable echoes that had been trapped in her mother's memories and then conveyed with convincing accuracy over and over again. Grace's head tilted to one side as she clinched one, tight fist against her breast; she sighed deeply, impressions of a lifetime bearing down with astonishing clarity.

⌘　⌘　⌘

"Grace? Grace. Are you all right?" Mildred's call and her knock on the door startled Grace from her reverie.

"Oh, yes. I'm fine. Come in, Miss Millie."

"I looked for you in the dining room but someone said you had torn out of there in the midst of a coughing bout. Are you not feeling well?" Mildred padded up to the chair where Grace reclined and leaned toward her.

"I'm fine, though dinner didn't agree. I suppose that's why the coughing fit," Grace admitted. "I'm afraid I ate too quickly, and besides . . ." She fell silent.

"Besides? Besides what, Grace?"

"Oh, nothing. I think I just got myself all in a dither because of those new folks who sat at my table . . . Maude *something* and her son. Henry, I think."

"Yes. I met them this afternoon. Maude Litzenberg is the woman's name. Poor thing. She's very unhappy about being placed here," Mildred informed.

"I gathered as much. She was quite abrupt with her son who looked to me as if he wanted to crawl inside himself to get away. All his ticks were very disconcerting. And she . . . well, neither Henry nor I could get a word in edgewise. Lordy, Miss Millie, those two have some settling down to do."

"I'd say," Mildred agreed. "Well, I'm sorry their discord upset your dinner, but I have a little surprise. I brought you dessert - a slice of apple pie."

"You are a gem, Miss Millie. You know how I love those sweets."

"I do, Grace. Now when you're finished just set the plate on the table. I'll pick it up in the morning. Can I get anything else for you?"

"Oh no, I'm fine now. I was just thinking about my mother. I guess that mother and son dispute at dinner made me realize how lucky I was to have had such a wonderful mother. Do you know she's been gone for thirty years, Millie, and I still think about her every day?"

"She was a good mother, then," Mildred said.

"A fact. She was. Thanks, Miss Millie. I'll see you in the morning. Think I'll enjoy this pie and then turn in before I think myself silly."

"Thinking's a good thing, Grace. You think all you want." Mildred smiled and turned toward the door.

"Did you know my mother was from Italy?" Grace interjected.

"I did not."

"Well, she was. She was thirteen when she came to this country with her parents and brother. Graci was her birth name. And she named me Grace."

"Well, isn't that something? How wonderful is that? You'll have to tell me more sometime."

"I will. I will."

"Well, sweet dreams, Grace."

"'Night, Miss Millie. Thank you for the pie."

"You are so welcome, Grace. 'Night." And with that, Miss Millie was gone.

Chapter Six

MILDRED

Mildred lived only a few blocks from *The Gardens* and walked to and from work every day except for Wednesday, hump day - the middle of the week for most people, but the end before the beginning for Mildred Watson. On Wednesdays she did her laundry, read, and prepared a few meals that she parceled into packets and froze for the days ahead. Squirreling away food had become a habit that served her well on evenings when she was too tired to stand up straight. The weariness, without fail, crept up on Mildred, often surprising her with its intensity, for during the hours she was working at *The Gardens*, she was filled with energy and purpose. She was never tired. She bounded down the long hallways, chose the stairs instead of the elevator, and rushed to apartments when lights at the nurses' station flashed a resident's request for assistance. *Those old folks need me; and they appreciate me too. I just know it.* Mildred bolstered her otherwise bleak life by reminding herself over and over that her job was perfect. She could give the one thing she had - herself . . . at least as long as she could hold on to her health and good senses. Money was always scarce; she knew she never would be able to afford to retire in a beautiful setting like *The Gardens*. She'd have to have a major turn in luck for that to happen. So, for Millie, the days melded into weeks, into months, into years, the routine strangely satisfying. The small dramas at the retirement community played out, a microcosm, Mildred assumed of bigger scenes, of more robust and loquacious players, and of much greater spectacles than she could imagine. In her small world, although she suppressed disconcerting reminiscences, she was content.

⌘ ⌘ ⌘

On the evening of the first day of Maude Litzenberg's arrival to *The Gardens*, Mildred could not avoid noticing the rise and fall of voices behind the old woman's apartment door. An obvious, contentious conversation between Maude and her son carried on much too long and ended when Henry charged down the hallway and out the front door of *The Gardens* as if he were an escapee. The behavior had halted Millie in her steps. *This is not normal.*

Mildred took it upon herself then, to slip by Maude's room to wish her a good night. She thought it only polite. Besides, she was curious. Maude's manner had been proper and staid when the two met briefly earlier in the day, but, by late afternoon, the poor, old woman rapidly had degenerated from seeming calm to hysterical. Her son, Henry Litzenberg, quite a severe man himself, had seen Maude to her room, closed the door, and, staff assumed, been able to soothe her anxiety; after several minutes, the tenor of their voices had lowered but the discourse between the two had continued, the barely audible, sing-song, give-and-take an imposter to the hateful vitriol the two were exchanging. If Mildred had known, she might have stepped in, but of course she did not. And that is perhaps why, when she knocked gently at Maude's apartment door, she was astonished to find Maude, alone, still dressed in the formal garb she had worn to dinner, quivering, and sniveling into a lace handkerchief.

"Why, Mrs. Litzenberg, whatever is wrong?" Mildred remained by the door, not wanting to violate Maude's privacy, yet wanting badly to step in more closely.

"Go away," Maude snapped. "Get out. I don't want you here."

"But, honey, my job is to be here . . . to make sure you are all right. Are you? It doesn't seem so," Mildred offered, her voice soft.

"I'm just fine. I'm absolutely first-rate, locked up in this accursed place. How the hell could you not see that?" Maude's words landed harshly, but because of Mildred's years of understanding misplaced abuse, they did not sting much. In reaction, she chose to do nothing for a moment. She simply stood silently and then took a step forward.

"I told you to go away," Maude snapped again. Her eyes had narrowed and a bit of bubbling saliva oozed from the corner of her mouth.

"Mrs. Lizenberg, Maude, I'm Mildred Watson. Millie. I work here. I work for you. And I want to help. Now, why not let me get a warm, wet towel and wipe away those tears?"

Maude's eyes widened and she stared at Mildred, the look on her face incredulous. "Why would you want to help me?"

"Because I'm supposed to." *Mama would want it. Mama would want it.* And in that moment, Mildred was cast back in time some twenty-odd years.

⌘ ⌘ ⌘

Mildred's father's sorrow for the loss of his wife and the tiny, shriveled stillborn morphed into an unspoken rage that no one, not even Millie, or her little sister Caroline, could mollify. He turned inward. Though he managed to hold a steady job, and was present, if only physically for his daughters, the change in him was profound. The once jocular, sociable personality disappeared and silence set in. He spoke only when necessary. He stopped drinking alcohol, coffee, soda, and tea. He lost sixty pounds. He read books . . . many of them. And, though quite aloofly so, he was kind. Millie and Caroline embraced his attainment of that milestone, an achievement that, before the event that changed their lives, had not seemed possible. He also silently cried. Millie observed from a distance, she saw up close, and though reticent to infringe on her father's sorrow, she did, offering him tissues, or water, or simply a pat on the shoulder. And as if by osmosis, his pain became hers as well. She shouldered it with dogged resignation. *Mama would have wanted it that way.*

Mildred's mute acquiescence to her plight allowed her to carry forward: she graduated from high school, attended a few classes at a local, university extension, worked part time for a neighborhood, veterinary clinic, and managed the home, such as it was, for the small, dreary, two-bedroom apartment barely had changed in the dozen years since her mother's death. She kept a wary eye on her sister, Caroline, whose skill at coping with her sorrow appeared nil. Though appropriate at home, Mildred knew her sister's behavior was quite the opposite when she was away. In time, neither sister could escape the gossip and innuendo as to Caroline's escapades with too many, young men who interpreted her pouty, introspective demeanor to mean permission. And apparently, she did not know how to say *no*. By the time she was eighteen, and Mildred twenty, Caroline was unexpect-edly pregnant, and woefully unprepared for a child of her own.

The sisters said nothing to their father, but when Caroline's condition became evident, aging John Watson understood that he could not see this pregnancy through. The decision was sudden, silent, and swift. *It's time for me to die.*

And he did.

John Watson did not commit suicide, not in a manner one might consider customary - no guns, knives, ropes, or pills - but he did see to his own demise, quite simply because he consciously willed it. He quietly crawled into bed on a dark, rainy afternoon, took a sip of Maker's Mark whiskey for the first time in many years, for the last time ever, and went to sleep. He never woke up. When Mildred found her father's body, stiff and gray, in the shadowy, morning light, she gasped. *I'm sorry, Mama. I didn't watch closely enough.* And then she sighed. *If only.*

Her final memory was of having looked intently into her father's sad, watery eyes the night before. *I want to know what you are thinking. Is it of Caroline? Is it of Mother? Is it about me? What, Daddy? What can I do? Mama would want me to stop your tears.* But she had said nothing, her words frozen.

And he was dead. In the end, Mildred believed the fault was hers. She had not intervened in time. She had failed her father as she had her mother. Smothered with remorse for her ineptitude, much more than for her loss, she cried for days . . . for days, until at last, the tears stopped dead, leaving her utterly hollow, too empty to feel. In time, how-ever, regret resurfaced, insidious and unrelenting, to join arms with her lasting grief, the two emotions her lifelong companions.

⌘ ⌘ ⌘

So it was. And on this evening, years since the passing of her parents, Mildred Watson was again gazing into the sad, old eyes of someone she could not possibly help. Not really. She could supply a superficial tissue or towel; she could offer a pat on the back; she could murmur words of comfort. She easily could do all of that; she could not, however, remove the anger and pain that clearly had morphed into a knot deep inside the old woman who stared back at her, eyes riveted, shoulders squared, and hands death grips on each other as if letting go would destroy her last, single essence of control.

"Maude?" Mildred tried once more. "As I told you earlier, I'm Mildred Watson, Millie, or Miss Millie, as some folks like to call me. I'm an assistant here at *The Gardens*. I'm here for you."

Maude's eyes lost their grip on Mildred's face as though the caretaker's words had stifled any, last resolve she had mustered to resist. She looked down at her locked fingers; her head bobbled forward and she exhaled a sigh so forlorn, Mildred visibly flinched.

"Oh dear," she murmured. Mildred tentatively touched Maude's arm. When the old woman did not pull away or hiss a *"Leave me alone,"* Mildred pushed further. "Let me help you get ready for bed. It's late. You've had a long day. Here, will you take my hand?"

Years of experience came in handy that evening. Mildred escorted Maude into her private bathroom where she helped her to the toilet; she slipped off her wrinkled dress, before sliding a long-sleeved, satin gown over her head. She wrapped a warm, velour robe over Maude's shoulders and then wiped her face with a warm, damp towel. When at last Maude appeared ready, Mildred gently led her to her bed, turned down the covers, and helped her climb in. Maude leaned back against the two, large pillows behind her and closed her eyes. For the first time all day, she was quiet - not ranting, not protesting, not blustering obscenities, and not crying real tears. Instead, she was still - silent and still like a fragile, porcelain doll that could break with the slighted provocation.

"Good night, Maude. Sweet dreams. Someone will be checking on you in the morning."

Maude opened her eyes, and then her mouth as if to speak, but she said nothing . . . not one word.

"Good night," Mildred said, again, this time more to herself than to Maude Litzenberg. She stepped into the hallway, pulling the door closed as thoughts of dread encompassed her. *I'm not sure I can, or even have the energy, to help this angry, ungrateful, old woman. She's such a different personality from Grace, sweet Grace, who makes assisting her so simple. I'm a bit intrigued by Maude though; she's a challenge.*

Chapter Seven

MAUDE

Maude lay in bed unmoving, as still as a dead one, although she did shift her eyes to the doorway as Mildred Watson departed her apartment, disappearing ethereally down the dimly lit hallway. *Miss Millie. What a silly name for a mature woman to call herself. She's simple, that one. She must be. After all she's a caretaker, merely subsisting I would imagine. Her salary is probably pittance. How unfortunate. And, oh dear, I'll be seeing the likes of her every day in this godforsaken place. Henry, you contemptible sham of a son, what have you done to me?* Maude's thoughts had darkened further. The interaction with Mildred had unsettled her, for although she vehemently had resisted the woman's assistance initially, she had recognized, to her chagrin, her own inability to manage one simple task for herself. She had been that undone. Had Mildred, *Miss Millie*, not persisted in lending a hand, Maude imagined she surely would be a fixture still in the large, overstuffed chair where Mildred had discovered her sniffling into her handkerchief. *Oh dear, what's to become of me?* Maude's thoughts drifted, and with them, she envisioned an array of faces - David, her husband - *dear, ornery Judge* - dead, alone, and rotting in the Cedar Knolls Cemetery somewhere east of Oakland; her physician, the shifty bastard, who had conspired surreptitiously with Henry to put her here in *The Gardens* as if it were some kind of sought-after Eden; Henry - *such a disappointment* - an unappreciative son with not one shred of decency, not one iota of loyalty, but a rogue, a turncoat, who clearly despised his very own mother. *Why else would he insist on sticking me in this hellhole?* And, Laura, that insipid wife of his, basking in Henry's accomplishments and luring his affections away, if indeed Henry ever held any regard for his parents at all. *He resented us, especially Judge. I just know it. Doesn't what happened so long ago prove it? And after all we did for him. He's ungrateful, a hateful, guilty ingrate, that's all.* Maude squeezed her eyes shut. *Go away, Henry. For God's sake, go way. If you don't, I don't think I can cope. I can't, not after all you've done to me . . . and to Judge, my dear, poor Judge.* Instantly Mildred's face appeared before Maude but fleetingly before disappearing and leaving one more - that of Grace Ainsworth, the old woman gagging, and coughing, and sputtering insults her way. Maude's imaginings were so absolute that she seethed. Visceral bitterness as to her newfound predicament, settled in her gut, a tight, nasty, binding lump she feared would never go away. In her mind, in contrast, the distress of the day could not be stilled. It was a hornet's nest of conflicted feelings, the last of which had converged with the striking face of Grace Ainsworth. *And, oh, for God's sake, we're residing under the same roof.*

⌘ ⌘ ⌘

Though, of course, Grace had no way of knowing, Maude's hostile glare had followed her as she had exited the dining hall. Maude had turned her head, tucking her chin down as she did, so that she could see over the bejeweled pair of half-eyes that more often than not *saved the day*. She had long ago abandoned her bifocals and with cataract surgery behind her, she could see well enough . . . that was unless she wanted to read, or pay her bills, or, God forbid, tinker with that little computer tablet Henry had insisted she have.

"It will open up a new world for you," he had insisted, but she had pooh-poohed his enthusiasm with a loud harrumph that could have awakened the dead. She had opened the tiny computer twice, stared at the screen that was a jumble of nonsense, and slammed it shut. *For Pete's sake, that Henry has the most ridiculous, hair-brained ideas. And now he's dragged me here . . . for another new world, Henry? And I thought military school would make you a gentleman. What a goddamned waste of Judge's good money.*

⌘　⌘　⌘

In the aftermath of Grace's hasty departure, Maude cleared her throat with a sound that was strident enough to draw stares from the residents at adjacent tables. "Well, what the devil? Why, my goodness, that Grace woman shot out of here without the decency to offer even a simple farewell."

"She seemed a bit distraught," Henry defended although the little woman's quick exit had caught him off guard as well.

"Right, Henry. Go ahead. Take up for her. Take up for someone you don't even know. Ignore the fact that her rudeness is quite astonishing and has upset me, if the truth were known . . . not that you give a hoot about your mother's feelings."

"Now Mother . . ."

"You know it's true, Henry. The least you could do is be sensitive to an old woman who's been snatched away from her beautiful home, a home of fifty years, may I remind you, and stuck like an orphan into this place. It's unconscionable, Henry, simply unconscionable what you have done to me."

Maude paused for a moment. "Just look at this. You've moved me into a den of barbarians." Her outstretched hands gesticulated wildly toward the room of elderly residents most of whom mercifully were otherwise engaged and ignored her ranting.

"Don't be dramatic, Mother. The woman was probably just feeling ill."

"Ill, *smill*. It doesn't make up for her absolute disrespect for me, and for you too, Henry, though I know good and well you don't have the gumption to speak your mind when confronted with an adversary. It's a good thing you aren't a defense attorney, for heaven's sake!"

"I'd hardly consider Grace Ainsworth an enemy, Mother, yours or mine. You only just met the woman, and the conversation here at the table could hardly be considered contentious or deep. For Christ's sake, Mother, get a grip."

Maude's eyes swam with tears. She wanted nothing more than to retreat to some safe and solitary place to cry, but her nature would not allow a capitulation of any sort to her son. Instead she lashed out, "Your contempt for me is blatant, Henry . . . blatant and unforgivable. You should be ashamed of yourself, but I doubt you'd admit for one second that you've crossed the line in forcing your poor mother into this . . . this *place*. Why, I have an urge to slip out of here right now and take a taxi home, damn it all to hell." She paused, sucked in a breath, and launched into her tirade once more. "After all I've done for you and that tedious wife of yours as well, by they way. And where is

Laura anyway? Couldn't be bothered to join you in packing up her decrepit, old mother-in-law?"

Henry's shoulder slumped forward, and he leaned toward his mother in hopes of silencing her outburst. "Mother, please," he hissed. "Not now."

"Not now? Not now what? Be silent, Mother? Is that what you want? Well, I won't have it, Henry. I simply won't."

Maude stood abruptly, knocking over her chair; she tottered for a moment as she scanned the room for an exit, and then ambled away. Henry, head down, could do nothing but follow.

⌘　⌘　⌘

As if they had not left Maude's apartment for dinner at all, Henry and his mother continued to spar when they returned; the animosity between them lay as thick as a shroud. Maude niggled her son relentlessly while Henry responded with mild rebuffs or restrained silence. The abuse continued with Maude chiding Henry for countless infractions, as she called them, from years before.

"At least my damned memory's still intact, young man. I don't forget a damned thing. You may think locking me away in this place is going to wipe the slate clean. Not on your life, son. Not on your life . . . because I remember things, big things, important things, like my David, your father, the attorney, *Judge*, the man who you could only aspire to become."

"Mother, enough."

"Well, it's true. Look at you. You don't hold a candle to the man he was. You don't . . ."

"Good night, Mother. I'll touch base tomorrow." Henry turned and strode toward the door, his mother's final, abusive words shadowing him long after he had left the building.

⌘ ⌘ ⌘

Alone, Maude sank further into despair. *Go ahead, Henry. Leave me here to die. That's what will happen, Henry. I know it. And it will be your fault. You will have killed me. You will have . . . you'll have killed me, once and for all, just like you did your father. And I can't imagine you've forgotten poor Judge's untimely demise.* For long minutes, deepening musings of misery and self-pity seemed Maude's only companions on her first night at *The Gardens*. She glanced around her apartment and shivered. *I don't think I'll be able to carry on here.* And she began to sob, as profoundly as she had on the sweltering, May morning eight years before when Judge's coffin had been lowered at last into a sodden, cemetery plot surrounded by only a few, silent souls who had cared enough to be there.

Chapter Eight

HENRY

Henry had had no intention of falling in love. It had not been a part of his plan. But, the girl was Laura - tall, slender, blue-eyed, and blond. She was perfect. She was perfect then.

They met on the steps of Sproul Hall, the imposing building awash in filtered, golden hues, the lingering colors playing hide and seek with shadows that had lengthened on another chilling, autumn afternoon. The fickle play with light and shade was nature's final game before dusk would darken the campus and capture the day. Laura had seen him first sauntering down the broad, concrete steps as though he owned them. His dark brown, unkempt hair dusted his shoulders and it blew ever so slightly in a cool breeze that carried in from the Bay. At the bottom of the steps, he stopped, adjusted his backpack, squinted into the lowering sun, and turned. Laura. He didn't know her name yet, but the moment he saw her, he knew he must. She was staring right at him and she smiled. That was all it took.

"Hello," he said, the word escaping before he could take it back.

"Hi. I'm Laura." She was not uncharacteristically bold.

A shadow shifted the moment Laura spoke causing sunlight to dance on her hair. He wanted to touch it, to touch her.

"I'm Henry. Henry Litzenberg. Pre-law."

She grinned. "Officially, I'm majoring in psychology. Unofficially, I'm undeclared."

Henry felt a sudden, unfamiliar flutter in his chest. *Oh shit.* "Well, Laura. Could I buy you a coffee, a beer, a glass of wine?" He paused. "Is that presumptuous? I don't even know your last name."

"I can fix that problem. It's Baxter. I'm Laura Baxter." She reached for her hair, twisting a strand around her fingers, and she smiled once more. "Sure. Wine or a latte might be nice."

"I know a place, just a block off campus. We can go there. Nothing fancy, but they have decent food and I'm starving."

"Okay, Henry. Let's give it a try."

⌘   ⌘   ⌘

As trivial as Henry and Laura's initial encounter might have appeared, it was an auspicious beginning and it changed everything. They secured a small table in the rear of Julio's Italian Restaurant, gorged on deep-dish pizza, drank beer and wine, and talked. It was easy. There were no lapses, no awkward silences, and no blundering comments. Instead the conversation was animated, intense at moments, and from time to time, a bit combative, though respectively so.

Clearly the two were very different having grown up under absolutely disparate circumstances. Henry's wealth, his years of military school experiences, and his current rebellion against anything traditional rendered him somewhat serious, perhaps too careful. His intellect disallowed shallow notions or random speculations; rather, he was staid and focused, but not without a wry sense of humor that colored his comments making Laura laugh. She, on the other hand was a free spirit, and in Henry's initial opinion, a dazzling, enticing sprite, almost inhuman. She was different from any girl, any woman, he had ever known. But if the truth were revealed, there hadn't been many anyway. No matter now. He was smitten.

Laura had grown up one hundred miles north of the San Francisco Bay area in a hamlet near the coast. She learned from her mother how to till a garden, pound abalone, and cook just about anything from scratch; her father taught her how to bait a hook, gut a fish, and heave a line from the rocky, Pacific shore without being jerked into the frigid waters and certain death as had happened to more than one, robust fisherman she knew. And she read. She read and she wrote, filling diaries and notebooks with stories, poems, or ramblings as random as the thoughts that spiraled into her mind for no particular reason. Her mother had insisted on home schooling her daughter until she was twelve, so with only one brother, ten years her senior, she studied and played alone. Laura combed the rock and sandy beaches, perched on bluffs to observe the pounding, often angry ocean, followed the dips and dives of countless seabirds, or curled up on her mother's porch swing, wrapped in a warm afghan to read. Her imagination was her best friend. It comforted her on dark days and enlightened her when need be. Laura Baxter's personality was a unique, complex combination. Though an introvert who relished her time alone, she never had been afraid to state her opinions, especially if she had been backed into a corner. And though her innate, quiet manner dominated, she was openly curious about the world. The physical world fascinated her most, but so did the people she naturally kept at bay. What was it that made human beings tick? Her speculations were fodder for her imaginings. She was both repulsed and attracted by the individuals she observed, and that, she supposed spawned an interest in psychology. She had managed public junior high and high school, existing on the fringe, but gaining notice for her intelligence. She graduated with honors and was accepted to UC Berkeley unconditionally. Though she knew she would be thrown out of her comfort zone in such an enormous, academic arena, she was excited, and especially so on the afternoon she and Henry Litzenberg became one.

⌘ ⌘ ⌘

A little bit tipsy, and high on an instant, intellectual connection, Laura and Henry strolled back to his place just before midnight. Neither hesitated. They kissed in the midst of undressing, hands reaching bare skin, the radiation of heat and lust unbearable until he pushed her gently onto his bed and moved over her body with lips and hands until he could no longer wait. He was upon her, inside her, and she reciprocated with her own cries of desire. They made love first passionately, unrestrained, uninhibited, and free of one iota of shame. They were the only two people on Earth. The second time, only hours later, was slow, poignant, and intensely emotional. Laura cried in Henry's arms before they fell into a restless sleep, arms and legs intertwined until dawn. From that day on, they were inseparable. For them, their love was sheer bliss; for others, it was a nightmare.

Chapter Nine

GRACE

Grace did not go to bed immediately after wolfing her treat - Millie's slice of deep-dish, apple pie - like a hungry teen; instead, she pulled the afghan more tightly around her, snuggled back in Frank's chair as if she were safely in his loving embrace, and glanced at the photo of her mother again. *Olivia Graci-Brown.* A smile danced across her lips and then she shivered as another memory crept into her mind. She closed her eyes.

At the cusp of her eleventh year, Grace was told what had happened. And why had her mother chosen that particular day? For Olivia, her reasoning had been completely logical; it was not clear to Grace though . . . nor, most likely, would it have been to anyone else for that matter. But Olivia was resolute. Grace was now eleven. It was time. *Carmine was eleven too, just days past his birthday. Grace needs to understand. Her eleventh birthday may be the beginning of a new year, but she cannot take it in stride, not for one minute. Life is too unpredictable.*

Olivia had been a complex woman whose logic could be confounding and whose rapidly changing moods indicated that she had questionable command of her emotions; on the other hand, however, maybe she was in complete control. Having grown up with change and chaos seemingly always on the horizon, her mercurial nature was, for her, normalcy itself. She was more comfortable feeling a bit off keel and had no problem towing others off balance along with her. Though Grace had wondered at her mother's erratic moods, unpredictable behavior, and confusing notions at times, she had adored her quick wit, generous spirit, and animated personality. The latter had cemented a deep and lasting love that never had diminished, even with death. Furthermore, and perhaps of equal importance, in addition to the affection, Grace had learned how to cope. And she remembered . . . did she ever remember.

⌘ ⌘ ⌘

Grace was officially eleven years old. Olivia observed her daughter as she brushed a few cake crumbs from the edge of the table into her open palm. They, along with confetti and melted ice cream dotted the tablecloth. All afternoon she had been hovering over Grace and seven other youngsters who had giggled through silly games, fawned over presents, and gulped down thick slices of frosted, chocolate cake and ice cream. But now, the children were gone . . . and Olivia's radiant smile had disappeared as well. Instead, her lips had tightened as she concentrated on the task at hand - clean up.

"Help me with this, Grace. Let's gather the cloth and shake it outside."

Without a word, Grace did as she was told and then she spoke. "Thank you for the party. It was fun."

"It was nice, wasn't it? Eleven. How did that happen, Grace? Eleven." Though smiling as she spoke, Olivia's face suddenly grew serious and her eyes filled with tears.

Grace was startled by the sudden change in her mother's demeanor. "Mama, what's wrong?"

Olivia glanced behind her as if someone were lurking there before she gestured for Grace to go back into the house.

"Let's go inside. I have something important to tell you," Olivia began. "I told myself that on the day you turned eleven it would be time, time to tell you about my brother - my little brother, Carmine."

"You have a brother?"

"Had. I had a brother, but I've never talked about him, not to you, not to anyone, except, of course, your father, may he rest in peace."

Grace blanched and fell silent. The mention of her father made her heart sink. Gilbert Brown had died three years earlier of pneumonia, an unexpected twist of fate for a man who had been strong, robust, hard-working, and in love with three things: his beautiful Olivia, his darling daughter, Grace, and his occupation as a mason. Grace had adored him, those feelings remaining still, but she had trouble remembering his face now, the contours blurred, the features remote or absent altogether. Tragically, the visage of Grace's hearty, loving father had paled with the passage of only a few years.

"Grace, are you listening?" Olivia demanded her attention.

"I am, Mama."

"Well, hear me out. This is important . . . and it's part of my history."

She began.

⌘ ⌘ ⌘

"It was a late Wednesday afternoon, the height of the workweek with the usual caravan of horse carts rumbling down Mulberry Street dropping off weary workers who had traveled miles and back for pittance. It was dusk. My papa had called me away from my chores to go find Carmine, the little rascal, who had rushed off with a band of pals and his birthday prize - a bulging, burlap sack filled with shiny, new marbles.

'Go find your brother, Olivia, and then get back to the restaurant straightaway to help your mother in the kitchen,' Papa demanded.

I remember staring at Papa's eyes, as black as ink, boring in on me with his command. I remember actually quivering. His whiskered jowls seemed to puff out with a flagrant anger that had no way to escape his body and he brushed the air with the back of his thick hand as if to say, 'Away with you, now, Olivia. Go.'

I was so afraid of him.

I had no way to know where Carmine was, of course, but I imagined him hiding in an alleyway. Many narrow alleys jutted out from Mulberry Street and teemed with activity. It wasn't unusual to see kerchief-garbed women hanging dripping laundry from pulley operated washing lines overhead or men lugging sacks of trash down fire escapes and tossing them into dented, metal garbage cans. Hugging the buildings' brick walls, a few vagrants smoked cigarettes and stared into space through weary eyes, while packs of children, dirty-faced urchins, dodged the adults, their squealing voices filling the air as they played tag or fooled around with tops, or balls, or marbles. That was in the daytime, of course. At night my papa wouldn't let us go near one of those alleys alone.

'Filled with riffraff,' he'd grumble.

I didn't understand what *riffraff* could possibly be then, but figured it out soon enough when I got older. But that's another story.

So I ran off down the street trying to avoid all the people who were loitering around vegetable stands, or pushing their ways into passageways to go upstairs. All the time I was calling for my little brother. 'Carmine! Carmine! Where are you, you little scamp?'

I had gone about two blocks when I heard a commotion - screams, cries, and demands - up ahead. I pushed my way through a thick body of watchers and stopped sharp. Wedged between the curb of the sidewalk and the heavy, wooden wheel of a horse cart was my brother, my Carmine, Mama's baby, my papa's prize. His head and chest were bloodied and his legs askew, splayed out as if they did not belong to the rest of his body. He was absolutely still, although his grubby hand still clutched the sack of marbles, only a few having escaped into the street.

I threw myself down on the sidewalk beside him just as a huge hand grabbed my shoulder and yanked me away. 'Get away, kid. Get outta here.'

I looked up into the ruddy face of a policeman and cried, 'He's my brother, my brother.'

I can't tell you my feelings at that moment, Grace, because I had none - not one that I could articulate, that is. I was numb. Carmine was not moving but his eyes were wide open . . . wide open as if he had been scared to death before he had time to close them. And then, my papa was there. He pushed me aside and fell to his knees beside Carmine who, he knew, was dead. '*Dio Mio. Dio Mio. No. Mio figlio,*' he screamed, and then he cursed the sky, his hand a fist, the features of his face twisted in agony."

Grace had grown absolutely still. Olivia's eyes were moist and her lips had sealed tightly as though she could not manage another word. And in that moment, Grace could imagine her mother, a young girl then, on her knees, tossed feet from the horse cart by her father who, when his curses had ended, had most certainly scooped his precious Carmine into his thick arms and cried unabashedly for all to see. Rapt, Grace listened as her mother continued.

"Papa carried Carmine's limp, little body all the way back to the restaurant and I trailed behind unsure what to expect next. I do recall the hordes of people though, parting like a Biblical sea to let my papa pass by. And for once, the street noises were strangely muted, some onlookers gawking in horror, their faces baring looks of sadness and sympathy for Papa, and for me, I would suppose, as I tagged along behind. Yet, Grace . . . and I remember this still . . . the slack jaws and wide eyes of many lookers revealed a patent display of relief. They had been spared. They need not bother to involve themselves further. Carmine's death was not their tragedy. It was ours.

And we were changed . . . Mama, Papa, and me. Mama grew quiet, her grief knotting inside. I know this to be true for at times her breath would catch and her body tensed so forcefully that she could not move; sadness was etched permanently in her face, and with unmitigated, self-imposed will, she wrapped herself in sorrow. Papa, on the other hand, became angrier still, the rage at life's unfairness his decisive death sentence though he could not have understood that then. None of us could. For me, I could only stand by and observe my parents' anguish, and in the watching, I grew up."

Grace's mother grew silent. Was the story finished? No. Olivia began again.

"Papa had insisted that Carmine be cremated. His little soul, Papa was sure, was immortal, the physical body nothing but a casing of sorts to protect the essence inside. Mama had wanted Carmine buried. 'I want to take him flowers,' she had wept. 'I want to visit him.'

Money was scarce though, a burial plot out of the question; Papa's demand won out and on one blistering, summer day, Papa closed the restaurant and the three of us marched away from Mulberry Street to the edge of the East River where Papa tossed Carmine's ashes, that had been placed in a loosely-tied, cloth sack, as far as he could into the murky, choppy water. Mama sobbed and I cried too, but I held on to a hope that somehow, some way, Carmine would make it home, back to his birthplace, to Italy. It was a silly wish, I know, but it gave me something to hang onto; it's all I had because with Carmine's passing, my parents departed too. Oh, they were present physically for some years more, but neither was emotionally present for me. It was as if they had moved away, both together and apart, their grief exact, their means of coping as divergent as head and tailwinds . . . and, I'm afraid, as unpredictable. I had just turned fifteen."

Olivia sighed. "So, I wanted you to know, now that you are eleven, the same age as Carmine was when he died so suddenly, that you must be alert, Grace. Aware. I want for you a long, productive life. It won't be perfect. You'll make mistakes, but just as I did, you will pick yourself up and carry on. Self-awareness is a gift, one that I learned early on, and one that poor, little Carmine never understood. Though I loved him, he was foolhardy and self-indulgent from very early on. My papa encouraged it, for Carmine was a boy, Papa's prince. And while I may have resented Carmine's freedom, I did not resent him. Never. You know, to this day, Grace, I still miss that little scamp."

⌘ ⌘ ⌘

Grace stirred in Frank's chair, the memory of her mother's tale vivid in her mind for some moments more before it faded to black. The clock next to Olivia's photo flashed midnight. "Oh dear, how quickly the hours have disappeared."

Chapter Ten

MILDRED

Mildred's trek home from her day at *The Gardens* was slow. The evening had cooled with the onset of darkness and a cruel, unrelenting wind kicked leaves and debris up into the air while tearing at the bun at the nape of her neck. Annoying strands of loose hair flew into her eyes and mouth, obscuring her vision and sticking to her chapped lips. She was irritated. An irrational sensation of impending doom closed in as fury flew over her. *Blast it all. I feel like I could fight a feather.* And she stopped. *Mother. Mother said those very words time and again; usually it was when Father was in a rage, or when he came home drunk . . . or not at all.*

Mildred recalled her mother hissing her exasperated ire in hushed, throaty tones as though she actually believed Millie and Caroline would not hear her. *"That John. He's going to be the death of me. Blast it all to hell. He makes me so mad*

I could fight a feather." But the girls did hear, exchanging wary glances, grasping hands, and slipping away together into the shadows. They were good friends then, Millie and Caroline, as close as sisters could be. But that was a long time ago.

Mildred pulled her jacket tighter with one hand, grabbed at her hair with the other, and hastened her pace. *Poor Mother. She was probably angry her entire life. And she died without ever getting it out of her system. How sad is that - a writhing woman, who was livid and virtually alone, dying in childbirth after delivering a corpse.* Mildred stopped again. She shivered, the unwelcome image of the shrunken infant vivid once again, and she glanced tersely behind her into the darkness. *Is someone following me? No. Just memories. Only memories. That's all. Think straight, Mildred. Think straight.*

⌘ ⌘ ⌘

Mildred's self talk could have been deemed unsound had she not noticed, only moments later, a shadowy figure at the door of her small bungalow as she approached. She started. Her body tensed and her heart raced as she peered forward. *What the hell? Who is that? Who the hell's on my doorstep?* Though she had wanted to shout out - something, anything - to address the person there, actual words failed her. Instead, her lips locked tight and a burning, acidic sensation crawled into her throat. *What am I about to face? And who?* But as she drew closer, she knew. *Oh, for Christ's sake. Well, I'll be damned. What is she doing here? It's my little sis . . . my old, little sis. It's Caroline.*

Mildred Watson had not laid eyes on her younger sister for some thirty-odd years. They had communicated from time to time - birthday cards, a note at Christmas, or a random postcard from Caroline who, in her entire life, had never settled. But suddenly here she was, all fifty-five years of her.

Mildred moved nearer. She noticed a stench first. Caroline smelled foul . . . a combination of whiskey, of stale cigarettes, of perspiration, of earth. She was wearing long-out-of-style, bellbottom jeans, a dingy, hooded sweatshirt, and a woolen cap pulled down to her eyebrows. Wild, curly, brownish-grey strands poked from beneath the hat in every which direction. She wore flip-flop sandals and carried a frayed backpack stuffed full of what Mildred assumed must have been the entirety of Caroline's belongings.

"Caroline?" Mildred's heart seemed to lurch in her chest. *What in God's Earth has happened?*

"Hi, Millie. It's me."

"I know. I know it's you." Mildred stared in awe for a moment before blurting, "How did you get here? What are you doing here? Where have you been? I haven't heard from you for months. And Adam. Where's Adam?"

⌘　⌘　⌘

Adam had been born to Caroline Watson in the same bed where her mama, with stillborn curled beside her, had died twelve years prior. Adam, in stark contrast to his shriveled, lifeless, would-be uncle, had not been silent, but instead had screamed out the minute his body was free of his bewildered, young mother's body. Loud, lingering, his infant cry implored immediate notice. From that moment on, his insistence on constant attention, positive or otherwise, had not deviated. It was as though craving attention was an inbred affliction he could not control. Nor could Caroline. And it became their burden. From the time Adam began toddling on chubby, little legs, he was a squealing, mobile menace who could not be left unwatched for a second. Though Mildred sought to insert some discipline into the chaos that became the trio's existence in the small apartment, Caroline seemed incapable . . . or perhaps, more accurately, unwilling to correct, let alone, punish her son at all. Instead, she catered to Adam's demands as if he were a tiny monarch.

Mildred's pleas for restraint, for rules, for some semblance of control fell on deaf ears. "Caroline, you simply must be more strict with the boy. He needs boundaries. He has to learn he isn't the center of the universe. You're creating a monster."

Mildred had bitten her lip after uttering the final word that cast Adam as incorrigible, but she was right. She knew it.

Caroline's response to her sister had been a blank stare, her eyes sad and dull as if all life had been sucked out of them by the sniveling, whining brat who did not understand the word *no* and who stood at that moment, a scissors in hand, cutting deep slices into the arm of a teddy bear.

Mildred, horrified by the sight, managed to have the last say . . . or so she thought. "Either you take control, Caroline, or you, and Adam, will need to find another place to live. I simply cannot tolerate this madness."

Two days later, on Adam's fifth birthday Mildred dragged herself home from a twelve-hour shift to find the apartment its usual mess . . . and vacated. Caroline, Adam, their belongings, and the constant bedlam that had defined the mother-child relationship in the tiny apartment clearly were gone, leaving Mildred in a sudden state of absolute panic. She was alone for the first time in her life. She dropped Adam's wrapped, birthday present on the floor, sat down heavily on the edge of Caroline's bed, and cried. She cried not for Caroline, and not for Adam, but for herself and for everything that in warped, unconceivable ways had led her to this place of absolute despair.

I let you down, Mama. As was almost a certainty in Mildred Watson's world, at any moment of angst, at any crux of change, at any chance that the unknown had seized control, she thought of her mother. *I'm sorry, Mama. Caroline's gone now, and Adam, too. I let you down. I should have taken care of them. You would have wanted that. You would have wanted that.*

That lonely moment, decades before, had become an indelible memory for Mildred. It could not be erased. Moreover, it had reassured her that her calling was clear. She was here on this Earth for one reason - to take care of others, at whatever cost to her. She did not question for one second that her conclusion might have been a bit askew.

And that was more than thirty years in the past.

⌘   ⌘   ⌘

"Caroline?" The question was in Mildred's voice because of the simple fact that for seconds, Caroline had squeezed her eyes shut, chewed on her lower lip, and said nothing. "Caroline, is Adam all right? Is he on his way here too?"

Mildred was comfortable asking the question, because she knew this much - Caroline and Adam had tag-teamed each other for years, verbally sparring with grave intensity over and over before, without fail, locking arms in unmitigated agreement. Either attached at the hip or playing cat and mouse, never had the two been too far apart. Mildred knew this as fact. Caroline's letters over the years always had included a tidbit or two about Adam's escapades. He was an adrenaline junkie whose antics and exploits often kept him in an alluring, exhilarating limelight, but whose wild abuse of caution had landed him in jail exactly three times. From a distance, embarrassed and chagrined, Caroline had been able only to stand back and watch. Mildred learned more, but only when Caroline found words to speak.

"He's gone, Millie." Eyes filled with tears, Caroline looked up at her sister. "He's gone like I knew he would be some day."

Caroline quickly looked down then and mumbled, "He killed himself, Millie."

Millie gasped. "How? What? What happened?"

"It was after he'd been released the last time. I was working again finally, and living nearby, but he avoided me. I saw him once after he was let go from jail. Once. But it wasn't Adam. No. Not *my* Adam. He had changed. The spark was gone, Millie. Somehow, somewhere inside that jail cell, someone, something stole Adam from me." She paused. "Last month a police officer knocked on my door. He gave me the news. Adam had been found, lying dead in his own vomit in a homeless encampment beneath the freeway. It was oxycodone, Millie. Drugs." Her face was forlorn. "His best and last, big high, I guess."

"Oh, Caroline." Millie voice trailed into silence.

"It's okay. It's okay now. I can manage. But I couldn't at first. Not at first. I left my apartment and have just been wandering the streets every day, every day for over a month. But today, this morning, I thought of you. You needed to know, so I'm here. I'm here because I knew you'd take care of me. You will, won't you, Millie? Like you used to?"

Caroline tilted her eyes upward as if the answer to her question floated in the air above her head. Her arms had fallen slack to her sides. She was a waif, a fifty-five year old ragamuffin, who had lost her greatest love.

As Mildred gazed at her sister, her throat tightened and her eyes blurred. She reached out, touching Caroline's shoulder. She had wanted to draw her sister close, but Caroline's body had stiffened immediately with that single touch. So instead, in a tone that revealed her love, Mildred simply said, "Come in, sweetie. Come in. Of course I'll take care of you. You're home."

Chapter Eleven

MAUDE

Maude had been awake for hours. She was sure of it, staring up at an unfamiliar ceiling in a strange, uncomfortable bed, alone. And now, she needed sleep, real sleep, sleep that would spin her into another realm filled with colors, with people, recognizable or otherwise, and with bizarre adventures and wacky fantasies too astounding to comprehend. She wanted to sink into a world she didn't know and yet, at the same time, did know; her dreams often took her into that space, leaving her, upon waking, breathless with relief, wonder, confusion, or, much more often, a desire to drift back where she could not be touched by a reality that had been closing in on her for years, for years, long before she lost Judge for the very last time.

The veracity of the matter was that she had lost her hus-band over and over, but she had never let on to anyone, especially those in her elite, social circle, that his brief disappearances, his painful indiscretions, his secret improprieties had soiled the perfect life she had imagined. Moreover, maintaining the façade of perfection had taken its toll. Maude was wrought with anxiety and a profound angst that gripped her with inexorable tenacity. Her only solace was that, without fail, David Litzenberg, her *Judge*, returned, though always with an aloof pretense that he had done nothing out of the ordinary and certainly nothing wrong.

But he was sorry, wasn't he? He always came back. Always. He always came back, even on that awful day when my life turned completely upside down. But, think about it, Maude, you have Henry to thank for that, don't you? You do . . . I do. I do, don't I? Maude's bitterness rose like a toxic bile into her chest. She gritted her teeth hard and squeezed both edges of the mattress with a boney grip that assured her she was not done yet. Not yet.

⌘ ⌘ ⌘

A soft knock on the door drew her uncomfortably from her ruminations, the likes of which, in recent months, more often than not, had left her silent and despondent. She was fearfully aware that she very easily could settle into a deep depression that on the one hand was quite alluring, but on the other, frightened the daylights out of her. So, she fought the blues with the one tool that had served her well for many years - hateful, spiteful anger. She wielded it out without discretion or forethought on whomever was handy. And generally that was Henry. *Henry, what a no-good excuse for a son he is.*

Expecting his face to peer into her room, she set her jaw and squeezed her eyes shut.

"Maude?" It was a woman. *Not you again. Go away.* Maude turned her head away from the door and sighed deeply, feigning sleep, but to no avail.

"Maude? May I come in? Breakfast will be served soon. Don't you want to join the others there?" The speaker clearly had entered the room.

"So there's no privacy here either?" Maude spat. "For Christ sake, I'm sleeping, can't you see that?" Her eyes remained closed, but she knew the voice was that of the woman from last night, Mildred, or Millie, something.

"Breakfast is served from . . . "

Mildred's sentence was severed. "I don't want any damned breakfast. I want sleep. Now leave me alone."

"As I was saying, Maude, breakfast is served from six until eight-thirty. No later. You're not going to want to go hungry until lunchtime are you?" Mildred Watson had been working at *The Gardens* for many years. She had been treated with kindness, and with respect; and she had been attacked with insults and contempt as well. Maude's attitude did not faze her. "Maude?"

"Oh for pity's sake," Maude squawked, springing into a sitting position so quickly Mildred was taken aback; she quickly regained the upper hand though.

"Well, now then. You are awake. Do you need assistance getting ready? May I help you dress?"

"Good Lord, no. Just leave me alone. I believe I've lived long enough to know how to put on my damned clothes, for Pete's sake!"

"I'll wait in the hall," Mildred said, backing away. "When you're ready, say the word."

Say the word. Say the word. When you're ready, say the word. And with that, Maude was shuttled back in time sixty years.

⌘ ⌘ ⌘

A lonely decade living primarily at a private girls' academy was behind her, a coveted Stanford education was behind her, a year in Europe - London, Paris, and Rome - was behind her and she was home, in the Marin County hill castle that looked over the San Francisco Bay. Though the dwelling was her parents' prized retreat, for Maude, being holed up there filled her with anxiety, the same childhood edginess that defined her early years. A nondescript assortment of nannies had come and gone, not one staying long enough to form a bond with Maude who was the only child of a vain and spoiled mother and an often absent father who when at home pranced the halls blustering his authority. And although Maude was lauded with every material possession possible, she was deprived of any real affection. Of course, she was paraded in front of her parents' friends often enough and fawned over in their presence, but beyond that, she was often alone, creating chaotic, imaginary dramas with her collection of dolls and porcelain figurines. It was not incomprehensible then, that when Maude was an adult, the memories of those times lay like fallow seedlings retarding her emotional growth. Though her schooling had been the best possible, and although she had fared well academically, she had grown into her twenties burdened with a plethora of childlike tendencies, not the least of which were being self-centered, entitled, selfish, prone to jealousy, and lacking one single speck of empathy for others. As a result, Maude's friendships were sparse, and shallow at that.

When at twenty-three, she fell into a deep depression, she finally gained a modicum of attention from her folks although the manner in which they showed their interest was mildly disconcerting to Maude, furthering her malaise. Her mother, fearful of would-be gossipers, shrieked her dismay at Maude's disheveled appearance, pleading over and over that she show at least an ounce of pride and clean up a bit; all the while, her father, with his typical, man-in-control demeanor, demanded she get off her lazy, entitled ass and obtain a job.

"You need to find employment somewhere. Put that degree to work. You cannot mope around here all day, Maude. It's not healthy. Look at you. Look at you," her father badgered, shoving her forward toward an enormous, ornate mirror that had been secured to a wall just inside the wide, front door of the residence. "Now, look, goddamn it," he demanded again.

Maude's eyes met her image, and his as well. He was glaring down at her, his lips pursed, a slightly bulging vein pulsating near his temple. Maude was not certain if he was angry or truly concerned. She hoped the latter, but really had no idea. She hardly knew the man. But she did as she was told, taking in the features of a face that had grown thin and gaunt. Her dark brown, almost black eyes seemed to have sunk even deeper than was normal in a face that was drawn and pallid save for an angry blotch of red on one cheek. Her pale lips, devoid of any color, were drawn shut. She was not sure she could part them if she tried for the fact was that she had nothing to say. Nothing.

It was her father who broke the silence. "Say the word, Maude. Say the word. When you're ready to snap out of this snit you're in, you just say the word."

And with that, he fiercely drummed a tight fist onto the top of a mahogany table that had been pushed to the wall beneath the gaudy, gold-framed mirror. Maude flinched, afraid the table might break into pieces right before her, the splintered shards irreparable and the destruction final and complete.

As her father bolted away from her, she stared once more at the young woman in the reflection. She felt battered as well, but she was not broken either. As sad as she had become, she suddenly was unwilling to crumble, not then. Perhaps in those unforgettable moments, when her father had made her look, to look and to see, she learned a truth. The direction her life would take was up to her now. She simply had to say the word.

⌘ ⌘ ⌘

Mildred Watson's voice, after several minutes had passed, shattered the old woman's reverie. "Maude. Maude, are you coming?"

"Yes, Mildred, yes. Momentarily." Maude's voice was soft, muffled, as though she were speaking from a great distance away, and perhaps she was, for she was convinced, that just beyond her reach, her father stood by nearly lost in a hazy fog, nodding in condescending approval.

Chapter Twelve

HENRY

Five months after their first, torrid encounter, Henry drove with Laura across the Bay Bridge that spanned the San Francisco Bay to the elite peninsula town of Los Altos Hills to meet his parents. He was nervous, not because he intended to confess his deep affection for Laura, the woman he planned to marry, but because his parents - his socialite mother and his father, the judge, both pretentiously lost in an insulated world - would hate her.

"They're going to love you," he lied, reaching over to squeeze Laura's bare knee. She was wearing a thin, peasant blouse and a mini-skirt, the current fashion that his mother had labeled vulgar and tasteless. Why Henry remembered that tidbit just then, he could not have articulated, but he recalled her words. *"Girls these days. They're asking for it, dressing like sluts, breasts exposed, and with their rumps barely covered.*

It's appalling, really. Thank God Judge and I don't have a daughter." He remembered his father smirking at his mother's comment, while rubbing his hands together as though the image she had conjured engendered anticipation for a nebulous prize; nevertheless, as was the norm, he nodded at his wife in silent, mock agreement. He had discovered, with Maude, it was easier that way.

Laura's voice jarred Henry's thinking. "I don't know, Henry. I'm actually feeling a bit anxious about meeting your parents. And that's not like me, you know, being worried about what people think; usually I don't give a rat's ass. But . . . well, we'll see. I hope they like me."

"I told you. They'll love you," he repeated.

They're going to hate her. Henry's thoughts annoyed him. *This is stupid. Who gives a fuck what they think anyway.* But he did care. He was in love. He intended to marry Laura Baxter. He planned to marry her, have children, and build a life together. All the while, he would develop his career, join a local, law firm, make money, bundles of it, and be happy. The introduction of Laura to his parents was only a minor hurdle to overcome before their lives, as one, would begin in earnest.

What Henry never could have imagined that bright, spring day, however, was that rather than celebrating a joyful beginning, an unforeseen and very palpable ending shattered the would-be tenor of the day. A bizarre, untimely, and dreadful occurrence changed everything. Maude, in shock, was devastated of course, while Laura stood by shaken and bewildered. But Henry . . . Henry's pragmatic way of thinking categorized the entire, ghastly event as just. It was an absolute and judicial culmination for a life that in Henry's view had been contemptible at best. Yet, in years to come, as though in eerie, absent control, with spiteful retribution, the life lived on. The atrocious event none of them could have foreseen that day remained intact for years, for all of them, the memory vivid and horrifying with the intensity varying only in personal incarnations.

⌘ ⌘ ⌘

Henry's MG rumbled over the cobbled, circular driveway to the front of the aberrant Southern Colonial manor that conspicuously stood, so out-of-place, in a community of more modern, sprawling mansions that either appeared to snuggle right into the hillsides or else were perched atop manicured ridges for all to see. His mother had wanted the classic manor though - her own *Tara*, tucked elegantly into a forest of Monterey pines, gnarly cypress, coastal oaks, with one, massive, weeping willow that had been trucked in, planted, and cultivated for years. The tree, misplaced as it was, became one of Maude's treasured acquisitions; she often teared up at its very mention.

With the giant, quivering willow as a backdrop that day, Maude Litzenberg met Laura Baxter for the very first time. Right before the large double doors swung open, Henry had whispered once more in Laura's ear, "Don't worry. They'll love you," but he understood instantly from the frozen smile on his mother's face that she would not.

"Hello, Mother."

"Henry."

Maude leaned toward her son, delivering an awkward, sideways hug. Henry stepped back as if he'd been scalded, but quickly regained composure so that he could introduce Laura.

"Mother, this is Laura Baxter, my girl friend."

"Nice to meet you, Mrs. Litzenberg," Laura said. She was inches taller than Maude, and though without intention, appeared to look down on the older woman as if in quiet condescension. She had meant to smile, but the serious, almost hostile expression that quickly had captured Maude's face, inhibited her. "Henry's said so many nice things about you," Laura managed to add.

Maude's reaction was cold, telling. She examined Laura from head to toe, pursed her lips, pulled in a deep breath, and said, "Come in then. Go through to the back veranda, Henry. We're having our luncheon out there."

Henry took Laura's hand for a moment before guiding her down a long, wide hallway that appeared to split the mansion into two distinct sections. Laura was almost afraid to look into the rooms that flanked the broad hallway, but took in enough to understand the decadence that clearly was its essence.

The hallway opened at its end onto a large, partially glassed, partially screened sitting area, the *veranda*, pristine in every way. Wicker couches and chairs were padded with thick, colorful cushions and adorned with pillows, plush and plentiful. A glass-topped, wrought iron table had been adorned with four table settings and a centerpiece of fresh, pink roses, delicate ferns, and baby's breath. The china, set in ordered perfection, seemed to radiate sparkles of light beneath a slow-moving fan, one of three, that aerated the expanse. Laura touched a loose fist to her chest and gazed in amazement at what appeared to be Maude Lizenberg's re-creation of *Gone With The Wind*.

"It's lovely here," Laura murmured. "Beautiful," she added, her voice finally taking hold.

"Yes, well, I . . . rather *we*, are quite enamored with our home. It really is a 'fantasy come true', isn't it, Henry? And certainly it's the envy of the community," Maude bragged.

"Yes, I can imagine it is," Laura offered, a miniscule smirk playing on her lips. "And, really, such an unusual home for coastal California."

"That's quite the point, dear. It was our desire to create a home that stood out in every way. But be clear, it's not *that* near the coast, for heaven's sake. We actually are several miles inland from the Pacific." As was her way from that beginning, Maude found a way to disagree with Laura repeatedly. It was her nature, in fact, to negate others at every turn whether it was one's opinion, character, taste, social status, or demeanor. Nothing ever quite suited Maude Litzenberg. Nothing. And to that end, she fostered a posture of arrogant superiority while secretly battling the horrid propensity for depression that had lain for a lifetime only skin deep.

Maude turned then, her head snapping quickly in the direction of the interior hallway. "Oh, dear, Henry. Your father is nowhere to be seen. He was supposed to be home an hour ago." She continued speaking toward the dark, empty corridor as though the man could hear her. "For Pete's sake, Judge, we have company. This really is quite rude. You should be here."

As if on cue, yet startling his wife, David Litzenberg, angrily pushed his way through the front door into the foyer of the house. He had ditched his gold Mercedes, slamming the vehicle's door as if it were on fire, and immediately had stepped back, surveying his near miss. And in that instant, irrational fury had gripped him with all its intensity.

The judge had wheeled the golden sedan within inches from the bumper of Henry's little sports car. David would not, for one second, take responsibility for the near accident, however. Rather, his illogical ire was directed immediately toward Henry. The usual, predictable blame game played out as it always had. *My inept, unconscious son . . . as usual, he's in the wrong place at the wrong time. Christ, he almost caused a collision.* It was David's position, one of decades of wielding authority and power in a court of law that had driven his need to judge and control in even the most mundane of circumstances. *I am the judge after all.* The pronouncement, unspoken though it was, was silently recited often, the assertion never altering. Having attained judgeship was David Litzenberg's greatest achievement and had become the lifeblood of his very being. And so it was, fueled by his sense of power, that he lashed into his son the moment he stepped foot into the veranda.

"For God's sake, Henry. You've parked that hunk of junk right in the middle of the driveway. I nearly slammed into it. Not to mention, I couldn't have driven by it to get to the garage if I'd wanted to. There's no space at all, goddammit." David was yelling at his son before he actually saw him. The man's voice bellowed his contempt. "Jesus Christ, Henry, do you still not have sense enough to come in from out in the rain? I had hoped you possessed a bit more brain power than you've exhibited."

David's cheeks had flushed crimson and bubbles of saliva had appeared at the corners of his mouth by the time his eyes, wild with emotion, finally settled on the stricken face of his son.

"Settle down, Dad. I'll move it." Henry's squared-off posture mirrored his father's, but he did not react further, serving his intention, it was apparent, not to anger David even more.

"Who are you to tell me, or anyone else, for that matter, to *settle down*, as though you have the right to demand such a thing? Your ridiculous, patronizing attitude, Henry, has no place here, not here in *my* house. You owe me an apology. And now." David's body began to quiver involuntarily, an ironic rebuff of sorts both to the man as well as to his irrational command.

"Now, Judge, it's not the time for a spat," Maude interjected as she sidled up alongside her husband and began firmly patting his arm. "We have company, don't you see, dear? And besides, I am sure Henry knows he's made a mistake. He'll move his car, now, won't you Henry?"

"Oh, for God's sake, Maude. Take your hands off me. I'm not a goddamned dog." Though David's words cut, they instantly fell flat when he noticed Laura Baxter for the very first time.

In the silent moments that ensued, Henry glared at his parents, his body taut and his hands flexing into fists before releasing once more.

If looks could kill . . . Laura stared at her boyfriend before her eyes beamed to the ceiling as though she were looking for an escape route. *What the hell have I gotten myself into?* Henry's voice, strained and deep, pulled her back into the reality that had her more than a bit discombobulated.

"Dad. I'll take care of the car, though at this point, moving it could probably wait."

David opened his mouth as if to respond but said not a word as Henry continued. "Actually, what's important to me right now is that I introduce my girlfriend. I brought her here to meet you. This is Laura Baxter. She attends Berkeley too - psych major."

Regaining some semblance of decorum, David extended his hand. "Pleasure to meet you, Laura. Psych major did Henry say? Are you going to become a real doctor some day or are you going to settle for some mediocre counseling job?"

"I'm not sure, yet, sir. There's time yet to decide."

"Time? You young folks always think there's time. Don't be so cavalier about time; it's a fleeting devil. And by the way, young lady, indecisiveness, in my view, certainly is no virtue."

"Judge, for Pete's sake." Color inched up from Maude's neck to her jaw.

Is she embarrassed by this jackass or pissed off? Christ, poor Henry. No wonder he hesitated to bring me here. Laura had no clue how to respond to the judge's retort, so she simply did not.

"Mother?" Henry addressed his mother, a question in the diction, but lost any other words.

"Yes, Henry?" And as if in a moment of weakness, Maude recognized her son's discomfort. "Yes," she said, "Let's move to the table for lunch. We'll chat more there."

⌘ ⌘ ⌘

Before any of the four reached the table, a rapid, loud pounding stopped them dead. "Oh good heavens, whoever could be knocking at this hour? Unless it's for a party or service appointment, no one comes way out here during the day." An awkward stretch of reticent concern ensued. "I'll go," Maude finally announced as if anxious to escape for a moment.

"No, Henry can go. One never knows who might be lurking outside these days. You stay put," David ordered.

Henry glanced sideways at Laura before striding down the hallway to the front door. He stood there motionless, listening. Whoever was beating on the door outside clearly was not going to stop, much less go away. Growing somewhat more anxious by the intensity of the commotion beyond the threshold, Henry hesitated longer.

"Open the fucking door, Henry. See who it is," David yelled from a distance down the hall.

Henry grasped the door handle and pulled. He was taken aback by what he saw. A middle-aged, disheveled woman, vaguely familiar, slumped, head cocked, next to an older, gray-haired man, who clutched her bare arm with a strangling grip. The man's expression was intense, exuding anger and loathing so visceral that it permeated the air with a putrid odor, an odd combination of foul halitosis, blood, sweat, and fear; the mingling of malodorous smells was an affront to Henry's senses. He caught his breath and stepped back. And as he did, the man lurched forward, his teeth gritted tight before he spoke.

"Get that son of a bitch out here right now," the man demanded.

"Excuse me?" Henry replied, recoiling as he did.

"I said, get him out here." The man took an aggressive step forward, dragging the woman with him.

Henry quickly stepped back, gripping the edge of the door to keep from falling. Adrenaline washed through him. "Who?" The word was barely audible.

"That no-good, philandering, piece of shit - Judge Litzenberg."

"I'm very sorry," Henry stammered, "but we have guests. You'll need to come back some other time." Henry's attempt to feign a calm presence failed miserably; his face had blanched and his voice cracked revealing a palpable, unanticipated terror. "Who, who in the hell are you anyway?"

"I'm this slut's husband. That's all you need to know. Now you either get that asshole out here, or I'm coming in to get the son of a bitch myself."

Panicked, Henry leaned his weight against the door attempting to close it, but the man outside resisted with an uncanny strength for someone his age. Henry was thrown backwards, his head slamming hard against the oak paneled wall. Overcome with sudden nausea, he slid to his knees; at that exact second, the man shoved his wife sideways onto the driveway where she lay motionless; a nasty gash at her temple began bleeding profusely, the crimson liquid oozing into the cracks between the cobblestones.

Henry attempted to stand, but in dizzy, semi-conscious confusion, slumped backwards; at that very moment, the trespasser charged into the entryway and lunged toward David Litzenberg who, having heard the commotion, had departed the veranda and was only feet away. The two men locked immediately into an awkward, violent hold, their hands grabbing, grasping, clutching, and at last, in mutual exhaustion, finally releasing. As they struggled to stay upright, in a sudden, epinephrine-powered surge of strength, the stranger catapulted David backwards onto the marble floor. The judge lay there stunned, eyes closed, unable to speak, with his breaths issuing forth heavy and forced for several seconds. And then, it was over. In a flurry of movement, the intruder produced a menacing Glock handgun, cowered over Judge David Litzenberg's prone figure, leaned downward, and pressed the black pistol hard into the judge's upper chest. He fired twice, the blasts deafening and decisive. And, in tragic, self-imposed retribution, amidst the thunderous concussion, the gray-faced murderer turned the gun on himself and fired, shattering his skull and scattering bloody, brain tissue in every direction. One, single blow into his own temple, had forced his body to rise awkwardly before it settled with almost mocking, deliberate lethargy into a gory heap only inches from the dead judge's feet.

In horror, Henry had watched the slaughter occur almost as if it had transpired in slow motion, but for years to come, as if etched onto an imaginary, rerunning reel in his brain, the rapid flashes of terror played on. He could not forget; nor would his mother, Maude, let him.

⌘ ⌘ ⌘

The aftermath of the murder-suicide was a continuation of the nightmare. Maude and Laura, upon hearing the gunshots, had clamored into the hallway only to be overcome by the unimaginable gore. Laura gasped a series of choking breaths that took her to her knees, while Maude screamed, the piercing shriek, so shrill that it reverberated into the lofty ceiling. Henry, forcing himself finally to stand, numbly pushed the two women far back into the dim hallway away from the dead bodies. "Stay put. I'm calling the police."

Through distrusting his ability to think one, rational thought, Henry realized he had to take control. *This is fucking insanity. What the hell just happened? Judge is dead. This crazy ass stranger is dead. And wait, there's a woman out cold in the driveway. Isn't there? Wasn't there a woman?*

His disjointed thoughts sought to distract him, but he resisted, physically pushing his mother and girlfriend farther back into the veranda. "Sit. Don't move."

He stepped back into the hallway and phoned the police while at the same time watching the women closely. They clutched at each other - touching, letting go, drawn, repulsed, both trapped in a dance of confused, horrified disbelief. They were undone, both of them, as the shadow of indelible shock settled in on their ashen faces. Henry stared at the two for minutes; he was connected to both as much as a person could be; yet, in this bizarre passage of time, he felt a strange disconnect as well. Or perhaps he willed it. *What's the payoff in getting too close? And what is the cost? Just look at this mess. For Christ's sake, how can anyone foresee how life's going to turn out? It's a fucking crapshoot, and I'm not sure I'm up for it.*

⌘   ⌘   ⌘

Though for Henry it seemed hours before police officers appeared, very little time actually elapsed. Two patrol vehicles and an ambulance arrived on the scene that was transformed immediately into a flurry of activity - a cordoning off of the driveway and entryway, photographs, taping around the bodies, fingerprinting, questions, answers, questions, answers, questions, tears, sobs, and accusations, not the least of which was directed at Henry.

"It's your fault, Henry. None of this would have happened if you hadn't been here, if you hadn't insisted on bringing that girl here, hadn't demanded that *Judge* be here too. It wouldn't have happened if you had been strong, if you had held that killer at bay, if you had been a good son . . . if you had been a man, Henry. Then it wouldn't have happened. My *Judge* would be alive." Maude, like a viper, spit her venom in the direction she knew it would hurt the most that day, but her false accusation did not die there. No matter the underlying truth - a quagmire of infidelities, lies, indiscretions, vengeance, and brutal retaliation - Maude placed the fault of her dear Judge's death in the hands of an innocent, non-suspecting being - her son, Henry, who, despite what Maude could have admitted, had lost something too. The culpability in the murder, she insisted, did not lie in the hands of an unannounced assailant but was Henry's alone. Judge, and his litany of excuses had played no part either. She had to believe that . . . she had to . . . in order to survive.

Chapter Thirteen

GRACE

"Morning, Grace." Mildred Watson, like clockwork, was at Grace's apartment door promptly at eight. "How are you doing this morning?"

"Oh, Miss Millie, I'm cranky as the devil right now. Can't seem to find those sturdy, walking shoes of mine, my damned hair has gone haywire, and I'm afraid, Miss Millie, that I stayed up half the night. Had a visit from my mother," Grace admitted.

Millie held her breath. *Wait a second. What is Grace saying? She had a visit from her mother? Oh dear, is she having hallucinations? Now this is a bit disturbing. Could this be the beginning of a new phase? Sometimes dear Grace is candid to a fault.*

Mildred had no choice but to mention her thoughts out loud. "Grace, sometimes you're candid to a fault. What do you mean you had a visit from your mother?"

"Oh, I don't mean she was actually here. Don't worry, Millie, I'm not completely off my rocker yet."

Mildred's response was a silent smirk.

"Just got her on my mind after our little chat last night. I did mention my mother to you last night, didn't I? Or did I imagine that too?"

"You did, Grace. You said she was from Italy."

"Oh. Good. Well, yes, she was. And last night . . . well, there wasn't a damned thing I could do about her. She was here . . . and stubborn, confounding, and as demanding as she was in real life, she settled in for a spell. I'll tell you, Millie, I could see her face so clearly in my mind's eye. She was a very beautiful woman, my mother - a real head-turner. Olivia Graci-Brown. Graci was her birth name. Did I ever tell you that's why she named me Grace?"

"I believe you did mention that, Grace," Mildred replied. She squinted at the old woman in front of her as if trying to adjust to the puzzled thoughts being voiced.

Grace fell silent; her head tilted slightly, and her features appeared to soften in the morning light that had edged its way through a crack between the window drapes.

At last she spoke. "Finally got to sleep after midnight," she confessed. "Guess Mother got tired of yapping about her life, or else . . ."

"Grace, are you telling me your mother actually was talking to you last night?" Mildred interjected. She was careful, but knew to be direct. Her pulse raced as she spoke. She had seen old folks go down fast - cognizant one day, confused the next; change was not always gradual. *Is Grace failing before my very eyes?*

"Damn it all to hell, Millie. Don't go shuffling me off to the loony bin just yet. Of course she wasn't talking directly to me. Not like you are now. But when I settled into Frank's arms," Grace hesitated, flinched as though caught somehow, and then sighed, "into his old, leather chair, that is, and when I closed my eyes, my beautiful, confounding mother waltzed right up to me, twirled me around, and in one swoop took me down memory lane - way back to when I was eleven. Hard to believe this old biddy was ever eleven, isn't it?" Grace chuckled, her voice cracking on *eleven.*

"Oh, I can picture you as a little girl, Grace. I bet you were adorable, as cute and sassy as you are now."

Grace sputtered, "Oh, Lordy, Miss Millie. Don't be silly."

The old woman's pretense of incredulousness in response to Mildred's comment was exposed with mute veracity when color rose to Grace's cheeks and she beamed. She had soaked in the compliment like warm sunshine.

"Well, do you want to talk about it?" Mildred offered.

"Not in grave detail," Grace replied, "but I can say this much. On my eleventh birthday, when I was tickled as the dickens to have had a party of my own, with friends and cake, and ice dream, all the things a little girl could want, my mother turned it all upside down. She had a way of doing that. We'd be going in one direction and she'd snap herself and everyone else around her into another. Never could get her bearings set for very long, my mother. And I'm not sure why." Grace paused as if contemplating a great mystery before she launched ahead with her story.

"Anyway, when I turned eleven, happy as a clam at high water, my mother ruined it all by telling me the saddest story - about her little brother, Carmine, being killed right smack in the middle of a busy, New York street. Run over by a big, old, wooden, horse cart. Killed the little guy on the spot. He was eleven. Millie, I didn't even know my mother had had a brother . . . not until my eleventh birthday, and then, she was hell bent on telling me the tale in blazing color. She told me first when I was eleven, but then again, just last night. It was quite disconcerting - both times."

"Oh, dear, Grace." Mildred touched the old woman's arm; the skin felt like crepe paper. "I'm so sorry."

"Oh, don't be. I mean don't fret about it. Lordy, Miss Millie, it was a million years ago. No need for the both of us to be in a tizzy."

"Are you sure you're all right?" Mildred asked. Her concern was real. It was common to find Grace lost in thought or napping upright in Frank's chair, her eyes closed and mouth open into a tiny *O*. She often shared a memory, embellishing it, Mildred was sure, so to entertain her listener. This was different, however. *A memory is one thing, a sighting another. And Grace may be confused as to what is the difference. Well, you don't need to remind yourself, Mildred, to watch more closely.*

"Oh yes. Of course I'm all right. But you know, Millie, do you know what has stuck with me?"

"What Grace?"

"My mother took the death of her brother and transformed it into a lesson. She was full of veiled messages, Millie. It was quite annoying."

"And what was this one? What was she wanting to teach you?" Mildred asked.

"Oh, something about the importance of self-awareness, I think. 'Don't be like Carmine,' she said. And then she declared, in no uncertain terms, 'Don't find yourself in the wrong place at the wrong time.' Lordy, Millie, I should have listened to that one a little better. With where I've wandered around in this lifetime, it's a wonder I've made it this far. Thank goodness I finally found Frank."

She paused and clasped her hands together before adding, "And, poor, little Carmine . . . how odd that a little tyke's legacy would be transformed into someone's notion of an important, life lesson."

"So for your mother, was this warning to you more important than her brother's death?" Mildred questioned.

"Yes, I think so. At least by the time she told me the story it was, because she had me, a child of her own, a little girl who had reached eleven, an inauspicious birthday in her mind, I guess, because it reminded her of Carmine - poor, little, reckless, dead Carmine. Oh dear, who knows what my mother was thinking, Millie? She was a mystery - a stunning, baffling mystery. And her message, though surely clear in her mind, was just as perplexing. What was as she saying? She was telling me to be responsible, to make my mistakes, but always to be responsible. Now that's a paradox, isn't it? What a bunch of malarkey, really, Millie. Don't you think? Olivia Graci-Brown has been gone for years and she still has the power to set me on my ear."

"Are you certain you are feeling all right?" Mildred was compelled to ask one more time.

"Yes. Yes, of course I am." Grace turned around in a complete circle, put her hands on her hips and said, "Lordy, Miss Millie. Now, where the devil are those shoes?"

⌘　⌘　⌘

When at last Grace was ready, Mildred escorted her to the dining hall more as a matter of precaution than of duty. *She is eighty-eight, after all and a bit sleep deprived as well, it seems. God forbid she might stumble and fall.*

A melding hum of ancient voices greeted the two women when they reached the wide entrance to the common area that was filled with round tables, each capable of seating six people comfortably. As was her habit, Grace circumvented the middle of the room, instead edging her way past the wall of windows to her front, corner table. Head down, she avoided the faces of other residents, some of whom were eating slowly, while others chatted to a neighbor, mumbled to themselves, or simply stared vacantly at the space before them. The exact scenario repeated three times a day, the list of players altering only slightly if an acute illness or unwelcome death took someone away or when a newcomer arrived. When one space emptied, someone new filled it almost immediately. In the course of her four years at *The Gardens*, Grace had watched the goings and comings, first with interest or curiosity, in time with mute acknowledgement, and finally with complete disregard. That was until yesterday when that Maude woman upset the apple cart.

When Grace had made it almost to her table, she suddenly stopped still. It was occupied . . . by one, single resident, Maude Litzenberg. Grace felt her body tense. *Oh dear, this day has begun a bit on the downside. The last thing I want to do is to socialize with strangers.* She stepped closer to the wall imagining by the mercy of a higher power to be able to fade into it unnoticed, but it was too late. Maude Litzenberg's chin jutted upward, she glared up at Grace, and as if unable to control herself, blurted, "Well, I see you're back. Wasn't expecting to see you again after your despicable behavior yesterday."

"Excuse me?" Grace managed.

"Well, Grace. It is Grace, isn't it? You must know that I found it quite rude of you to bolt from our good company - my son's and mine - yesterday without even a simple *pardon me* or *good-bye.* Astonishing it was, don't you think?" Maude paused. "Well, you must know, Grace, I was quite undone by your lack of courtesy."

Grace's eyes widened with the verbal assault and though she wanted more than anything to offer an appropriate retort, she was speechless. She simply slid into her chair, picked up her napkin, wadded it into a tight knot, and clutched it until her knuckles were white. She sat absolutely still while averting her eyes from Maude, in silent hope she might disappear.

And suddenly she was thirteen.

⌘ ⌘ ⌘

"What is it I hear you have you gone and done now, Gracie Brown? I swear you're going to drive me to drink."

Olivia stared at her daughter as though the girl were a stranger. She extended a flat palm directly toward her, the gesture displacing the would-be words: *Stay right there, at a distance young lady.*

It was an odd moment. Grace's mother adored her. That was a fact. Then why was she admonishing her so? What had she been told? Grace's lip trembled, but she did not cry. Instead, she looked down at her hands that were absently clutching a rolled hunk of the hem of her plaid, wool skirt. *I haven't done anything bad.*

Another woman looked on, her fingers clinched together as if she wanted to pray but had forgotten just how. Instead Sister Mary Theresa's pursed lips parted and she dug into Grace like a wildcat.

"First of all, the homework was half completed, scribbled in pencil on a wrinkled sheet. Unacceptable! And Grace daydreamed throughout the entire lesson. When I asked her a plain and simple question, her response was an insolent 'Huh?' - as though that is an appropriate way to speak to a teacher. But that's not the end of it. When I told her to stand up and acknowledge to the class her misbehavior, she would do nothing of the sort. Instead she bolted from the room, slammed through the classroom door, and ran down the hall to the bathroom where she hid in a locked stall. It took a custodian's precious time to dismantle the lock so we could get to her. What is wrong with you, Grace Brown? Your behavior is despicable. You were rude to me, to your classmates, and it looks to me now, as if you are equally rude to your mother who has been kind enough, it appears, to come to your rescue." Sister Theresa actually stomped her foot and snarled, the sound she emitted inhuman to Grace's ears.

Grace could look at neither woman. Her mother, she imagined stood by in quiet acquiescence to the nun's tirade, but surely she did not believe. Not Olivia. Her support of her daughter always had been steadfast, unquestionable. As for Sister Mary Theresa . . . Grace had only wanted to escape her uninspiring, mind-numbing drivel, her condescending demand for apology, and her apparent, blatant need to control the youngsters around her. The sister's reputation had preceded her, and soon after she arrived at the Catholic academy, every student learned the hard way that she relished the power her tongue and innuendo wielded. The day at hand had singled out young Gracie Brown. She would not forget.

When, at last, silence dominated again, if only for a few seconds, Grace began to breathe shallow, little breaths that morphed into hiccups. The humiliation of having been disparaged by the religious teacher in front of her mother and classmates was complete.

"Take the girl home. Some time for quiet reflection is in order, it would seem. But do with her as you wish," Sister Mary Theresa directed Olivia. "The look on your face however, Mrs. Brown, tells me all I need to know. No wonder the child is incorrigible."

Grace looked up into the dark eyes of her mother. They reassured her of everything she always had understood. She would be safe. *Thank goodness, no matter what, Mama believes in me.*

⌘　⌘　⌘

It was over then, the strange and distant memory. Grace felt the warm touch of Mildred's hands grasping her shoulders. She glanced sideways to catch her eyes, but they were focused elsewhere.

"My goodness, now, Maude, let's begin again. Good morning, ladies."

Maude cleared her throat, took a sip of tea, and sputtered, "Oh, good grief. Good morning, Grace."

"Good morning, Maude," Grace responded. "It's your second day here. Onward and upward."

"One can only hope," Maude snapped, setting her cup down with a thump.

"Well, enjoy your breakfast, girls. Get to know each other," Mildred said before adding, "I can assure you of one thing, Maude, and believe me it's true. This sweet gal may just become your friend if your let her, and that, believe it or not, could be your own saving grace. Oh look, breakfast is here. I'll be back to check on you."

Maude and Grace both watched Mildred sashay away, skirting tables until she reached the lobby. It was only then that they took a chance and looked at each other as if for the first time.

Chapter Fourteen

MILDRED

For the first time in many years, Mildred Watson was in a quandary. She had no idea what to do. Her sister, Caroline, had arrived out of nowhere, from somewhere; God knows, it could have been anywhere. But she had appeared there, camped out on Mildred's doorstep in the dead of night, simply waiting, waiting and waiting, for what would come next. That was the nature of her little sister, a vagabond - a modern-day gypsy - who, in almost forty years, had never stayed in one place for more that six months. She couldn't. Mildred was certain of it. From the instant Caroline had fled their parents' apartment with her young, five-year-old son, Adam, in tow, she had not settled. She had flitted from one stop to the next, one transitory employment to another, one relationship to yet one more, all the time assuring her big sister in scrawled notes and through stained, smeared, postmarked letters that she was all right, that Adam was well, that they were on to the next, best thing - *thing* taking on gargantuan, inexplicit, and worrisome import in its vagueness. With every correspondence, Millie was conflicted both with a fleeting sense of relief, as well as the burden of acute anxiety. *Where are they? What are they doing? How are they surviving? But they are okay, aren't they? Caroline wouldn't lie to me. Not about that.* So the months and years passed, one after the next to the point that both Caroline and Adam were blurred images that resided in Mildred's less than credible visualizations. *God only knows, I have no idea what Adam even looks like now. He's a man . . . and he's had some troubles.* Mildred had been apprised of that much. Twice she had received a postcard, and once a dirty envelope containing a note written on a paper napkin - *Poor Adam had another brush with the law. He'll be in for eighteen months, hopefully less, with luck. He's a good boy . . . just headstrong. You remember, Millie. Will be in touch. Love you, Caroline.*

But now Adam was dead. Only the night before had Mildred learned that abject fact. Without him, Caroline surely would be adrift, with no anchor, however insecure, to steady her course, erratic though it had been. Mildred was positive of that. Though she had no firsthand knowledge, of course, her sister and nephew must have existed in a complex, almost Oedipal relationship for they were together, or never too far apart for years, reliant on each other, yet both surely and innately craving independence. Having never known a father, Adam absurdly may have sought an archetype in prison and conceivably he developed some semblance of individuality there; or perhaps he sought his freedom in drugs. No matter the backstory, his destiny played out, and despite the contours of the pair's journey, in contrast to her son, Caroline never found, for one second, a means to be self-sufficient. Adam was the only man in her life who had remained a constant, Mildred surmised, and now that he was deceased - stone, cold dead of a drug overdose - Caroline was lost. *And that is why she's here now. It is, isn't it? Is that why? Without Adam, am I the next, best thing? Oh my sweet Mama, I'm not certain I am up for this challenge.*

⌘　⌘　⌘

Early that morning, Mildred had left her sister sprawled out in an almost comatose sleep on the living room couch, her cat, Midnight, eyeing the woman from a safe distance. He had growled his disapproval as if to inform Mildred that his private space had been invaded as well. The two women had spoken only briefly once inside the house the night before, when in obvious exhaustion, Caroline's head had slumped to her chest the moment she sat down. With her tangled hair jammed into her dirty collar, and with her mouth agape in a contorted scowl, poor Caroline had appeared the spitting image of an inebriated, homeless vagrant.

"Need sleep, Millie," she had slurred.

"Of course, of course. Take the couch here. I'll get blankets."

By the time Mildred had returned from the linen closet, Caroline had been sound asleep. Covering her gently, Mildred had been overcome with myriad unexpected feelings of anger, sadness, angst, and disgust. And love had been present too - a distant, amorphous affection that could not be denied amid the loathing for this sudden and foreboding disruption that was certain to complicate her life.

A quick note placed on top of Caroline's filthy backpack explained that Mildred was working at *The Gardens* until nine that night. Food was in the refrigerator. The shower was available. *Make yourself comfortable. The cat's name is Midnight.* The last two lines had been added almost as an afterthought.

⌘ ⌘ ⌘

Work never had seemed more appealing than it did to Mildred that morning, perhaps because there she was in her element. That fact was unquestionable. Taking care of the clients whom she considered patients and friends, challenging and otherwise, gave Mildred purpose. And hadn't she begun the day on a positive note? She had left Maude Litzenberg and Grace Ainsworth alone at the dining room table, having averted a brewing confrontation by stepping up to Maude and firmly asserting that it was time to *begin again*. And somehow, her words had taken hold. The two, old women had exchanged strained, but polite, greetings and Mildred had stepped away, silently praying that decorum would rise to the fore. Fortuitously at that same moment breakfast had been served, a hearty meal that could not be ignored and that re-directed the women's focus, at least for a time. When Mildred had glanced back from a distance some minutes later, Maude and Grace were eating breakfast and actually gazing at each other with something other than contempt. Relief had swept over her. *They're going to make it. They are.*

Mildred was responsible, at *The Gardens*, for the west end of the fourth floor - six, quite lovely apartments that were the final homes, she would imagine, for those who lived there - currently two men and three women, including Grace and now, Maude. The other woman was Lilly.

Little Lilly Littleton had been at *The Gardens* longer than anyone, having moved in on the day the facility opened. She was ninety-nine and probably weighed one hundred pounds at best. Though Lilly was as wrinkled as a dried, apricot pit, with sunken eyes and thin, curly hair the color of periwinkle, she was amazingly spry, with a keen head for numbers. She had been a mathematics professor at a lo- cal, junior college for thirty years when, at seventy, she lost her loving partner, Gladys, and with that passing any enthusiasm for life. Yet, Lilly clung on, ambling behind her walker, always prompt for her meals, and though willing to acknowledge others around her with a nod or two, was as silent as a ghost. She seemed always to be counting, her tiny fingertips touching, separating, connecting, and then releasing as if in each tap was a calculation or a solution to an equation that finally could be solved. Mildred adored the little woman.

And there were the two gentlemen - Ralph Fisher and Louie, *the lover*, Lawrence. They were as different as chalk and cheese. Ralph had been a Presbyterian minister for more years than he could remember, devoting himself to God and his church above all else. At least that's what he maintained. And perhaps that was true. He had never married and before moving to *The Gardens* had lived a Spartan life, alone, in a small cottage adjacent to his beloved house of worship. He was ninety-two and more anxious and ready than anyone else at the retirement community to meet his maker. In fact, Mildred thought the old guy harbored a bit of resentment that he hadn't been snatched up to heaven already. He often looked skyward, his lips squeezed in displeasure, his arms crossed, with one foot tapping, tapping, tapping in wait. Despite those lapses, however, his manners were impeccable, his dress and hygiene flawless, and his faith unflappable - the perfect gentleman. "I want to be ready and presentable when it comes my time," Ralph repeated often. "God isn't about to let any old slouch up there in his neighborhood."

Mildred wanted to believe.

In stark contrast to Ralph, was Louie . . . Louie, the would-be lover. He was eighty-five, but with a firm, though distorted, perception that he was the same, strapping chap he had been when he was thirty. And amazingly, though the years had left him wrinkled and somewhat sallow he had

retained a rugged handsomeness. Moreover, he still imagined himself the Casanova he had been for much of his life.
To that end, the ladies at *The Gardens* had to watch their
steps around the old guy. A pinch or slap on one woman or
another's backside was Louie's daily ritual that resulted in
reactions that ran the gamut from giggles, to face smacks,
to out-and-out curses in retort. Besides that, to the vexa-
tion of more than a few residents and staff members, Louie
Lawrence's categorical fondness for his manhood, not
simply his manliness, was the root of unmitigated, often
ribald, unrefined gossip. The fact was that he held an un-
precedented attachment for his more than ample, personal
plumbing. The truth could not be denied, for quite often,
he had his penis, concealed or otherwise, firmly in hand. In
the course of her caretaking, Mildred had observed Louie's
genitalia more than once and silently admitted she wondered about him. *Louie must have had been quite the Romeo in
his time. My goodness! He must understand though that here is not
the time, nor the place for shenanigans. Does he not understand
that?* Despite the efforts of Mildred and other staff to sub-
due the man, Louie was like an incorrigible teenager. He
appeared quite out of touch with the fact that he was a senior citizen, a man who should be prone more to napping
than cavorting. Still, he persisted, seeming to thrive on the
thrill of the shock especially when confronting a resident
like poor Lilly Littleton who shook with disbelief when he
exposed himself or Grace Ainsworth who took the man's
behavior in stride but was convinced that Louie was a confounded pervert.

"Lordy, Miss Millie, that Louie is quite depraved, isn't
he?" Grace had espoused her opinion more than once.
"He can't seem to keep the damned thing under wraps."
Though generally extremely reserved, Grace quite pointedly had had her say.

As a result of the goings-on, with her perceptive, pro-fessional acumen heightened in Louie's presence, Mildred had, on more than one occasion, gently reprimanded the old man for being inappropriate.

"Now, Mr. Lawrence, save the personal touching and displaying for a time when you aren't in the company of the other residents. Can you do that? I'm sure you wouldn't want anyone to feel uncomfortable."

He had looked at her with sleepy eyes and winked. "All right, Miss Millie. I'll be good, but I sure don't want to be. Where's the fun in that?" His words had settled uneasily as he weaved his way down the hallway, chuckling all the way.

Mildred had watched him go, assured she had made her point clear, but in the long run, any reprimand meant nothing to Louie Lawrence. He never would have believed he was not as handsome and enticing, head to toe, at eighty-five as he had been at twenty-one . . . and that astounded everyone, including Mildred. *Why burst his bubble though? Let him enjoy his illusion. He could be gone in the blink of an eye.*

The harsh veracity that death held a grim and tenacious grip on each door at *The Gardens* was fresh in Mildred's mind. Only two weeks prior she had entered the last of the six apartments under her watch to find the cold, grey corpse of Mable Moore. She had been only seventy-three, at the facility for less than a year, but overwrought by sad-ness. She had lost a husband, a daughter, and her home; her career as a registered nurse had ended, as well, when she virtually had been shoved, at the age of sixty-six, out the door. She had been too old, administrators in power had told her, to keep up with the pace. Once at *The Gardens*, Mable had seemed to settle in, but she had been alone, ignored by two, grown sons who, Mable had insisted, were busy men. She had piddled away the days staring out the window or poking at the material stretched across an em-broidery hoop with a dull needle for hours on end. And then it was over. Mable had given up. Mildred was sure of it, and, if asked, would have offered that the cause of death, undeniably, had been a crushed and broken heart.

⌘ ⌘ ⌘

At nine o'clock sharp the dining hall was shut down, tables cleared and stripped of their linen coverings, and lights dimmed. Any dawdlers were firmly escorted to a spacious, ornately decorated lobby where they awaited assistance from a staff member or stood staring at the metal, elevator doors until they whooshed open, the sound hissing like a heavy, deep, and melancholy sigh. The ancients would file in then, poke a familiar button - two to six - and stand silently until it was their floor to exit.

As was her routine, Mildred accompanied the west-wing residents to the fourth floor. Then she escorted the group down the hall depositing each resident at his or her door-way with firm orders to settle in for a spell until lunch. Lilly, Grace, and old Ralph Fisher never uttered a peep of pro-test, but Louie was stubborn.

"Oh, Miss Millie, last place I want to spend the next three hours is stuck in that dark hole. Why don't you and me skip this joint and head out for little snort at Whiskeys on Fifth. They open early, if I recall."

"Now, Louie, you know I can't do that. And neither can you. Why we'd be apprehended at *The Gardens'* front door the minute we got there and you know it," Mildred coun-tered. "Besides, *Whiskeys on Fifth* is gone. Closed down last fall. Place is empty now."

"Well, I'll be damned. I could have sworn I was belly up to the bar, two-fisting it, only a week ago, Miss Millie. Believe I was there with Lilly and Grace as a matter of fact," Louie asserted, his hands searching blindly inside the deep pockets of his trousers for his treasure.

Mildred ignored his fondling and played along. "Well, that probably is a nice memory, Louie, but you'll have to leave your recollection at that, my friend. Today everyone is going to stay put on the fourth floor. Right here until lunchtime."

"You're ruining all my fun, Miss Millie," Louie pouted before his hands stilled and he blurted much too loudly, "And who the devil is that way down the hall there, Millie? Now that's a fine filly if I ever saw one. She new here?"

Mildred followed Louie's gaze to the last apartment on the left, the one directly across from Grace's. Maude Litzenberg stood at her doorway looking nothing like she had earlier in the dining hall. She now was wearing a short, wool jacket over a floor-length, satin robe, had donned a large, floppy-brimmed, straw hat, and clutched a red, leather purse close to her heart. Her head bobbed from left to right as though she was deciding on a direction. *Looking for an escape route?* Mildred's stomach lurched. *Oh good grief. Where does Maude think she's going? And how did she change clothes so quickly? Didn't I just see her at Grace's apartment door? Damn that Louie. He could sidetrack a freight train.*

Chapter Fifteen

MAUDE

Maude had survived. Breakfast with the rather quaint, and more to the point, maddeningly standoffish Grace Ainsworth had ended. *Thank the good Lord.* Mildred Watson, that annoying caretaker who insisted on referring to herself as Miss Millie, *of all things,* virtually had forced the two women into conversation that morning though Maude was certain that Grace had been no more inclined than she to converse, especially after Maude had made her feelings known initially. *I guess I told her.* Nevertheless they had exchanged strained pleasantries while sipping tea and dabbing at a much too hearty, morning meal. *Lord, have mercy. Surely I'm not expected to consume all of this mess.* The thought of actually doing so had made Maude flush with discomfort. Her tablemate, Grace, had seemed equally repulsed. She had poked at her milky, scrambled eggs and had gnawed on a sliver of tough bacon, but had not eaten another bite. *No wonder she's such a wisp. Maybe with luck she'll blow the hell away, straight out of here, and out of my sight . . . the devil with the likes of that prissy, damned hag.* It was a hateful thought but was consistent with Maude's overall mood. She was furious at Grace for existing, at Mildred for meddling, at her detestable daughter-in-law, Laura, for not giving a hoot in hell for anything except unearned prestige, and most of all, at Henry for snatching away her freedom and virtually incarcerating her at *The Gardens*, where he knew she'd be looked after as though she was just another, old, demented invalid. Every stinking aspect of the reality she perceived made her blood boil and she had no idea how to escape the heat of her rage. *Damn it all to hell. I've been bamboozled . . . by the whole, damned bunch of them.*

⌘ ⌘ ⌘

The moment Mildred had escorted both Maude and Grace to their apartments after breakfast Maude digested the fact that she and the Ainsworth woman were neighbors, their doors only one wide, carpeted corridor apart. *Why she's close enough to spit on.* Maude swallowed an irrational chuckle as she actually imagined watching the spittle fly, but she wisely retained her civility by remaining silent. *Oh dear, how ghastly would that behavior be?* Nevertheless, she felt agitated. *These living accommodations will never do. Never. I'll need to think of something. Something. Oh dear. I simply cannot tolerate the attitude of that woman with her sickening smirk and proper airs. No. Being near her, living this close is not acceptable. No. And I've been so lovely to her. I have. I'm sure I have. Oh my word. Henry, you cretin, what have you done to your poor mother?*

⌘ ⌘ ⌘

Enough, for Maude, was quite enough. A resolute determination had materialized instantly in her otherwise confused and angry mind. Only she - *an old, abandoned woman* - could have understood how quickly the resolve had taken hold.

In the brief space of time that it had taken Mildred to direct each of her wards to their living areas, Maude had slipped out of her clothes, donned an elegant, satin dressing robe and a warm, wool jacket, certain that she was attired appropriately for her journey back to her *Tara*. Standing in the hallway, pocketbook in hand, she reasoned. *It's high time I move back home now. I've been in this awful place much too long.* Her head bobbed left and right, searching, wondering. *Which way? Which way?*

"Maude? Are you planning to go somewhere?"

Oh my word, it's that Millie, that nosey Miss Millie again.

"Maude?"

Go away, can't you? You're a meddler. You're a royal pain in my backside.

"Maude. Let's get you back inside your room, honey."

Honey? You can't call me honey. Only Judge does that. Only Judge. How dare you steal his endearment for me . . . how dare you. Judge will be so angry. I hate you Millie.

Mildred touched Maude gently at the elbow and deftly angled her back into the apartment.

What are you doing? Let me go. I'm going home, back to Tara, to my beautiful Tara.

Mildred had no idea, of course, what delusions were rearing in Maude's psyche . . . none at all, but she was astute enough to understand that Maude's agitation had reached a tipping point. The old woman's eyes were wild and dilated, the black pupils seeming to meld into the ebony irises as though they were one; at the same time, her eyes - two, identical, glassy spheres - quavered in rapid, disconcerting unison. Her cheeks were mottled - pale with spidery blotches of blood red. And her hands were cold, icy to the touch. Her entire body trembled. Even beneath the warm, woolen jacket, Maude quivered like a fragile feather in a hostile breeze.

Maneuvering the old woman's body was not easy, but at last she was seated again, slouching awkwardly in the very chair she had demanded Henry have delivered to *The Gardens* the day before. Mildred looked a Maude with sad concern. She had seen this before - angry, new residents that could not, for one second, accept their fate. It was as if they were dead on arrival. And not one lasted long. Either they retreated into their private worlds where comfort was defined by their own, muddled fabrications or they gave up altogether, passing away quietly when no one was watching. *Oh, please, Maude, don't let this be you.*

Mildred was convinced Maude would require a sedative in order to sleep and, in time, regain her composure, if indeed she ever would, but that necessitated a visit from the house physician. Mildred quickly paged the doctor and then stooped down beside Maude's chair to wait. She took Maude's hands into her own and began to rub them tenderly; at the same time, she began to talk. The content of her words were not important. In fact, Maude likely was not even listening, but Mildred understood the significance of sound, of a voice. It was a presence, undeniable and real. So Mildred began, "I had a visitor last night, Maude, and what a surprise it was. My younger sister showed up at my door . . . completely unexpected. I haven't seen her for a very long time. Guess she'll be a staying for a while, but really, who knows? Maude, her name is Caroline . . ."

Chapter Sixteen

HENRY

Henry was apprised immediately of his mother's condition. One of two physician's assistants who had been hired by *The Gardens* as first line responders for medical emergency incidents among the residents, made the call.

"Your mother, Mr. Litzenberg, has taken a turn this morning. We have not yet determined the cause of her sudden disorientation, but we are concerned. She is resting comfortably at the moment, having been examined and sedated by the physician on call. We wanted to inform you as to her current condition, however, so there will be no surprises when you stop by today."

Henry's body tensed. *Oh for Christ's sake. She's manipulating already.* He cleared his throat noisily before responding. "Look. Well, actually, I had not planned to visit my mother this afternoon. Frankly, I was exasperated as all hell - excuse the language – after dealing with her intake yesterday. It was an unblessed nightmare and took up my entire day. And now, as a result, I am buried neck deep in work. I'm litigating an important case for a prominent client of mine and simply don't have time for this, especially today."

"I see. Well, perhaps early in the morning then? Having a family member present, you know, a known and friendly face often diminishes the severity of such episodes. It lends a sense of familiarity. Adjustment can be difficult for new arrivals and from what I understand, your mother was very upset about being admitted to our facility."

"That is an understatement," Henry growled. "Look, I'll see if my wife can stop by, though she's busy as well, but, like you say, it would be a familiar face."

"That would be advantageous for Mrs. Litzenberg, I'm sure."

"Well, don't be too certain about that. Old Maude has never been a fan of Laura, my wife. Never. Look, what you need to know is that my mother is an expert manipulator, plain and simple. Whatever she's been up to is probably all a big act. She was indulged her whole life by her parents and then by my father. Believe me, Mother or not, the old woman knows how to get what she wants." Henry caught himself. He had wanted to say more, to reveal more, if for no other reason than to cover his own, reluctant ass, but he knew better. *Those poor do-gooders have no idea about Mother. She's as cunning as a cobra and packed full of poison. She'll instigate a sneak attack on anyone who gets in her way. And if she sets her mind to it, she'll get rid of any person she considers a bother . . . and without fail, she'll sway someone else to do her dirty work. God forbid that she'd be at fault. How well I know that goddamned scenario. Transparent? Straightforward? My mother? Hell, no.*

"You'll let us know then? About who will be by and when?" The physician assistant's voice had become direct, cold, and distant.

"I'll get back to you," Henry muttered, his voice barely audible. A prolonged silence ensued before the connection went dead.

⌘ ⌘ ⌘

"Damn!" Henry repeated the explicative out loud to nobody. "Damn. Damn it all to hell." And then he fell quiet as his eyes quickly scanned his desktop. It was strewn haphazardly with myriad papers; his multiple computer screens brightly displayed a database of financial records, a brief in progress, a letter. The preponderance of work he had before him had, five minutes before, been challenging, stimulating, doable. He had felt energized by his innate ability to sort through the minutia and to focus on the big picture, to see it through, to succeed, to win. He had been doing so for years.

One phone call, however, had brought his efforts to an abrupt standstill. It was as though his mind had become paralyzed, incapable of focusing on the business at hand. His brain, quite simply, had betrayed him. He clasped his hands, placing his nose onto his interlaced fingers, and stared blindly at the space before him. And instantly, he was yanked back in time. He was a young boy again . . . barely ten.

⌘ ⌘ ⌘

"Henry, get your butt inside now," his father had bellowed from a deck overlooking the enormous, perfectly square swimming pool; Henry had been floating on a bright, red, air mattress, the emblem of Stanford's *El Palo Alto*, a block *S* encasing a coastal redwood tree, a cushion to his bronzed belly.

His head popped up in recognition of the deep voice that, as usual, conveyed displeasure, or worse. Even at home David Litzenberg was unwilling to abandon his judgeship, surveying his domain with a critical eye. He donned his authority like an invisible mantle, and used it without mercy to keep both his wife and son obediently under control. Maude kowtowed to her husband's demands and opinions by offering not one statement of disagreement or reproach, but much more often, with cunning as sharp as a blade, she got her way by skillfully fawning over her *Judge* as if he were a god. Henry had watched his parents' ever-predictable dance and had attempted to mimic the steps at first, but he could not. He simply could not. So he grew sullen, as quiet and distant as he could be without sparking his father's ire or another of his mother's emotional crises.

And it had worked . . . until that unforgettable day. "I told you to get your butt out of that pool. Now." David Litzenberg's hands were knotted at his hips, his legs spread wide in a masterful pose of intimidation.

Henry was at his father's side in a flat minute. "Yes sir?" he asked.

"Get dressed. Then come to my study." That was it. Not one other word was spoken, not even a greeting. *Hello, son. How's it been going?*

Incredible. Henry's stomach tightened and he gritted his teeth to repress the response that was strangling him. *You miserable asshole; you couldn't care less about me.* The fact was, that Henry had not laid eyes on his father for four, full days.

⌘　⌘　⌘

Minutes later, with the demeanor of a frightened hostage - hands moist, mouth dry, heart rate rapid - a flushed, ten-year old Henry approached the double, oak doors of his father's study. They were ajar. From his vantage point, he could see David Litzenberg, the judge, sitting stiffly in his high-backed, leather chair, hands flat before him resting on the sheath of a thick notebook; though his head was downcast, his eyes scanned the room as if he were preparing to deliver a verdict. And perhaps he was.

Henry tapped on the door and then entered slowly. He had no idea what was coming, but instinct, and experience, told him whatever his father had to say would not be pleasant.

"Sit, Henry."

Without responding verbally, Henry slid into a darkly upholstered, round-backed chair as he had been instructed and stared directly at his father. At that exact moment he heard a rustle behind him. *Mother.*

Maude moved toward a chair identical to Henry's. He watched her somewhat mesmerized by the figure that was his mother . . . and yet was not, for she was far from motherly . . . quite the contrary. She always had maintained a reserved distance, never, to his memory, caressing or cuddling him as he had seen other mothers do with their children. Nor had she interacted with him often - no story telling, book reading, or even simply chatting. That, Henry had learned, was the nanny's job. Maude had observed her son however, though always from afar as if she was afraid to get too close. Sadly devoid of normal, nurturing instincts, she froze in Henry's presence, woefully cognizant of her shortcomings while, at the same time, terrified of what her child possibly might do next.

Settled in her husband's study, Maude again ignored her son altogether; she sat quietly, her lace and satin dressing robe swishing eerily as her body shifted. She was so thin she appeared anorexic, her face pinched and angular, her lips parched beneath a smear of garnet lip color, and her ebony eyes dull, lifeless. Henry, though only a child, was repulsed and a tiny bit frightened. *She looks like a ghost. Her face is so white. Is she sick? Is she dying? Why won't she look at me?* Henry's thoughts had not been without merit. He had not seen his mother for over a month. Either he had been at summer camp, day camp, equestrian lessons, or otherwise engaged by the cranky, rule-driven nanny who ran his life, or, he had retreated to his bedroom to read or to the pool to float aimlessly for as long as he was allowed. His mother, equally, early on, had been engaged in busying activities - bridge, bunko, the spa, or a rare, evening outing with *Judge.* In recent weeks, however, she had remained at home, sequestered in her suite, simply existing.

Though he had been curious, Henry had not asked to see her; nor had he been allowed near her bedroom door. It was as though the woman that had identified herself as *Mother* no longer existed for Henry at all. And he had been bewildered. A ten-year-old child could not have understood that Maude had fallen into one of her prolonged depressions again, her emotions unable to counter the raw reality of life with her *Judge,* for the fact was that although he lavished her with every material item she could have wanted, he was unfaithful, a philandering, self-absorbed cad whose judgment regarding his notorious, personal affairs was lacking indeed.

But no matter *that* on this day.

David Litzenberg held fast to his belief that he was infallible, and certainly not liable for his wife's unhappiness. Instead, the depth of Maude's despair would be heaped, at the discretion of Judge Litzenberg, on the shoulders of their young son, Henry. David had reasoned that the boy was in the way; he was, after all, a sullen, willful, unloving, unappreciative child whose behavior easily could have been at the root of his poor wife's misery. *Clearly.* It had been a simple task for David to convince Maude he was correct.

On the day in question, then, on the day that Henry would never forget, David informed his son that the imposed, fall entrance into a distant, military school, the institution that would teach him manners and make him a man, that place, had been advanced a few months.

"I have arranged for you to be admitted into your new school earlier than scheduled, Henry. Tomorrow. You will leave here tomorrow. It will be best . . . for you, certainly for your poor mother, for all of us."

Henry tensed and his lip quivered; he bit into the soft tissue. *Stop. Stop.* He was not sure he would not cry. Consumed with sadness, anger, and confusion, he stared at his father, fearful of speaking, afraid to make a sound.

"Go to your room now, Henry. Your nanny has been instructed to help you pack. Get dinner after you are done. Then sleep. Tomorrow will be an adjustment. You need to be ready." Judge Litzenberg's orders were a clear indictment.

But . . . why? I don't want to go. Why? Henry swallowed hard. *I guess I have been really bad.* He glanced quickly at his pale, rigid mother, the lifeless soul beside him. Her mouth was drawn, taut, and her eyes were closed tightly. She did not see Henry at all. She wasn't even watching.

Good-bye, Mommy. See you, Judge . . . sometime, sometime, maybe when I'm a man some day. Maybe I can see you then. Henry stood and marched away from his parents. He did not turn back. He did not waver. In an instant his young life had been changed forever for his mother's *Judge* had decided. He had issued a sentence that would not be revoked. Henry's stomach pitched, for he understood a damning truth. He had not uttered one word in his own defense.

⌘ ⌘ ⌘

Henry had not moved while the memory of that day reeled through like a movie. *Damn, I remember it like it was yesterday. Shit. And now? What a fucking paradox this is. The mother that did not want me wants me now. She needs me now . . . and right now so it seems. Christ. What an unbelievable mess.*

"Well, I'm not going there today. I'm not." Henry's words were audible but there was no one to hear. He reached for his phone, connected with Laura, and launched in, "Laura, need a favor. How's your day stacking up?"

He detected a deep sigh. "What's going on, Henry? Is this about your damned mother?"

"You guessed it."

"What?"

"Some nurse from *The Gardens* called. Mother's not adjusting. She's become disoriented, I guess. They've sedated her, but the nurse thinks she needs someone there with her. I am up to my ass in work today. Yesterday nearly sank me. Could you stop by . . . just for a few minutes? I think the nurse is expecting you." Henry held his breath.

"Oh, hell, Henry. I knew this would happen. I knew it. You put your mother in a facility and then can't be bothered. I'm left to pick up the pieces."

"Look, I'll get over there but not today. Look, honey, I could use some help here."

"This time. This time I'll go, but don't make this a habit. Your mom detests me, Henry. She's never done one goddamned favor for me. She treats me like shit and I'm expected to go fawn over her like we're best pals. It's ironical, really, isn't it? All of a sudden she wants the person she doesn't want."

"I know. I know. *I understand at the deepest level.* Look, I'll make it up to you."

"Yeah, right. A trip to Paris maybe?"

"That's actually not a bad idea," Henry offered.

"Damn it, Henry. Don't patronize me on top of everything else. I told you I'd go check on old Maude. I'll be in touch."

"Thanks, Laura. Really. I love you."

"Yeah, I know. Love you too. Will call when I'm done dealing with this shit."

In the moments that followed, Henry engaged in some harsh self-talk. *You're an ass, Henry, dumping Maude's problems into Laura's lap. Can't blame her for being irritated, but hell, I have work to finish.* Focus was elusive though. His concentration had been broken. Regrouping at all would take some time, but he did have that. He did have time. *Thank you, Laura, for coming through.* His heart shuddered. Though he and Laura had had their quarrels, never had she let him down - not when they met, not when *Judge* was murdered, not in raising their children, not with his once shaky career, and finally, not now. Why his mother despised Laura, Henry would never understand. She was the best thing that had ever happened to him.

She is, isn't she?

Chapter Seventeen

GRACE

After the uncomfortable breakfast alongside Maude Litzenberg, Grace was content to be alone in her apartment again. Though the days she spent there were solitary, each one melding into the next, she was far from lonely. She truly relished her privacy, perceiving her fragile autonomy as a precious gift. At last, for eighty-eight-year-old Grace Ainsworth, time seemed to have relinquished its wretched control once and for all . . . even though, at some level, she was cognizant that the years still ticked on. At her age though, for the most part, she didn't give a good goddamn about time at all. *The devil can deal with it.* Besides, she had countless, delicious memories to keep her company - warm, sometimes baffling visions of her mother, Olivia, and, of course, thoughts of Frank, the essence of her husband still lingering uncannily in the room as if he never had left her completely after all. And, yes, though Grace resisted the intrusions as mightily as she could, Percy Rawling paid a visit now and again as well . . . the damned old boy a proverbial *thorn in her side.* He was as persistent in death as he had been in her young life when he had determined not to let her out of his sight until he was satiated with the thrill of another conquest.

Percy Rawling had pursued Grace relentlessly even in the face of blunt rebuffs by Olivia who told him in no uncertain terms, "Don't come around here any more, Percy. You're too old for my Gracie, and on the wrong track. We're looking for something better. Yes, we are, aren't we Gracie Brown?"

Grace could envision Olivia even now, and she quivered as she had way back then, at the power her mother projected when confronted with anything, or anybody, she considered a menacing threat. Without a doubt, Percy Rawling had fit into her thinking. *There is no way that riffraff, carnival barker will have his way with my beautiful daughter. If Gilbert were still alive, why he'd dare that rascal to round of fisticuffs and run him right out of town, no doubt about that. But Gilbert's gone, God bless him. Damn it, Gilbert. It wasn't fair that you left like you did.* And though Olivia had been buoyed by the thought of her late husband, her eyes stung with tears. The unfairness of a random illness such as pneumonia taking such a strong man, her lover and friend, had been a knife in the gut. She never had recovered from Gilbert's unexpected death and a few folks had paid the price of her pain as a result, not the least of which was Percy Rawling.

To Grace, Olivia had been equally as firm in touting her outrage toward the man, "Grace Brown, you are not to see that Percy creature. It's time to choose wisely, young lady. Haven't I always taught you that? He's the wrong person; it's the wrong time. You listen to me and you listen like there's no tomorrow because I do know a thing or two. I do. You have a lifetime ahead of you, Grace. Now, mind me."

That was all it took. Rebellion blossomed like a field of wild dandelions. Grace had been smitten. *No one is going to tell me what to do.* Grace's thought became a mantra.

She had met Percy by chance when she was only seventeen, he twenty-five, at the annual Alameda County Fair. With arms tangled through those of two, clutching girlfriends, she had spotted him first - a handsome, muscleridden, young man demanding to be heard and pulling anyone willing onto the midway to be further enticed by carnies and clowns. Grace had never seen anyone with such earthy appeal. She was certain her mouth gaped wide open when he looked down at her from the pedestal where he stood perched and said, "Well, look at you, pretty lady. I believe you've taken my breath away." His smile was unsettling, wide, yet pouty, and his eyes, as green as sea glass. She knew in that moment she would not resist.

And for weeks, she did not, ignoring her mother's warnings, discounting her own exasperating bouts with a pestering conscience, and yielding to the lure of an unsettled wanderer who, unbeknownst to Grace, was a prisoner to his desires. The thrill for Percy Rawling was in the hunt, in the capture, in the kill. After that, he was spent.

To that end, theirs was a thwarted affair from the beginning, two disparate souls who could not possibly have understood the other's motivations, the other's needs, the other's expectations, but who launched into a reckless game of *hide and seek* or, to be more precise, one of *truth or dare.* The result of their rash and careless play was a heartrending failure for both of them.

After two months of clandestine encounters - in the dim corner of a carnival tent, in a steamy, borrowed, co-worker's car, on a patch of dry leaves beneath a long-dormant maple, and more sordid still, in the dark shadows of Olivia's own, private home - the inevitable happened. Percy's kisses and caresses, his wanton words of affection and promise, his masculine yearnings proved too much for young Grace Brown.

On a warm evening in late spring, Percy made his move. He had been circling Grace for hours, watching her from a distance as she went through her day. He had made plans and knew she would do exactly as he'd instructed. When Olivia departed for a meeting in town, Grace slipped out of her house and ran off to meet him.

"Down by Old Mill Creek," he had told her. "Bear off County Road 87 onto Lindsey Lane. It'll lead you right to me. I'll be waiting. It will be perfect, just you and me," he had promised. "Have you ever watched the sun go down, hand in hand with someone you adore? Have you? Well it's going to happen. This will be your night, Grace Brown. I promise."

Percy's strategy did not take long to play out. No sooner had the sun dipped behind a distant hill, than a dilapidated, wicker, picnic basket was shoved roughly aside and Percy advanced on her. Grace did not resist, at least not at first. She had not known how, and so, she had not, not until his caresses roughened and he restrained her to the point she could not move.

"Let me go," she hissed, but her plea was flouted. Percy's lust was too intense for either of them. He molested her aggressively . . . and then it was over. His heaving abated finally and he collapsed against her breasts, breathing heavily into her ear.

"Get off," she croaked, her voice disobeying her in her intent to exhibit a shred of grit. "Get away. Away." She twisted from him and began tugging at her clothing - a ripped blouse, soiled skirt, and panties tinged crimson. She began to sob. *Oh no, what have I done? I'm so stupid. I'm ruined. Mother was right.* Her thoughts of Olivia and of her own misjudgment, mute to Percy, were searing to Grace. Pressure grew behind her eyes, in her ears, inside her nose. *My head - it's going to explode.* She stared at Percy, not really seeing.

"Now, Grace," he responded, pushing her sideways and grabbing her arm with ruthless force. "Calm down. Get a hold of yourself. This is not the end of the world. What did you think was going to happen, anyway? Damn it, girl. What's wrong with you?"

The words were throwaways.

In the following moment's silence, Percy released his grip on Grace. Startled, she flinched. He threw back his head as if to mock her, and then he grinned though his mouth, this time, had dramatically altered. In place of the usual, arresting smile was an alien sneer - ugly and repulsive.

Grace glared at Percy as if he were a stranger. "No. No. Away," she shrieked. And she ran. *Have to get away.* She slid once on the muddy embankment, but regained her balance and fled through a thicket of wild gooseberries, needle grass, and nettles onto the dusty, country lane that forked away from the county highway. She did not look back, only down, farther down at slender legs, now scratched, burning, and oozing blood, and at bare feet, painfully cut, encrusted with mud. A scream caught in her throat; she made no sound. Instead, she was silenced, appalled at what she had left behind and mortified in the face of what lay ahead.

Half-heartedly, Percy had attempted to grab Grace once more before she bolted, but his hand was left empty, flailing, flailing. "Get back here," he yelled, but the cry was unheard. She was gone. *Oh hell, who cares? She's another dumb broad.* He yanked on his jeans before settling back with a smirk and a nearly full, quart bottle of cheap, malt whiskey. *She'll get over it. She'll be back. They always come back.* He was certain he was right, though Grace's reaction had been startling, unlike any of the others. *What the hell is her problem?*

Christ. What did she expect? He was convinced he had made love to the girl. He had known just how to handle her. The fact was, however, that he had not; instead he had taken her, roughly and callously on a rough, horsehair blanket spread on the mucky bank of Old Mill Creek just as a brilliant day had clouded over and slipped into dusk. He pondered for a moment. *She's too naïve, too young. Not worth the trouble.* He tilted the whiskey bottle upward letting the warm liquid burn his throat as he swigged. *Oh hell, baby hooch, there's nothing like you to soothe a man's soul. Take me home my sweet, amber heaven. Take me home.*

And it did.

Percy Rawling's bloated body was found two days later at the edge of Old Mill Creek. It was lodged between an ancient box elder and a young, black willow sapling its spindly branches wrapped around Percy like an angry lover. Nearly comatose with intoxication, and mercifully, likely unaware, Percy had been pinned into the muck during the fury of a deluge that pushed Old Mill Creek over its banks for two days. A lone hunter's two Beagle dogs sniffed out the find just as the water had receded and a hot sun began marinating the dead body in a coating of slimy, steamy silt. The decomposing corpse stank to high heavens.

Grace learned of Percy's death as the rumor mill churned. She said not a word though her girlfriends ogled her, silently imploring a reaction that never was forthcoming. In regard to Percy Rawling, Grace had become steel. Even when Olivia pointedly asked, "Did you hear, Gracie, about what happened to Percy?" she only nodded, too afraid to say more, too anxious to hear more, and unable to forget.

It was understandable. Her mother had been home when Grace, filthy and panicked, had stumbled into the house two nights before. Olivia had been waiting, frantic with worry. Though furious with her daughter, with astute and caring devotion, she had attended to Gracie's scratches and cuts. Those would heal. The pain inside, on the other hand, would not. Olivia was certain of it . . . and though she had, on a base level, wanted to curse and cry, "I told you so," she did not. Instead, she pined for Grace's losses - her innocence, her self-respect, her virginity. Because that was enough, because it was too much, Olivia did not lash out. *What would be the point? Lessons have to be learned, don't they? And isn't it true, we punish ourselves enough. Experiences, good and bad, stay locked inside us forever.* She understood at the deepest level, for Olivia Graci had been a young girl once too.

The alarming news of Percy's demise on the muddy banks of Old Mill Creek dissipated in short order. He was a nothing. No one had really known the man. He had been passing through, a rambler, drifting with the tide of his fortune. He had been an untethered rover unable to secure body or soul, and his conscience was broken, faulty to the core. Grace believed that to be true with every ounce of her being, and as a result, retained her own emotional self-control. She did not confess the veracity of that calamitous tryst for many years, crying only in relief when she realized she would not carry the man's baby. Her relationship with Percy had been a mistake, but she had survived, perhaps by the grace of God, perhaps because of a spurn of the devil. No matter, it was behind her. She would move on . . . and she did, anchored only by a phantom memory that, when she least expected it, slipped in to harass her. *Seventy years, you bastard. And you're still badgering me.* Grace had cursed the son of a bitch for years, but he had returned time and again, tormenting. *Oh, for Christ's sake, Percy, enough of you. Get the hell out of my poor, tired brain. I have better things to do with my time. Go away, would you? For heaven's sake, you're going to be the death of me.* She sat very still feeling anxious and annoyed. *Percy, go on now.* And at last, her wishes won out.

The thoughts of Percy Rawling dissolved into nothingness, swept away on an abstract tide of angry recriminations.

⌘ ⌘ ⌘

So here she was - settled in with her mother's ancient afghan tucked around her legs, resting like a cozy cat in Frank's chair. His face, handsome until the very end, took precedence in her mind's eye. *Ah, Frank, how I miss you. Did you remember the day we met? Before you left me, did you ever think about that day?* She sighed deeply and her lids closed.

1951. Grace Brown spotted Frank Ainsworth strolling up to the ticket booth at the Roxy Theater as though he owned it. He had tossed the jacket of his gray suit over his shoulder and peeked out from under a darker grey Stetson Whippet hat at the young girl selling tickets. He smiled. She blushed. *And why wouldn't she? He's the most handsome man I've ever seen.* Frank was tall, but it was his features that had captured Grace's attention - jet-black hair, a chiseled jaw, full lips, and brown eyes lined with long, dark eyelashes. *Lordy me, I can see them from here.* Grace was certain she was gawking. He wore perfectly creased trousers, a tailored, white shirt, black tie, and gleaming, patent leather loafers. He was the embodiment of perfection to Grace's eye but a man who would not look twice at her, she was sure - not at her with her boxy, linen coat, long, near ankle-length, cotton skirt, and flats. *Flats! For heaven's sake, I'm not even wearing high heels.* Yet, despite her misgivings, he turned toward her. *Oh dear, he's caught me staring.* She quickly looked away, motioning at the specter of another person to hide her embarrassment. She was mortified at having been caught being so bold. *It's simply not lady-like.* Her heart pounded. *Can he tell?*

It didn't really matter because he began to saunter toward her. *Is he coming this way?* She looked quickly behind her. *Surely he's not walking to me . . . of course not. He's meeting someone who's behind me.* She turned to look again. Not one person was within ten yards of her. *Oh, dear.* She turned back . . . and he was there, two feet away, grinning like a Cheshire cat and gazing down at her as if he had discovered a treasure. And perhaps he had.

"Hello," he said. His voice was like chocolate.

She looked from side to side and drew in a breath. "Oh, hi. Hello, I mean. Uh, do you know me?"

"I'm afraid I don't."

Grace was perplexed. *Well, what are you doing here then?* She finally stammered, "Are you seeing *The African Queen?* I just adore Humphrey Bogart."

"I was hoping the Roxy was still playing *The Day The Earth Stood Still,* but found out it was replaced just yesterday. *The African Queen* should be fine though. Want to join me? I'll buy you a Coke." He stared directly at her.

"Well, I shouldn't, really. I don't even know you." *Oh my, those eyelashes.*

"Oh, come on. Don't worry. It's a public place, the theater, for crying out loud. And, I promise, I'm a gentleman. Were you meeting someone else?"

"Well, no, but . . ." Grace glanced from side to side. There was no escape, and if she had been able to articulate a complete sentence she would have had to admit she didn't want one.

"I'm Frank," he said. "Frank Ainsworth . . . home from a stint in the Army and now selling real estate . . . have my own firm, Ainsworth and Associates. Have you heard of it?"

"Well, yes, I believe I have."

"So good. You know I'm reputable, then. And, well, Miss, I'd love to accompany you to see your favorite actor, Mr. Bogart, but don't think I can do that until I know your name." He smiled broadly again. Grace was certain her heart skipped two complete beats.

"It's Grace Brown," she said demurely. She bit her lip before offering a tiny smile.

"Grace. Ah, a beautiful name." He paused and then added, "Well, Grace Brown, shall we go? We don't want to be late, do we?"

That was it. He escorted her into the Roxy, bought her that Coke and some popcorn to boot, and together they fell in love with Humphrey Bogart, Katharine Hepburn, and each other. Six months later, after winning the approval of Olivia Graci as well as Frank's mother, Louise, they married in a tiny, stone and ivy-covered, Episcopal chapel on the outskirts of town.

In a stunning display of chic and good taste, Grace wore a long, taffeta, beaded wedding gown just one shade darker than absolutely pure white; in contrast, Frank was attired in an elegant, dark, charcoal tuxedo, accessorized perfectly to accentuate Grace. *They are so lovely together, a striking couple, and so in love.* Louise Ainsworth's thoughts were not singular to her. Heads around the chapel nodded in joyful appreciation. For long moments, Louise clasped her hands close to her breasts and smiled brightly. All the while, she watched her son's marriage to Grace transpire in a simple, but poignant ceremony that to her seemed over before it began. And as for Olivia Graci, when she observed from a short distance the adoring couple at the entrance of the chapel after their vows had been exchanged, after they were officially husband and wife, she openly wept. She was that happy.

Grace's remembrance of that expanse of time was a like a dream, the most remarkable day of her life. And it was for Frank as well, for over the years, he often reminded her. "Remember, Grace? Remember, honey, the day we got hitched up finally for good.?" He would chuckle a bit at his backwoods vernacular and then ramble on. "Remember, my Gracie, when you became my bride? Oh Lordy, sweetheart, what a day in our lives."

She imagined his smile, she heard his laugh, and she settled back into Frank's chair, as though cuddling in his arms one more time. She sighed deeply . . . but then, in a sharp instant, she felt a chill.

She opened her eyes immediately and shuddered, taken aback by a startling, dark, and intense visage only inches away from her face. Maude Litzenberg was leaning over her, gawking at her as if she were dead or perhaps not even real. Grace gasped. She reeled away from Maude in shocked repulsion.

"Maude? What in the hell? What are you doing here?"

Maude stepped back as though she had been stung. But she did not retreat far. Instead she stood silent, leering, hands gripped together, fingers entwined as though she were praying for a new start or for a means to an end. And then she began to cry.

"Oh, for Pete's sake, Maude." Grace squeaked. "What the hell's gotten into you?"

Chapter Eighteen

MILDRED

After the doctor sedated sad, confused Maude Litzenberg, she fell into a light sleep, snoring with raspy regularity with every third breath. Mildred felt comfortable leaving her in order to check on the others on her wing. As was not unusual, Louie Lawrence was at his apartment doorway peering in both directions as if waiting for the same, trusty, 8:15 transit bus he had boarded for years when his graveyard shift had ended at the mill; it would take him home. And on this day, certainly not out of the ordinary, he held a felt fedora in one hand and his penis in the other. Fortunately, for Mildred, floppy pajama pants, a striped polo shirt, and a long, fuzzy sweater concealed the latter.

"Morning, Miss Millie," Louie smirked.

"Good morning to you, too, Louie. Are you waiting for someone?"

"Oh, no, not me. Nobody's coming to see this old boy . . . besides everybody I ever knew is dead or long gone." He chuckled as though he had cracked a shrewd joke, rearing back his head to reveal a coated tongue and missing molars.

"Well, don't you think you should go inside and take a nap or check in on *Days of Our Lives*; it's your favorite."

"I'm tired of that confounded soap opera, Millie. I'm confusing the characters and half the time can't figure out whether they're coming or going. Besides, the broad I liked most, that harlot with the massive bosom and big teeth, well, she took off to Texas after some rich, oil tycoon. It's not the same without her. I swear, Miss Millie, I miss the devil out of . . . whatever her name was, confound it."

"Well, why don't you go back inside and read. Do you have today's newspaper?"

"Read the damned thing cover to cover this morning. Maybe it was this morning. Was it?"

"I really don't know, Louie." Mildred stood her ground, unwilling to leave Louie alone in the hall. *God knows what he'll get into next.*

"Well hell, guess I'll go back inside and sit. Nothing else to do, and I'm damned good at it." He paused. "Hey, need to ask you, Miss Millie, what happened to that new gal in town?"

"Well, we do have a new patient on the wing. Believe you might have seen her at breakfast," she replied, knowingly. She astutely understood Louie's somewhat pathetic intent in asking.

"Thought so. A looker. I caught a glimpse."

"She's a very nice lady, Louie. But today, she's a little under the weather, so keep a distance, you hear?"

"You know me, Miss Millie . . . always a perfect gentleman." He rubbed his crotch energetically before turning abruptly and retreating into the dim room behind him.

What a character. I can't forget to warn Maude to be careful. Louie has no clue about boundaries. Mildred moved farther down the hall and tapped softly on Ralph Fisher's door.

"Come in," he said, his voice gravelly.

"How are you doing, Ralph?" Mildred smiled. "Everything okay?"

"Just peachy, Miss Millie. Been reading a little of the word of the Lord."

"That sounds like a lovely, late morning pastime," she offered. *Not something I'd do, but bless his heart, without a congregation, guess he's ministering to himself. Nothing wrong with that, I suppose.* "Can I get anything for you, Ralph? A juice? A snack?"

"Oh, no, Miss Millie. I'm as content as a cucumber, happy as a lark, pleased as punch. Think I'll catch a few *Z*'s and then get on down to lunch. It's mac and cheese day."

"I believe it is. Everyone's favorite." And Ralph was one of Mildred's favorites. *What a sweet man.* "Have a nice nap, Ralph. I'll be back around noon." She pulled his door closed and moved next to Lilly's studio.

Lilly Littleton was counting, her tiny fingers flying a mile a minute. Mildred didn't have the heart to interrupt. *Look at her there, in her own calculated paradise.* Lilly's head bobbed up and down, left to right, as though trying to keep up with the fingertips that tapped, retreated, tapped, retreated. It was somewhat enthralling to watch the frail, little ninety-nine-year-old woman in a world of her own, as independent as a hog on ice, her motion unstoppable. *Lilly really is remarkable. I bet she been self-sufficient her whole life . . . just like now. Surely she doesn't need me spoiling her utopia.*

Mildred stepped away from Lilly's door and slowly began to walk toward the other end of the hallway. As she moved forward, her sister, Caroline, came to mind. Caroline, a woman who had meandered, unsettled for years, was a polar opposite to Lilly who must have managed control to the nth degree her entire life - that is until her companion and sweetheart, Gladys, died and Lilly came to *The Gardens*, all on her own, to grieve and to figure out the next steps. *My God, Lilly has been here for years and she's still figuring, her analytical mind ever at work. Amazing.* Mildred smiled. *The human spirit never ceases to astound me.*

⌘ ⌘ ⌘

As Mildred continued down the hall in order to check in on Grace and then, of course, on Maude, she felt a flutter of panic. *Caroline. I wonder how she's doing? Still sleeping? I must give her a call. I will. I will. Later. First, Grace.*

Mildred noticed immediately that the door to Grace's apartment was half open. *That's unusual.*

"Grace?" No sooner had she uttered the woman's name than she heard the sound, a stifled blubbering as if someone were strangling. "Grace, are you all right?"

Mildred stumbled into the room, strangely darkened with the drapes pulled, and came face to face with Maude Litzenberg, the woman crimson-faced and reeling as if she were intoxicated. "Maude. What are you doing in here? What are you doing here?" As was an old habit that often surfaced when she was surprised or frightened, Mildred repeated her question. "Maude, what . . .?"

"That's what I'd like to know." Grace's voice cracked. "For Pete's sake, Miss Millie. Why is she here?"

"Oh, I'm so sorry, Grace. I have no idea. I have no idea what happened, how Maude got here, why she's here. Maude, why are you here?" Mildred addressed both women hoping for a quick end to what *The Gardens* administrative staff looked upon very unfavorably. Residents were not free to enter the apartments of others without permission and surely Grace had not, out of the kindness of her heart, invited Maude inside to chitchat. Besides, hadn't Maude been sedated? Hadn't she been sleeping? Not an hour before, Mildred had left Maude snoring soundly in the wing-backed chair she had had transported from her very own *Tara.*

Maude gazed at Mildred with glazed eyes before she bobbled sideways, collapsing in a slow motion heap onto the floor beside Grace's - *Frank's* - chair.

"Oh, my heavens. My heavens. I'll need some assistance. Grace, are you all right? Are you?" Mildred's words were a rush.

"Yes. It startled the daylights out of me though when I opened my eyes and saw her standing there. Lordy, Miss Millie, she was not even a foot away, staring at me as if I were an alien or something. Startled the daylights out of me," she croaked again.

"I can imagine. I certainly can imagine. I'll be right back, Grace." Mildred spun quickly toward the door and into the hall. In moments, she was back with a burly orderly who assisted in pulling Maude gently into a wheelchair where she slumped to one side with her head lolling forward and her hands falling limp in her lap like sodden rags.

"Let's get her to her own apartment," Mildred instructed the orderly. She looked quickly at Grace. "I'll be back in a few minutes, Grace."

Before Grace could respond, as if miraculously raised from the dead, Maude reared her head back and snarled, "Grace, I want to talk to you. I need to talk. Can't you understand that? Why are you treating me this way? Did Henry tell you to ignore me? Did Judge? Oh no, Judge. Not Judge. He's gone, isn't he? Isn't he? Grace? Answer me."

Maude's head fell forward once again, bobbing several times before it stopped still. A dribble of saliva slid from the corner of her mouth and glided down her chin before seeping into the wrinkled folds of skin on her neck.

Mildred, Grace, and the orderly, like an unlikely three-some of conspirators, stared at the stricken woman in naked amazement. Grace's mouth was agape. "Oh, Lordy," she finally uttered.

"To the word, Mrs. Ainsworth," the orderly replied as he steadied Maude's shoulders with his large hands; then to Mildred, he added, "Ready?"

"Yes, let's move her. Careful now. This situation is more tenuous than I had imagined. I sure hope someone from the family is on the way." Mildred spoke more to herself than to the man assisting her. He had no possible way of knowing anything about Maude's family, or about her past. And really, more to the point, did she?

Eerily, in that moment, a blurry image of Caroline's face materialized in Mildred's consciousness. It was the same, pale countenance Mildred had observed when she left her sister sound asleep that morning, curled up under an old blanket like an orphaned child. *I'll be on my way, soon, Caroline. Don't worry. Before you know it this shift will be over and I'll be home.*

Chapter Nineteen

MAUDE

Thanks to the efficiency of the kind orderly on Mildred's wing, Maude was wheeled back into her apartment with no further incident. In a quick minute, a physician's assistant arrived to evaluate her condition. Maude was slouched in the same uncomfortable-looking posture she had assumed when she had fallen into semi-consciousness in Grace's room. She was quite a pathetic sight, slumped in the wheelchair like a half-filled grain sack; she made no motion, as though she had settled complacently into that awkward position for the long haul.

"She can't be comfortable, or secure, for that matter," Mildred commented to the physician's assistant.

"No, of course not. Let's move her. Gently now - to her bed."

Mildred pulled down the thick comforter, blanket, and sheet, fluffed two pillows, and turned. "There. This should be a pleasant nest." When she looked back toward Maude, the orderly and the physician's assistant were holding her firmly and, *on three*, hoisted her into bed. She did not gain consciousness; instead, she flopped back like a child's Raggedy Ann doll and lay perfectly still. The only movement was a slight twitch at the left corner of her mouth. Mildred pulled up the covers and tucked Maude in with such tenderness an onlooker might have believed she could break. And perchance such an assumption was right. For if the truth had been revealed, it already was too late. Maude had been broken eons before, deep down inside, the hidden, veiny cracks from the initial blows continuing to splinter in every which direction.

⌘ ⌘ ⌘

The sedative Maude had been given finally took hold and she slept, unmoving and soundless, except for the tiny snore that resumed with every third breath. Mildred cocked her head, listened, and silently tallied as Maude inhaled. *One. Two. Three. Snort. One. Two. Three. Snort. Now isn't that cadence uncanny?*

"She looks so peaceful, now," the orderly whispered.

"She does. She should sleep for some time. We'll need to keep a close watch though in case she wakes again." The physician's assistant spoke directly to Mildred.

"I will be in and out to check on Mrs. Litzenberg all afternoon, of course, but I am responsible for other residents on my wing as well."

"Oh, I understand, and I'll be back in myself, but I'd like you to stay with her for a bit right now, just to observe. Hopefully someone from the family will be here soon to sit with her. I spoke with her son earlier. He, or maybe his wife, will be coming if they can fit a visit into their busy schedules. I sure hope so, although the son was quite evasive. The attitude was bothersome, really. I'm not convinced anyone cares enough . . ."

The physician assistant's comment was severed. "Oh, for goodness sake. People care as much as they dare. It's just that old Maude has never made it easy for anyone to give a good goddamn." A tall, blond woman had entered the room silently and stood examining the three facility employees as if they were defective. "What happened, anyway? Her son said there was an issue."

A brief, awkward silence ensued before Mildred spoke. "Mrs. Litzenberg awoke in quite a belligerent frame of mine, refusing breakfast, wanting only to sleep. I finally convinced her a bite would do her good so I accompanied her to the dining hall. Once back from the meal, however, she became very disoriented, confused, and demanded she be shown the way back home."

"Belligerent?" The woman chortled. "When is she not belligerent? Seldom, let me tell you, very seldom. And as for being confused . . . that condition has been ramping up with random regularity for some time. Why do you think Henry put her in this place anyway? She's become a constant worry to him, but more to the point, she's a goddamned burden to all of us."

"And you are?" The woman's rant had fueled Mildred's ire. Her checks flamed red.

"I'm Laura Litzenberg, the son's wife." She sneered in the direction of the physician's assistant and tugged at the visitor nametag pinned on her jacket. "See. I'm legit. Old Maude, here, unfortunately, is my very own mother-in-law. What a joy that relationship's been for too many years to count."

Mildred, dumfounded by the toxic venom Laura spewed, skewed her lips into a tight *O* and clinched her fists. *My heavens, Mildred, calm down. Protective instincts shouldn't provoke violence toward this woman, dreadful though she seems.*

"Look. I'm here. I'll sit with Maude for an hour or so. At least I won't have to make small talk. She looks like she's pretty much dead to the world," Laura babbled. "Just get me a chair, would you?" She spun around in a circle and spied Maude's wing-backed chair. "Well, I'll be damned. She coerced poor Henry into bringing this thing all the way over here. He's such an annoying pushover sometimes. Great, so, I'll sit here. Go on. Do what you need to do," she spat, flipping her hand outward in a dismissive gesture.

"Would you care for some reading material?" the orderly offered. Mildred stared at him, astonished that he had any words to give, for she could not have managed one more remark.

"Oh, hell no. I have my iPad and iPhone. Those should keep me entertained. Don't have a clue how we ever lived without them," she said, clutching her tablet as if it were a prize. "Now let's see, two hours to kill. Guess I'll see who's checked in on Facebook." Laura clearly was speaking only to herself, for the others already were retreating into the hallway like wounded soldiers.

Laura gazed once at Maude who lay unmoving in her bed and sighed. *God, that breathing is annoying. Maybe she should do us all a favor and just get on with it.*

She opened to her Facebook page and quickly updated her status: *News Flash! I'm stuck for the afternoon in a retirement community - an honest-to-goodness old folks' home - babysitting my mother-in-law. Wow! Goes to shows how thrilling my life is these days!*

"Let's see how many likes I get for that one," she mumbled aloud before scrolling on down to catch the latest. She did not glance up at her mother-in-law once.

⌘　⌘　⌘

Maude dreamed. The sedative had, at last, begun its work. She had not been able to survive its pull after resisting, resisting . . . and now she was powerless, caught like a fish in a net, breathing still, but unable to move, knowing surely that she would die. She would die if someone did not come for her. And who would do that? No one. No one ever had.

So, was it really a dream or was it a revived reality . . . the latter perhaps? Deep in an almost comatose sleep, Maude allowed the images to come alive, vivid and real. The world that her mind was shaping was foreign; at the same time it was familiar - a paradox of her own, demented making.

"Mommy! Daddy, come get me." The tiny voice was not even a whisper; it gurgled in the back of her throat.

She lay at the far end of a concrete culvert that extended the length of the driveway leading from the main road to her parents' estate aloft a hill overlooking the San Francisco Bay. Her head throbbed, she had bitten her tongue, and her arm was twisted awkwardly behind her back, broken by a force so strong it had taken her breath away. She remembered that. She remembered being unable to breathe as some boy, the councilman's son, the law partner's kid, one of them, or someone else maybe - a blond, wild-eyed adolescent - had held her firm. A thick palm had been rammed into her upper chest and long fingers had encircled her neck before clamping onto her lips, silencing any sound; another hand had tugged down her panties and pushed wide her legs. And she was raped, roughly, cruelly, and then abandoned, injured and alone. She was a child in a ditch . . . eight years old.

When it was over, he had run; she recalled the sound of his panting breaths and pounding footsteps, audible for only seconds before he was gone. She opened her eyes to a slate sky and a sliver of sun that she watched disappear behind a stand of eucalyptus, their leaves rustling ominously in the wind. She could smell them too, though she could not have been able to identify the pungent odor - mint, pine, and camphor - as familiar as fog and as heavy. Just as heavy.

She lay still, not because she wanted to, but because she could . . . not . . . move. An indeterminate pain, deep inside, throbbed, throbbed, throbbed. The deep cut in her tongue had filled her mouth with blood - warm, metallic, suffocating. She wanted to yell out . . . to Mommy, Daddy, somebody . . . but her swollen lips would not part. Tears welled in her eyes and she cried, panting and hiccupping in a strange, rhythmic pattern . . . pant, pant, pant, hiccup . . . pant, pant, pant, hiccup, over and over until she fell exhausted into a state of unconsciousness.

Little Maude was located hours later by a member of an impromptu search team that had been formed when the girl finally had been discovered missing. Her mother was aghast when she saw her daughter draped over the shoulder of a deputy sheriff. In the first instant, she had presumed the child was a corpse, and she held her breath until she knew for certain how she should react amid the small, murmuring crowd that milled around in awkward anticipation. Rewarded with relief, the watchers began a tittering hum when they realized the young, eight-year-old girl was alive. The family, however, unbeknownst to the others, harbored more reticent emotions. Though Maude did not die that evening, many times in the years that followed, she wished she had. She internalized a fabricated notion that her childhood demise would have been easier on everyone and grew bitter with resentment when neither one of her parents ventured to argue otherwise. Not even in the immediate aftermath of the assault, did Maude receive deserving comfort.

"For heaven's sake, Maude. How could you have gotten yourself into such a predicament." Those were the first words Maude heard from her mother at the hospital after the broken arm had been set and the doctor had confirmed that she had been molested sexually, her little body ravaged, but healable, restorable. Those had been the doctor's words of choice: healable, restorable. Maude had never forgotten them.

· "She'll be normal in no time. Kids bounce back," the physician had declared.

"Who was it?" Maude's father had demanded, glaring from the end of the hospital bed, his arms crossed, his cheeks crimson. "Who did you let touch you?" When she had been unable to answer, he had abused further, "You deserved it then, acting like a silly, little twit at the party, insisting on cavorting on the dance floor among a horde of teenagers twice your age. And we'll never know who did this, will we? I'll never be able to prosecute because you're not bright enough to remember."

The comments never had been erased from Maude's memory. Never. She was stupid; she was silly; she was a twit. Throughout an entire lifetime, Maude believed. It became her truth.

Six weeks after the incident, when the cast had been removed and the bruises had paled, Maude's parents enrolled her in an elite private girls' school two hundred miles south of San Francisco. She would live there. *I'll be the burden for someone else now. Mommy and Daddy have had enough of me; they will be happy when I'm gone for good.* Maude churned with emotions she could not identify. She only understood the feelings - a burning tummy, stinging eyes, and pounding deep, deep in her chest. *It's hurting. It's hurting. I think I might pop open and die.* And in that moment, in her childlike attempt to understand her fate, she determined with absolute certainty that she must have earned exactly what a stupid, silly twit deserved. Her punishment - being sent away from her family - she decided, was nobody's fault but her own.

What even Maude did not comprehend until much later in life, however, was that neither parent accepted responsibility for not watching closely enough, for not reacting deeply enough, for not showing one modicum of affection that could have changed the course of their daughter's life. As a result, as though in contempt for a dysfunctional family and a broken child, irony cast its wayward influence, seeming to mock them all in the years to come. Though Maude was lauded with every possible possession and opportunity, her parents were distant and cold, and she reciprocated, taking all she could and giving nothing in return. When she married her boyfriend, her future *Judge,* at the age of twenty-one, they eloped, the ceremony a secret until she decided to tell, and when Henry was born three years later, the parents received one, single, phone message - "You have a grandson, Henry David." Communication continued to be spotty even as the parents grew old and frail. When finally they died, both of cancer, two days apart, Maude did not cry one tear although she did embrace the comfortable inheritance with an air of smug retribution. Instead of mourning, she flounced into her role as the attorney's wife, the judge's spouse, and the eager socialite. It was as though she lived outside herself. Inwardly, however, as if the absurd had reached its highest, finest peak, Maude became the epitome of the detached and hateful mother she had grown to detest, her behaviors as engrained as the blood that flowed through her veins.

And life carried on.

Though it had seemed a duty to bear a child for her husband, the outcome was an instant disappointment to Maude. From the moment he arrived as a squalling infant, the couple's son, little Henry David Litzenberg, was an absolute annoyance and, in time, a burden too great to bear. The boy's every misstep threw his mother into a tizzy, elevating her temper or pushing her over the brink into debilitating depression. They all suffered - Maude, the child, and the husband who very early on sought relief from his chaotic home life in the arms of and between the legs of countless, accommodating women. His improprieties did not remain clandestine, however; in fact, they became notorious fodder that fed the gossip mill and contributed to Maude's further, emotional decline.

"This is no way to live," she had screamed over and over, the verbal renditions of her angst varying to the degree of her husband's sexual misconduct or to her inability to cope with a growing son who, though a typical boy, was alien, his behavior maddening, unacceptable. Maude's warped sense of justice clouded her judgment when, in a pretense of protecting the fragile bond that was her marriage, she placed blame for her mercurial disposition on the difficulties of raising a son.

"I simply cannot cope with the boy any more, David."

"But Henry's only a child . . . and the nanny says . . ."

"I don't give a hoot what the nanny says. And what would you know? You're never around." She paused, her eyes welling with tears. "If you cared about me, if you cared at all, you would do something. Can't you see? I'm at my wit's end."

Maude's *Judge* eagerly made arrangements. If he had been candid enough to reveal the truth, he already, without his wife's knowledge, had been investigating myriad possibilities for extricating both he and his wife from the annoying boy. Henry was sent away to an elite school, just as Maude had been. She was free of her son for years . . . yet, in a not unsurprising reprisal for her callousness, she never could escape herself. As her husband's career flourished, she maintained a façade of life in perfection, but when the parties were over, when special events were hailed as successes, when the door was closed behind the final guest, she cried herself to sleep. An onlooker never would have known. But in her darker days, after Henry had been sent away and when her husband found companionship God only knew where, she suffered in lonely silence. *Well, what did you expect, you stupid, silly, twit? You've reaped your just reward. Who cares about you anyway? Nobody. Nobody.* The negative self-talk had led Maude to contemplate suicide more than once, but she had staved off her demons every time . . . and she was not certain why. Perhaps it was the little girl inside, the spoiled one, the fragile one, the broken one - not *healable,* not *restorable* - who only wanted to see if life would ever turn around.

Chapter Twenty

HENRY

It was late afternoon before Henry's laser-focused thinking allowed room for consideration of his mother's wellbeing again. The moment Laura had agreed, however reluctantly, to go to *The Gardens* to check on Maude, he had relaxed a bit. *God, how could two women be so different?* That had been his last thought before plowing back into his work.

The brief he was preparing could not wait another day. His client's parents had passed away leaving every asset, savings included, to their only daughter; the son had been excluded completely for reasons Henry really did not want to know. He preferred the backstory remain in sole, proprietary custody of the burly man who had limped into his office a few months prior loaded for bear. The man had hired Henry for one reason that he stated in no uncertain terms: "I plan to get my fair share of that goddamned inheritance away from that bitch . . . not that it's a fucking fortune, but I want what's coming to me. I'm not going to stand back like a pansy and not put up a fight. You're going to help, damn it all too hell, aren't you? I got money."

Henry had been afraid to refuse. Certainly he had not been drawn in any personable manner to the rather disagreeable man, and the thought of intimidation of any kind was off putting as hell, but the guy seemed genuine enough. Henry did ascertain that he was an Iraq War veteran with, as he put it, "Enough shrapnel in my goddamned body to build a fucking cannon." Beyond that, Henry assumed a bit of post-traumatic stress was in play as well, for the fellow had fidgeted throughout each of their encounters, his hands constantly touching, releasing, touching, releasing any item that was within his grasp. Furthermore, all the while he had talked and listened, the man's eyes had darted in arbitrary fashion about the office as if he was anticipating, at any moment, another bombshell to explode and alter his life one more time.

Fortunately, Henry's client's father had had a fly-by-night, would-be attorney prepare a document, a watered down Will that surely would not hold up in court. *How stupid can some people be?* A Living Trust might have alleviated what Henry was certain would be a final, unpleasant confrontation between siblings, but that document did not exist, setting Henry in a powerful position to prevail. *I just want this damned case over and done before there's bloodshed.* Prior brief encounters between the brother and sister had been tense, hostility boiling like molten lava. He did not want to get too close or they'd all be burned. And knowing the family's secrets was not an option. Henry had learned early on in his career to stay clear of sentiments and emotions for they could be toxic both to him and to a legal action. His intention to avoid a courtroom battle and to complete his argument in the judge's chambers had morphed beautifully into an actuality that would play out in his favor. No problem. His client would be given his fair share, the sister would go on her way, and Henry would bank the hefty percentage he charged for his services. It was that easy.

⌘　⌘　⌘

He basked for a split second on the anticipated outcome of the case at hand before reality set in like a club to his temple. *Oh, shit. Mother. Guess I'd better check in.* Before he could pick up his cell to call Laura, *Taps* bugled its sad refrain into the silence of the office. Henry stared at his phone that he had set on a table some distance away. It would be her, Laura. He knew it. Although the sound of his ring tone was always the same, a melancholy rendition of *Taps*, he invariably knew, in some inexplicable way, when she was the person calling.

"Why in the hell do you have *Taps* for your ring tone, Henry? It's ridiculous and morbid," she had argued more than once.

"I don't know. *Taps* is different, meaningful - the end of the beginning, or maybe the beginning of the end," he had chuckled at his lame attempt to be erudite. "I'm an estate attorney. I deal with dead people. It fits. Besides, no one else would ever pick it."

"Hell no, they wouldn't," she replied. "It's the craziest, damned thing I've ever heard. You are so unbelievably weird sometimes, Henry. Honestly." She had shaken her head with disdain. "*Taps*, for fuck's sake."

Laura never had been one to mince words. She said what she thought, embellishing her dialogue with a variety of profanities that ran the gamut. *It's no wonder our kids have been reprimanded so many times for saying fuck or goddamn it at school. They hear that fucking language every day from their mother.* Oh well. No matter. He put up with Laura's foul mouth because she used it in glorious ways otherwise. The simple thought caused his sensibilities to stir as if all systems were on automatic pilot. *Shit. Get a grip, Henry.*

"Hey there," he mumbled into his phone. "I was just thinking about you, about calling you."

"Yeah. I bet you were." The voice was not happy.

"Look, I'm sorry you had to serve a sentence today, honey, but you understand, don't you? It was crunch time here at the office, especially after my stint at *The Gardens* with Mother yesterday." He paused and added, "And I appreciate it. You." He corrected his word choice.

"It's done, Henry. The duty's fucking done. I'll fill you in when I get home."

"Is she all right? Mother?" He had no idea why he had to clarify who *she* was, but *Mother* slipped out before it could be retracted.

"She's okay, I guess . . . bitchy as ever, but not quite with the program. I left her calling for some woman named Grace. I have no clue who that is, but *Grace* had better show up or Maude is apt to flip out completely," Laura replied, her voice rising.

"Oh, shit. It doesn't sound good."

"Hell, no, it's not good, Henry. Your poor mother - your, crazy mother, Henry - well, you'll see."

"Is she being looked after properly?" he asked somewhat inanely.

"For what you're paying for that place, I sure as hell hope so." Laura paused, settled. "She's being cared for, Henry. She demands it. She gets it. Nothing has changed in that regard. Look, I'm in my car. See you at home. I'll explain."

"Okay. Honey? Thanks. I owe you."

"You sure as hell do that," Laura blurted. She hung up without saying good-bye.

⌘ ⌘ ⌘

Henry got an earful when he arrived home only minutes after his wife.

"So, I was quietly sitting there in Maude's chair. I can't believe you dragged that damned thing all the way over to *The Gardens* for her, Henry. For Christ's sake, like that swanky facility doesn't have nice enough furniture." She stopped herself, refusing to digress further.

"Anyway, I was there, sitting with my tablet and cell, trying to entertain myself while Maude slept. Have you ever heard her sleep, Henry? She breathes funny, and she snores. Not loud, but it's definitely snoring. She breathes a bit and then she snores, she breathes, and then snores. It's annoying."

"Maybe she has sleep apnea or something," Henry interjected. He had no idea where Laura's story was going, nor why he had felt obligated to defend Maude's snoring. *Sleep apnea. For Christ's sake, Henry, everybody snores. You do. Laura does. The whole damned world snores.*

Laura continued. "So, it had been a couple of hours. I was bored and, hell, Facebook and Instagram can only entertain for so long. I walked to the doorway of your mother's apartment, hoping to find an assistant or orderly to relieve me when all of a sudden Maude shot up in bed like she'd been sprung from a trap and started yelling. 'What are you doing here? Where's my son, and where are my grandchildren? They were all here earlier. We had lunch downtown on the Plaza. What did you do with them, Laura? Have you sent them away? I bet you have. Damn you. Why have you hidden them from me again?' And she began to cry. Wow. You can imagine my shock."

"Why didn't you call me when this happened?" Henry asked.

"I did, Henry, the minute I could. Damn it to hell, it got kind of crazy in there." She stopped, angry. "Do you want to hear this shit or not?"

"Sorry. Go on." Henry acquiesced.

"Well, some assistant, Mildred, I think, came hauling ass up the hallway when she heard Maude screaming. Of course, she wasn't very pleasant either, asking what happened and how had I provoked Maude into such a state of frenzy. That attitude didn't sit well, I can tell you. So, I told the bitch, look, she just woke up, sat up like she'd risen from a tomb, and started hollering at me."

Henry had no idea how else to respond. "Go on."

"Well, Maude was crying and then she was shaking her finger at me like I was a bad child. She accused me of stealing your heart away, of hiding the kids. 'Probably in some dungeon,' she said. Christ, Henry, it was insane. That attendant, Mildred, got your mother settled down, but not before Maude told me to get out. 'Get the hell out of my room, Laura!' she screamed. And then, do you know what she did, Henry? She spat. She spat at me. And, damn, can the old girl ever launch one. But that's when I said *enough*. I was getting the hell out of there. Last thing I heard was your mother screaming at the top of her lungs. 'Get that bitch out of here. I want Grace. Get me Grace. I want Grace and I want her now!' Christ, it was so damned bizarre. Henry, I think your mother has gone over the brink. I really do, and I'm not up for helping revive her. Christ, maybe old Grace can - whoever the hell that is."

Chapter Twenty-One

GRACE

Grace jolted awake. A series of shouts and shrieks, so out of place here on this wing of *The Gardens*, had roused her from a brief nap. *There's a commotion. I can hear it. Good grief. Is that woman, Maude, having another conniption fit? I suspect she is. She's way across the hall and I can hear her hollering from here. What in the hell is wrong with that woman?* Grace's speculating quickly got the best of her; her entire body tensed. *Should I do something?* On the one hand, she so badly wanted to know more and leaned forward, peering at the partially opened door of her apartment as if she might actually be able to observe what she assumed could be Maude's complete and final breakdown. On the other hand . . . well, it was probably better to keep a distance. *Mother told me over and over to stay away from hostile, negative people.*

⌘ ⌘ ⌘

A sudden, unexpected image of Percy Rawling swooped into her consciousness causing her to shiver. It had been during that ill-fateful period of Grace's naïve and impressionable life that Olivia had scolded . . . and she had lectured. In a very un-Olivia-like manner of speaking, her mother had said, "You play with shit, Grace, and you're going to get covered with the nasty mess; it'll stink like the devil. Stay away from that awful man." And although Grace, at the time, had not listened well, she remembered her mother's warning as if she had proffered it only the day before; Olivia's words had become indelible because they were true. It was no wonder that Grace was wary of Maude Litzenberg, the cross and arrogant woman who had taken up residence across the hall. *Maude is angry through and through it seems to me. Why, she was mad as a hornet at her son yesterday, I could tell, and today, well today, right here, after sneaking into my room, she looked fit to be tied. Lordy me. What on Earth is wrong with that woman?*

Grace stood. She sat. She rose again, and then she plopped back down. She gazed at the space before her unseeing, and then seeing, the vision as clear as day. Her mother, Olivia, was standing right in front of her, shaking her finger and chastising, "Don't be a Nosy Parker, Gracie. Nobody likes a busybody."

"But, Mother . . ."

"Don't *Mother* me, young lady."

And Grace was hurled back in time.

⌘ ⌘ ⌘

Sister Mary Theresa glared at Grace. The little girl had turned eleven the week before, and to the nun's way of thinking had returned to school after the weekend a different child. Instead of sitting quietly, hands folded, mouth closed, eyes focused on the chalk board at the front of the room as was required, Grace squirmed in her seat looking right and left, up and down, her hands moving from the desktop to her hair, to her knees, to her lap, to each other, squeezing together until her little knuckles blanched. The nun observed Grace for a full minute. *Why she's like a curious, little monkey, can't sit still . . . ants in her pants.*

Of course, Sister Mary Theresa had no way of knowing that only days before, Grace's mother had divulged to her daughter the saddest tale, along with an ultimatum: "Don't be foolhardy, Gracie. Watch everything that goes on around you. Stay alert. For goodness sake, don't be like Carmine."

So, naturally, the normally obedient, respectful Grace did as her mother had instructed; she became overtly attentive to her surroundings. God forbid, she should end up like Carmine. Her mother's little brother had been killed, crushed like a bug on a busy, city street, because he had been woefully unaware of any hazards in his environment. He had been careless; he had not thought ahead; he had been his own worst enemy. The tragedy had shattered the lives of Carmine's parents, but it had altered his sister, Olivia's life as well, quelling her youthful verve. She immediately understood her duty; she would attend her mother and father as grief consumed them. Beyond that, she vowed to stay alert, to be ever vigilant, and to prepare for the unexpected as her parents had not. In an attempt to control what she could not see coming, Olivia created her own chaos, her mercurial nature feeding into an existence that continued to be wrought with doubts and uncertainties, the majority of her own making. It was as though she felt most comfortable when turmoil of any kind was within a finger's reach.

Olivia had attempted to pass on to her daughter, Grace, the same propensities, beginning on the very day Gracie turned eleven when she warned her to be ever aware of her surroundings, but her effort ran aground, thwarted by an angry nun who harbored her own need to control.

"Grace Brown, what are you doing? And why are you being so nosy? It's none of your business what goes on around you. Don't be a meddler. Sit still. Eyes forward. Behave, you little busybody." Sister Mary Theresa's habit pressed up against Grace's desk so close Grace easily could have studied the tight weave of the black fabric if need be. Instead, she closed her eyes. Myriad odors emanated from the garment: soap, garlic, chalk, musk, and dust. Grace began to cough.

"Stop that. Stop that right now. Straighten up." Sister Mary Theresa placed her hand on Grace's shoulder and held it firmly. She gripped the child with needless force as if daring Grace to move an inch.

As though in obstinate contempt for the nun's demand, Grace began to slide down in her desk, lower and lower until her chin touched the desktop. And then it happened. The sister grabbed Grace by the arm, pulled her from her seat, and marched her to the front of the classroom. She pushed Grace up against the dusty chalkboard and drew a circle on the board. "Put your nosey little nose in that circle. Now."

"But it's too high up."

"Tiptoes, then. Stand on your tiptoes."

"But . . ."

"Not one more word out of you, Grace Brown. Do as I say. You'll stay there until your mother comes to retrieve you and take you home. Poor woman. I have no idea how she puts up with your impudence."

Grace was certain she heard muffled tittering as her classmates looked on behind her.

"Silence. All of you," Sister Mary Theresa admonished.

Not one student made another sound although Grace's ears were filled with it - a thumping, rhythmic whoosh that imitated the rapid beating of her heart. Yet the pulsations were not enough to alleviate the almost palpable burn she felt of thirty-five sets of eyes riveted on her back, all watching to see if the little girl would waver before a parent came to her rescue.

As could have been expected, Olivia Brown kowtowed to Sister Mary Theresa when she entered the classroom to claim her daughter. "I am so sorry, Sister. I don't have an answer for Gracie's poor behavior."

And then she saw her child, face crimson and pressed against the dusty chalkboard, her hands gripping the chalk tray, for balance, for she was on tiptoes. Tiptoes. "What is going on here?" Olivia cheeks bloomed pink and her heartbeat quickened as she lunged toward Grace who nearly collapsed in her mother's arms. "What's going on?" she asked again, the voice lowered this time, almost to a growl.

"Grace was misbehaving terribly. Her punishment was to stand at the board, back to the class." Sister Mary Theresa offered no further explanation.

And Olivia did not ask for more. Instead, she put her arm around Grace and escorted her out of the room in a hurry. Other than the slam of the door behind her, there had been not one other sound.

⌘ ⌘ ⌘

As Grace thought back at the incident, she recalled the humiliation, but more importantly, she remembered her mother's love. In the aftermath, Grace had been allowed to explain her feelings, her reasoning, her actions, and especially her anger at the nun who had abused her in front of her classmates. Olivia had listened well; she had not judged. But she had not let Grace fully off the hook. An apology was written and Grace returned to school the very next day. That was it. End of story . . . although it wasn't, not really, for Sister Mary Theresa lived on in Grace's memory, tormenting her from time to time just as Percy Rawling did in his own annoying way. Grace wondered why those two, in particular, had never left her memory completely.

Isn't it odd about people? Those two. Sister Mary Theresa and Percy Rawling were as different as night and day, and yet, they were the same. At first glance, Percy was handsome and suave, but beneath the skin he was evil, as mean as the devil. And Sister Mary Theresa . . . she bore a veneer of grace and goodness, but underneath, not far from the surface, a ribbon of sheer wickedness ran into her core. Somebody must have hurt them both when they were young because they were damaged goods - deplorable and so godforsaken callous deep down inside. How did it happen? I wonder. And why can't I get rid of them once and for all?

"Oh dear, Grace, stop brooding. It's a mystery. Time to let it go." She murmured the words aloud, but then she was silent, listening. She tilted her head to one side and smiled. She was sure she heard her mother's voice from far in the distance.

Olivia was advising as she always had, "Don't fret, my Gracie. No need to worry. Soon it will be over, the mystery will, and then you'll know. Don't fret, dear Gracie. In the end, everything will be perfectly fine, but until then, be aware. Be mindful. I've warned you to be since you were a child. Eleven." And the voice was gone.

⌘　⌘　⌘

Grace closed her eyes again but only for a moment. Mildred appeared at her door.

"Miss Millie?"

"Oh, Grace. What an afternoon. I might have to lean on you for a little help."

"With Maude." Grace's had not needed to question; she knew the answer.

"You guessed it. She's still asking for you."

⌘   ⌘   ⌘

Maude had been moved from the bed to her chair where she sat erect, chin up, eyes scanning the room as if searching for the unknown. She wore a blue, satin robe and was wrapped in a plush, pink blanket. And in her hand was her designer, patent purse. She was ready to go.

"Finally, you're here," she blurted as Grace walked into the apartment on the arm of Mildred. "It's about time. You can go, Mildred," she added rudely. "I only want to talk to Grace. She's the one. Not you. Now leave us be. We have to make our plans, don't we Grace?"

Grace said nothing. Somewhat bewildered, she glanced at Mildred as if looking for a signal of some kind.

Mildred's expression appeared a bit wounded, but she nodded her head and said, "Let me get you a chair, Grace, so you'll be comfortable. I'll be right outside . . . if you need anything?" The question was a promise. Mildred had no intention of leaving Grace alone with Maude unattended, but she had to be careful. Maude was a tinderbox. She might be perfectly safe if left untouched, but if provoked, she could ignite with fury. So, with game plan intact, Mildred exited the room, but remained stationed right outside the door like a sentry. From her vantage point, she hoped she could hear almost every word the two old women would say to each other; more to the point, however, she would be at Grace's side in a flash if need be. And she would be there for Maude as well. The poor woman was fragile as well as volatile. Whether she cracked into pieces or exploded was anyone's guess. It was going to happen though, one or the other; Mildred was certain of it. And she knew to be watchful.

⌘ ⌘ ⌘

"So, Maude. This day . . ."

Grace's first words were interrupted immediately.

"This day had been horrible, as was yesterday, as was last month, as was last year, as has been my whole damned, miserable life, Grace."

"Now, Maude."

Again, Grace was cut short. "It's true. I have not a friend in the world. Not one. I've been abandoned, you see, and I have nothing. I essentially am nothing." Maude's eyes glistened.

Grace paused, considering an appropriate reply to what she deemed an overly dramatic rant. "I can be your friend," she finally attempted.

A reaction was immediate. "Don't lie to me. Don't you dare! People just lie, lie, lie, lie . . . and I hate liars." Maude face instantly darkened.

Grace was taken aback by not only Maude's bitterness, but by her crazed visage as well. *My heavens, she looks possessed.* Grace felt an instant urge to retreat, and quickly too, but she did not. Miss Millie had asked for her to speak to poor Maude. The last thing she wanted was to let Miss Millie down, so she stayed put. In an effort to elude Maude's obvious near-hysteria however, she softened her voice and tried a new tact. "Miss Millie said you wanted to talk to me, Maude. What did you want to talk about?"

"Miss Millie! I hate that damned name. It's so silly to call an adult woman Miss, isn't it? *Miss Millie*, this and *Miss Millie* that . . . call her Mildred for goodness sake, Grace."

"*Miss Millie* is an endearment, really," Grace tried to explain. "She likes it."

"I don't give a damn what Mildred likes. She's a fake like all the rest of them."

"Like who? What do you mean, Maude?"

"She doesn't care one bit, not one bit, about me. No one ever has. Never. Oh, they pretend to, or pretended to - *Judge*, Henry, that horrible Laura. She was here, you know. Did you see her? The nerve of her . . . and now she's gone . . . taken my grandchildren God only knows where. And where is Henry anyway? Was he here today? Tell me, Grace, was he here today, or was that last week? I've forgotten how long I've been in this godforsaken place. Do you know? I'm so damned discombobulated I don't know where to turn. And I don't know the way. I thought maybe you might help. I thought maybe you could show me the way home. Can you? Could you take me there? Something about your eyes makes me think maybe you could help me break out of this awful asylum and go home where I belong. Can you?"

The look on Maude's face was beyond forlorn; it was stricken. She was afraid, clearly, and so, so sad. Grace was not quite sure what to say or do. *I'll stall until Miss Millie returns. She'll know what to do. I'll just play along for now.* "Before we go anywhere, Maude, can you tell me about Judge? Who's Judge?" she asked. "And Laura?"

That was all it took. A full hour later, Grace knew more than she ever had wanted to know about Maude Litzenberg, but at least she began to understand. Maude laid her history bare, blabbing on about her indifferent, unloving parents, their wealth, her nannies, and her feelings of isolation; she was a very lonely child. But that didn't seem to matter to anyone until she was eight, only eight, and brutally blindsided . . . raped by a kid she didn't even know. She swore it was true, yet Grace had to wonder. *Is it?* Maude was insistent, "I can remember. I can. For the first time in my life, I had everyone's attention, but that didn't help. My life only got worse. I hate to say it, Grace, but sometimes I'm sorry my sordid, damned story didn't stop there."

Oh, Lordy, she sounds so sad. "What happened next?" Grace blurted, suddenly rapt.

"The next thing I knew, my parents sent me off to boarding school, as far away as they could. They didn't want me around, I guess, to remind them that they had a little girl who already was completely ruined," she said, her voice cracking with the word *ruined.* Her arms crossed her body and held there, a protective pose.

Grace waited, her own heart pounding after Maude's reference to rape. *So we do have a connection of sorts, though such a dreadful one.*

"I am smart though." Maude was off again. "After that ridiculous boarding school was finally behind me, I attended Stanford, graduated, and traveled through Europe . . . all by myself." And then Maude admitted a truth. "During those years, I took all of my parents' money I could - and there was a lot - but I virtually was estranged from them. They didn't even want to see me on holidays, Grace. Not even then."

In the end, she made them pay dearly, or so she hoped, although niggling in the back of her mind, was the crushing conviction that until they died, her parents truly could not have cared less. Nevertheless, Maude's attempt at reprisal remained intact. Her folks were informed by phone that she had eloped with a boyfriend they did not know, and later still that she had borne a child. Little, baby Henry was the grandchild they never were permitted to see. Never.

Grace was beginning to think her head might burst with all the crazy history, but she sat quietly and listened more.

"I had no idea how to be a mother," Maude continued, "or a wife, for that matter. *Judge* was a lawyer who was very successful. He shot straight up the ladder in his profession .

. . but the son of a bitch left me behind like an afterthought. And it hurt in more ways than one. I suffered, Grace. I can't begin to tell you."

Grace thought surely Maude was off on another tangent, but she instantly spit out the name one more time.

"*Judge*. His name was David, but to me he was *Judge*. The bastard was a real, honest-to-goodness circuit court judge - smart, successful as hell, but a womanizer, a philandering fool. But he's dead now. Dead as a damned doornail." Maude's mouth twisted into a tight, ugly snarl, trapping her rage for a moment before she carried on. "He was murdered, you know. Shot dead by some maniac in the foyer of our very own home, my *Tara*." And in an instant, Maude switched gears as though *Judge* had never existed at all. "I should tell you about my beautiful house sometime, Grace; it's a mansion, and it's my dream, tucked into the coastal hills. And in front is a huge, huge, willow tree - all my idea - the trunk as wide as a barrel." Maude's eyes beamed to the ceiling and her mouth fell slack. "I just want to go home." Tears welled and slid down onto her wrinkled cheeks where the trapped moisture glistened in the crevices like forgotten diamonds.

"But, Maude, you're safe here," Grace managed.

"I don't give a fig about safe, Grace," she shot back before leaning forward and continuing in a hoarse whisper. "Let's get the hell out of here, Grace, like that crazy Alice, the one that went to Wonderland, or maybe Dorothy who swirled off to Oz to meet the wizard, or better yet, Bonnie and Clyde; wouldn't that be an adventure? Can you shoot a machine gun, Grace?" She paused and smirked at the little woman who was staring at her dumfounded. "Better yet," she said again, "let's get out of town like Thelma and Louise. Remember those two, crazy gals? They were friends like we are now. We are friends, aren't we? Aren't we? So, let's do it. I'll drive and you can go along for the ride. Come on, Grace, let's get out of here, Let's do it, before they take us away for good. You know they're going to do it - lock us up, and throw away the key."

Chapter Twenty-Two

MILDRED

Not often did Mildred think twice about why she still worked at this particular place, at *The Gardens*. After thirty years on the job, however, on this day, one that had been particularly hectic due primarily to dear, cranky, old Maude Litzenberg's never-ending needs, she did. *I've been here a long time.* She felt drained and a tiny bit anxious although she couldn't pinpoint the exact reason why, and no matter really. Her feelings were secondary to her duties and though a few burned-out associates, long gone now, had warned Mildred that she counted too, she shoved that notion aside. *Others first.* She was a caretaker, only months shy of sixty, but she understood as clearly as she breathed, that the role she had assumed as a child was essential to her wellbeing. Nurturing was at the crux of her nature, ensconced like a permanent wrinkle in her character and emblazoned by her practicality. She was a no-nonsense giver, expecting little in return, aside, perhaps, for a smile and a *thank you* once in a while. Her express purpose was focused on tending the elderly folks at *The Gardens*, most of whom, in all likelihood and somewhat sadly, were simply anticipating, or perhaps fearing, the end.

It was late afternoon, when Mildred slumped onto a leather office chair to gather her thoughts, most of which lay comfortably dormant in the back of her mind. A few others, however, had been churning incessantly with nowhere to go. Central to her thinking were three women - Maude, Grace, and Caroline - in particular, Caroline. Though this day had been consumed with the needs of the residents, her sister, Caroline, had been present as well, a bird perched on her shoulder, the claws digging in. *She's sleeping, I'd imagine. She was absolutely exhausted when I left her.* Mildred had placed a call, but the phone had rung and rung. Unanswered. *She'll need me, of course. When the time comes, I'll be there.* And in that sliver of time, Mildred's tension calmed. *Caroline won't mind waiting. I'm where I need to be, doing my job.*

Caregiving, for Mildred, was instinctive, an identity shouldered with a sense of pride. She was good at it. And it filled her up . . . with what? Not happiness exactly, not ecstatic joy, but with something more subtle. She was content. *And isn't that everything?* Contentment was peace. *Contentment is peace. And I'm holding on to it for dear life. No doubt about it, I'm in this job for as long as I physically can manage it. Why for goodness sakes, not having these old folks to take care of, I imagine, just might be the end of me. They give me purpose.* She sighed deeply and stood up, gripping the chair for a brief moment to steady her achy legs. Satisfied she was ready, she then strode back into the hallway ready to meet head-on whatever, the hell, was coming next.

⌘   ⌘   ⌘

Sometimes Mildred felt as though she were herding sheep when it was time to gather the men and women on her wing together for an elevator ride down to the dining area for meals. Left to their own devices, once out of the security of their apartments, three of the four, long-term residents, Lilly, Ralph, and Louie, were apt to wander away in the blink of an eye - Lilly, her skinny fingers flying, meandered the halls and nodded like a parakeet at multiples of anything she thought she could count; Ralph sauntered aimlessly, finally pressing up to any, clear window, standing still as a stump, and scanning the skies for a glimpse of his redeemer, the one he was sure would come take him home; and Louie . . . well, Louie might disappear anywhere. He loved closets and cubicles, the staff and nurses' station, or the small, visitors' waiting room tucked just behind. In this space, without quick intervention, he had been caught more times than Mildred could count, revealing his genitalia, concealed or otherwise, to any individual who noticed him there. Mildred had done her fair share of explaining and apologizing for the old guy's lack of discretion. However, without fail, the unsuspecting observer would blanch in shock or else turn crimson with rage.

"What in the hell is that old fart doing?"

"Gross!"

"Turn your head, Annie. Don't look."

"Oh, for heaven's sakes!"

In every instance, Mildred, or another staffer, hastily scooted Louie out of harm's way, while Louie simply chuckled in the aftermath, delighted that his knack for scandalizing had garnered attention, dubious though it was. In Louie's mind, that was enough. And he gloated. *It doesn't take a genius to see I'm still up to snuff.* Mildred never was able to ascertain if Louie was fully aware of the potential consequences of his lewd, idiosyncratic conduct, but so be it. He was not about to change . . . and he wasn't going anywhere.

"What are they going to do . . . haul me off to the slammer?" Louie had reasoned rather astutely when confronted with his misbehavior. His logic made sense. He was months past eighty-five, too old to prosecute for indecent exposure in a confined and costly, residential setting. And more to the point, he was too ornery to care. Besides, staff members, and residents alike, took Louie's antics in stride. They had learned, with time, to turn a blind eye . . . literally, the choice, plain and simple.

Besides those three characters, Mildred cared for Grace. *Bless her heart.* She was the only resident who, without a word of protest, followed instructions. For years, she had trailed in the shadow of her husband, Frank, following his lead, while still holding his hand. *They were the dearest couple.* After Frank's unexpected death of a rare, coronary embolus, it had taken some time for Grace to find her own way, and she had floundered a bit; yet the little woman knew who she was. *Someone must have set sweet, little Grace on solid ground . . . her mother, perhaps? I've never seen anyone like her, able to roll with the punches no matter how hard the blow.* Mildred had grown in awe of Grace's uncanny ability to cope with change the greatest, of course, being the loss of her husband. In the two years since his death had occurred, Mildred had not been able to strike away the image of Grace and Frank together for the very last time. Frank, the still-handsome, once-robust gentleman, dressed in his signature, satin-lapelled, smoking jacket, dress slacks, and slippers, had died without warning, and without a sound save for one, last, ghastly gasp the moment he expired. Mildred had not been there to hear his last breath, but Grace had, and when she felt she could no longer bear the pain alone, she expressed the horror, albeit through tears, only to Mildred . . . to Miss Millie, the one soul she knew who would care enough to listen.

Mildred had found the two on her evening rounds. Frank, was sitting upright in his leather smoker with the daily news caught in his grip; his head had listed slightly to the left and his eyes, still open, appeared to stare down at Grace, a sunken heap on the floor beside him. She had been motionless as well save for her hand that gently, but ceaselessly, had patted her husband's knee as though she hoped he might revive if touch were enough. But it was not. Frank's body had been escorted out of *The Gardens* a few hours later. Only then had Grace cried, as love and loss, joined as one, intertwining together into the greatest grief she had ever known.

"He was such a lovely man, Miss Millie . . . a stubborn, arrogant bastard who was wonderful and so, so kind. Isn't that a paradox? But he loved me. Frank Ainsworth stole my heart and now, God bless him, he's gone and smashed it into tiny smithereens." She had paused before adding, "I don't know how in the world I'll survive without him."

Mildred had stayed with Grace all night long. After that, the two women were bound inexorably in a friendship that needed not one explanation to anyone.

⌘　⌘　⌘

Mildred thought often about the fragility of life. Of course she did; she lived with it every day. And though loss and grief abounded, not all was sad. On the upside, her experiences at *The Gardens* had afforded her friendships, amusements, challenges, and delights. New residents brought with them families and friends, a carousel of characters rotating through to color each day. Life was interesting at *The Gardens*, stimulating, demanding, and frustrating too. She thought of Maude, the newest, most vexing resident in her care. *Maude.* Mildred was in a quandary about the poor woman. *And where will this story end? I have no idea, but we'll see, won't we, Mildred. It's impossible to know what tomorrow will bring. God only knows what troubles old Maude will get into next.*

And in that very moment, as though fate were a listener, the bellowing scream of a female shattered the silence, the intensity of the screech reverberating against the walls of the hallway. *Maude? Grace? Lilly?* Mildred bolted into a sprint in the direction of the commotion.

Chapter Twenty-Three

MAUDE

Maude screamed. She had not been able to cry for help when she was a terrified eight-year-old, but now, eight decades later, with unrestrained might, she shrieked as loudly as her feeble voice would allow, the sound amazingly strident for such a sad, bewildered, eighty-year-old woman. Her initial reaction upon seeing it, *it* being Louie Lawrence's long, floppy penis, was a pitiful yelp, the sound not much louder than a whisper, but when he ventured through her doorway, grinning from ear to ear like a jovial clown, she let loose with a screech that could have aroused an ancient mummy.

He did not get far. Mildred was upon him like a lioness protecting her cub. "For goodness sakes, Louie, put that thing away and get your butt out of Maude's apartment. Now."

"Ah, Miss Millie, I was just introducing myself. You know I don't mean any harm. I'm all heart." Louie backed into the hallway as he spoke, while at the same time, tucking his personal prize under wraps where it belonged. "You know I'm a lover, not a fighter. Besides, this new gal is a firecracker if I ever saw one." He swiped at his forehead as if checking for fever.

Mildred shook her head. "Louie, settle down. You cannot do this. You cannot. It's harassment, sexual misconduct. Wrong." She guided the old man back to his own apartment, gently shoved him past the doorway into the shadows, and whispered, "That nice woman, who's very dignified and proper, by the way, could press charges if she had a mind to. Do you want that kind of punishment for such foolishness?"

Louie face went slack, his eyes darting. "Well, I'll be damned. That sure would be a revolting comeuppance, now wouldn't it?"

"It would, Louie. So, watch your Ps and Qs. Go lie down now. Get your mind on . . . on something that's not going to get you into a load of trouble. Behave. I need to go back to Maude now. And I mean it, Louie. Stay put."

⌘ ⌘ ⌘

Mildred reached Maude's room at the same moment Grace tipped her head past the edge of the doorjamb of her open door. Her eyes were wide, searching the hallway as she questioned, "What now, Miss Millie? Maude again?"

"Yes. Well, yes and no. It was Louie introducing himself to the poor woman . . . in typical Louie fashion, of course."

"Oh dear, I can imagine," Grace responded. "Louie is quite a pervert, isn't he?"

"Well, he does have his moments. Sorry, Grace, I need to make sure Maude has recovered," Mildred said, somewhat dismissively.

"Do you need my help?"

"Oh, no, Grace. You've done enough for Maude today. My heavens, you were with her for over an hour."

"I was, and what an hour that turned out to be. I'll have to fill you in later, Miss Millie. That Maude is wound up like a ten-day clock."

"Yes she is. I bet you got quite an earful. I admit I was privy to a bit of the conversation from out in the hallway. We'll talk later. Rest now, honey. Dinnertime will be here before you know it." Mildred turned her back on Grace then and walked to Maude's door. She tapped lightly before stepping forward.

⌘　⌘　⌘

Maude was sitting in her chair, the pink blanket wrapped tightly around her in cocoon-like fashion. Her dark eyes glared.

"Took you long enough," she snarled. "But at least you found me this time."

"Well, of course, I found you," Mildred answered, ignoring Maude's barb, the reference to *this time* not, of course, registering at all. She expected another retort, but Maude grew silent, the features of her face almost visibly tightening. *She's brooding again . . . about Louie? The past? Her future? I have no idea.* Mildred could only carry on, and in doing so she feigned normality, though instinctively she knew it was an abject attempt at best.

"How are we feeling, Maude? Better this afternoon? Are you less groggy than you were earlier? Some darn medications can take their sweet time wearing off, can't they? I see you had a nice, long chat with Grace. Did you enjoy that? She's such a sweet person, isn't she? Are you feeling more comfortable around her now that you're better acquainted?" Mildred peppered Maude with arbitrary questions, not really expecting a reaction, much less an answer. Her one-sided conversation filled the air, however, and she hoped it would detract from any lingering retention of Louie Lawrence's wayward intrusion. She was to be sorely disappointed.

"Who was that man?" Maude suddenly blurted.

"Who do you mean?" Mildred was careful.

"I mean that man who accosted me. You know he was up to no good, don't you? He and that god-awful organ of his were up to no good. Who was he, and where is he now? He got away, didn't he, just like last time. I knew it. They always get away." Maude tugged at the edges of the blanket pulling it tighter.

"That was Mr. Lawrence, Maude. He's a resident here."

"Well, he needs to have his head examined." Maude paused a moment before her carping continued. " I had no idea you allowed deviants and hooligans to live here, right here on this property next to civil individuals like myself. Have you lost your good senses, Mildred? Have you no standards whatsoever?"

Mildred could have responded, but she thought better of it. Instead, she bit her tongue, literally, her teeth digging into the tender flesh. *I'm not in charge here, Maude. I'm an employee, just a worker, trying to take care of folks, and it sure as hell isn't easy coping with the likes of you.* Unexpected anger bubbled inside, but Mildred quashed it in an instant. She had no intention of provoking an argument that surely would further incense Maude, so she stood silently by, although the woman's antagonistic words still stung like a flat-handed slap in the face. *What a piece of work.*

Maude closed her eyes. What she could not see would not bother her. Right? That included the awful Lawrence man as well as Mildred who stood by, hovering. Maude could feel her presence, unwelcome, annoying. *Go away!* The desire to shout out had never felt so real, but the words fell silent, lodged in the back of her throat like a lump of vile and smothering sputum. She swallowed hard. *If I keep my eyes closed, will she disappear?* Maude wanted nothing more. It had worked before . . .with her parents, with Henry, with Judge. Met with any confrontation, real or imagined, from the time she was a child until this very moment, she simply had closed her eyes, silenced her words, and stopped even the slightest movement. She had learned over time to become stone - hard, unfeeling, and heartless. It was her salvation. An escape. A distraction. In a world that always had been baffling and for Maude, profoundly unkind, softer sentiments were not to be tolerated. Anger and incivility had become her coat of armor. How else would she survive?

Minutes passed. Maude was steel. And in time, she was rewarded for her stalwart callousness. She heard a rustling, the tap of a heel, a sigh. Mildred, *Miss Millie,* Maude was certain, had walked out of the room without a word. Silence. *Blessed silence.* Now she would wait, but not for long. *Is Grace coming? If she is, she'd better hurry. I can't postpone this journey for long. What would be the point? My heavens, really, why wait at all?* Whether her newfound friend accompanied her or not, Maude's mind, as fuzzy as it had become, was made up; she knew exactly what she planned to do. She would not waver. *No mam, I'm not shillyshallying, not any more.*

Chapter Twenty-Four

HENRY

Henry stared at his wife. Who was she? He wasn't sure he knew any more. Laura certainly was not the idealistic, young woman he had met years before on the steps of Berkeley's Sproul Hall, the girl he had loved from his first glimpse of her, blond hair shimmering in the waning, California sunlight. No, she was not that girl, for she had grown up, not in the *Where-have-the-years-gone?* kind of way, but in a more profound sense. She had matured, and she had hardened, the years and experiences of their lives layered on like coats of lead paint. Henry's thoughts flipped back across time. *Damn, she's plowed through it all: Mother's venomous first reaction to her, followed by rude, annoying, ongoing hostility - continuous salt to the wounds; my bull-headed, opinionated father whose pretentious, inflated ego cost him royally. Will any of us forget Judge's gruesome murder? Hell, Laura witnessed that shit first hand. Plus, us: my career, demanding as hell, not to mention our own ups and downs. The births of our kids weren't a party for Laura. Long labors. Difficult. And so soon after were her parents' drowning, their skiff yanked out to sea by an ill-timed, sneaker wave - too young, but so long ago. And now Maude's latest antics are dragging us along into her personal hell. No wonder Laura is cynical sometimes. Life sure has thrown enough crap our way.*

His gaze had not left her. Even with all the history, she was still beautiful, a sometimes toxic, enigmatic woman who still made his hands sweat, who could not be put in a labeled box, who loved him, and their children, with un-wavering vivacity, and who spoke her mind, lacing her ver-nacular with profanity befitting the crew of a frigate.

"I can't help myself, damn it," she had told him many times. "A little swearing just fucking works." He had learned early on not to disagree, and furthermore, not to judge. His lovely Laura was not going to change.

And he was stuck with her, having lived for twenty years in the most wonderfully insane and yet perfectly seamless relationship he could imagine. She was an absolute walk-ing, talking paradox – stunning, devoted, energetic, unpre-dictable, headstrong, and dreadfully candid. She had never let Henry escape from facing himself head on, as she did this day.

"So what the hell are you going to do, Henry? Your mother is most certainly losing her shit. Seriously."

"I'll go there tomorrow."

"Henry."

"I'll go tomorrow. She'll be okay. She has people looking after her. Besides, I don't want to be spat on," he chuckled.

"Oh for fuck's sake, Henry." But she grinned anyway and returned a snicker. Having Maude spit at her earlier that day had been maddening. It felt good to make light of it for a moment though she felt slightly guilty in doing so, for Henry's mother was in a serious decline; the situation was not going to improve. Laura was sure of it.

⌘ ⌘ ⌘

At eight thirty the call came. Henry's cellphone vibrated on the kitchen counter as it moaned *Taps* out into the room.

"Better get the damned thing, Henry. It's probably a client, or someone from *The Gardens*, or God forbid, your mother."

Henry reluctantly moved toward the phone, read the screen, *Unknown Caller*. He left it untouched.

Two minutes later, it rang again. *Unknown Caller*.

"These damned robocalls!"

"Answer the damned thing, Henry. Tell them to go to hell. Whoever it is will keep calling otherwise."

He rolled his eyes, picked up the phone, and snapped, "Who the hell is this?"

Silence.

"Oh, for God's sake. I'm on my way."

Chapter Twenty-Five

GRACE

The dining hall uncharacteristically hummed with conversation when Grace reached her corner table in the early evening. She slid into her chair and sat, back to the wall, surveying the room as she often did to see who was absent, who was a newcomer, who was chatty, who had fallen silent, and who didn't appear to know where they were at all. Those, the feeblest ones, almost took her breath away. *Why have they been the chosen ones to end up this way with their skeletal bodies harnessed into wheelchairs, their teary eyes unfocused or lids closing? And what are they thinking? Or are they? Are there memories inside? Surely there are, but I wonder.* She felt oddly lucky, at eighty-eight, to be cognizant, still, of the world around her. *Though you do have your moments, don't you, Grace?* A tiny smile played at her lips.

⌘ ⌘ ⌘

The residents from her wing had trudged into the room together but had parted immediately - Lilly to a table with equally silent seniors, all, more likely than not, counting the hours; Ralph to his chapel mates, the balding lot bowing in prayer; and lecherous, old Louie to a group of giddy women who blushed when they saw him saunter over their way. He was a nuisance, they all knew it, but he was attentive and gregarious, his catalogue of compliments expansive and colorful. Grace had watched the interactions from afar, not wanting to judge, but falling into the trap anyway. *That Louie is quite the degenerate. Lordy me. Those silly ladies need the attention, I guess. For heavens sake, they're carrying on as if they were teenagers again. Good grief.*

Grace watched the goings-on for only a few minutes before she grew bored and irked by the foolishness playing out before her. It was solely her opinion, of course, that the behavior was foolish. She was well aware of that. Simply being a watcher, however, made her uncomfortable and she recognized why. She comprehended fully her innate preference for quiet and reserve. She squirmed in her chair and glanced away from Louie and his court of blue, white, and grey-haired octogenarians. Meaningless chitchat and pointless banter such as theirs annoyed her primarily because she was not good at it; such interactions gutted her energy and depleted her spirit. She'd rather be alone. Such a predisposition had been hers for a lifetime and she knew why. Olivia. Her mother. Olivia Graci Brown's mercurial nature, her dramatization of even the most mundane of events, and her proclivity for rash behavior and reckless repartee had become a model, for Grace, of what she did not want to become. Oh, she loved her mother dearly, and even attempted to emulate her softer side, but when Olivia's impulses got the best of her, Grace wanted to hide.

⌘ ⌘ ⌘

Lovely Olivia, at times, lost all sense of control. She knew it . . . and she was oddly stimulated by it. In fact, it was natural for her, as familiar as her reflection captured in a mirror. The trouble was, she did not always see it coming. When circumstances provoked her though, she became hell bent on setting things right . . . on her terms. And pity the poor soul who got in her way. Such had been the case since adolescence, since the death of her little brother, Carmine, since her mother's silent withdrawal, but more to the point, since the revelation from her father, Giovanni, that she was not his child. Crushed with grief over the loss of his only son, Giovanni had lashed out, first at his wife, Sophia, with a stinging, flat-handed slap to her face and an abusive curse, "*Puttana*! Why did you not watch my son more closely?"

When his menacing hand rose again, Olivia jumped to her mother's defense. "*Babbo*! Father, stop." She grabbed his arm, her fingernails digging in, and forced her slight body between the short, plumpish figure of her stricken mother and the angry hulk whose black pupils glinted fire and tears.

"Move away, *cagna*," Giovanni ordered.

"I will not . . . and you will not call me a bitch. I am your daughter, *tua figlia*." Olivia's dark eyes glared in defiance.

"Ha!" he snorted. "You are not. You are not my daughter. I have no daughter. Never in my life have I had a daughter." Spittle gathered at the corners of his mouth. "Ask your mother. Ask her." He pointed at Sophia with a fat, quivering finger before deliberately spitting a mass of bloody mucus onto the floor. He stood for a moment, his body shaking, his eyes darting as if he were trapped . . . and he bolted from the restaurant kitchen into the alley, and then onto Mulberry Street, disappearing into a motley crowd of laborers and domestics trudging toward home.

Olivia swirled around to face her mother whose cheek bore the red outline of Giovanni's thick hand. "What is he saying, *Mamma?*" she squeaked, for her voice had failed her in the aftermath of the hideous disclosure. Her stomach lurched.

Sophia lowered her eyes and clinched her hands into tight fists; her shoulders slumped forward. She finally grabbed ahold of the back of a flimsy, wooden chair for support, but she said nothing.

Olivia tried once more. "What is he saying, *Mamma?* What did he mean?" This time her tone was firm, cold, and sonorous, defying the queasy feelings deep inside and disregarding a pounding heart. She waited, agitated by her mother's silence. Her skin began to tingle as if it crawled with an alien, disgusting vermin that had appeared out of nowhere. "*Mamma?*"

At last Olivia learned the truth. "Gio, Giovanni is your father, Olivia, but he is not your father." Sophia's voice was flat, controlled. She paused.

"What are you saying? How can that be?"

"You are the child of Angel, Angel Graci, your father's brother. I loved him very much." She sighed. "But he left me when he discovered I was pregnant. And your father, your uncle really, took care of me. He took me in. He made me his wife, and quickly too, to save me from humiliation and shame that surely would have been my fate had he not legitimized your birth. Giovanni loved me, you see, all along, but I had been blinded by my own infatuation, my own lust, and my own recklessness. I owe your father everything."

"And Angel, this father of mine, where is he?"

"I do not know. When we left for America, he already had traveled to Rome. That is all I know. That is all I will say. There is nothing else. Do not ask more of me. I have no answers. I understand nothing of this life." It was Sophia's haunting truth, revealed in halting, broken English. The only sound that followed was a wretched groan. Sophia's hand rose to her face, her fingers pressing delicately on the swollen, crimson welt blooming on her cheek.

Olivia stared at her mother as if she had never known her, and perhaps that was accurate. *How could my mother hide such a secret? How could she? And he? Father. Now I understand. No wonder he has never loved me. He resented me. No wonder he has been distant, detached, and mean. Always. No wonder. I'm not his. I've never been his.* And yet, though her thoughts tormented her, in her father's, *her uncle's*, footsteps, Olivia fled from the restaurant into the busy street where she walked alone amid an undulating mass of humanity, an aching heart the only suggestion that she was still alive.

⌘ ⌘ ⌘

Grace had no idea about this history, about the source of her mother's angst and volatility, until much later, in the waning days of Olivia's life . . . and no matter really, because, for Grace, her knowledge of the woman's complicated past would not have changed a thing. Her mother was, most definitely, untamable, unapologetic, and most importantly unforgettable . . . as she was now, having maneuvered her way into Grace's thoughts like an illicit, crime boss. Just like that, in the dining hall of *The Gardens*, Olivia appeared and Grace became a child again, cowering in an alcove at the top of the staircase as another drama played out, the scene directed and choreographed by her very own mother - one more time.

It was not surprising. Grace heard her mother scream a string of obscenities, all in Italian, before throwing something - in this case a cast iron skillet - against the wall. Only moments before the only sounds resonating throughout the house had been the lively, Baroque timbres of Vivaldi, Olivia's favorite composer, and appropriately so, as his exuberant, flamboyant style was a perfect fit to her own. But poor Antonio was cut short, the cord from the radio ripped from the wall socket.

"Enough of you." Grace heard her mother yell. "And you too, Gilbert. How dare you sneak home early, tracking that damned, sticky mortar with you, and scaring the living daylights out of me."

Grace's father, Gilbert Brown, was a robust, hard-working mason, renowned for his skill, a talent sought out by folks of great economic means. He never lacked work, laboring well into the evenings and earning more than enough money to keep his beautiful wife, Olivia, and his little girl, Grace, comfortable and secure. They lacked for nothing and the love the three shared was impenetrable, or so they assumed.

"Why are you home so early, for God's sake?" Olivia shouted again, pushing her husband back out the front door and onto the brick porch. "Take off those filthy shoes. Look at you." She shoved him gently, but he fell backwards, his head banging into the stucco wall. He staggered forward, kneeled down, and on all fours, began to retch.

"Gilbert? What in the hell is wrong with you?"

"Sick," he mumbled. Strings of bile-colored vomit slid onto the bricks and settled between his wide, calloused hands.

Olivia stopped short. She reached for Gilbert's cheeks and forehead. "You are. You are. You're burning up with fever." Olivia yanked at his shoes, tossed them aside, and attempted to lift her husband. He was dead weight.

"Come on. We need to get you inside. Help me."

Gilbert struggled, and though unsteady, was able to stand upright. Using all the strength she had, Olivia guided him to their bedroom, turned down the blankets, and helped him into bed. He fell into a restless sleep, his head lolling from side to side as though some demon inside was denying him precious rest. He lay in bed, oozing perspiration while, at the same time, shivering in uncontrollable spasms. His chest heaved.

Olivia convinced herself that Gilbert would feel better by morning. *He's strong. He just needs sleep. Tomorrow he will be back to normal.* She was wrong. In the afternoon of the following day, his fever spiked even higher and he was whisked away by ambulance to a local, city-run hospital; in the evening, while Olivia dozed in a chair beside his bed, his condition worsened until it was too late. No manner of close monitoring had been enough. Only minutes before sunrise, he was gone. The official cause of death, Olivia was informed after a state-ordered autopsy, was organ failure, all due to a bacterial infection, a complication of the pneumonia that had been diagnosed shortly after his admittance. In all the time since he had slipped into that agitated sleep the day before, he never awoke, falling instead into an unconscious stupor.

There had been no time for good-byes.

Olivia handled her grief as only she could. She scrawled her signature on the necessary death documents, ordered a cremation, gathered her sleepy daughter from a neighbor, and walked into an empty house.

"Go to sleep, Gracie."

Grace looked at her wide-eyed. "I can't."

"Try. For God's sake, try." The anguish in her mother's face was a warning to obey.

Grace trudged to her bedroom, lay on her bed, but did not sleep. She would not have been able to anyway, because all hell broke loose. Downstairs, Olivia's shock, her sadness, her utter devastation gave rise to chaos only she could create. She took every plate and bowl, every piece of glassware, and every precious item of crystal she could amass, stacked them on the kitchen table, and one by one, threw them against the wall. Each time she hurled a glass or china plate, she either shouted a curse or internalized a prayer. She threw until she was exhausted. And then she stood back. The pile of broken glass, china, ceramics, and crystal, slumped into a perfect angle of repose, was five feet wide and crawled up the wall to a precarious peak. She surveyed the destruction and was satisfied, for it emulated the person she was at that moment - broken, completely shattered, her heart cracked in two. Tears welled and she sobbed for long minutes . . . and then it was over.

⌘ ⌘ ⌘

She began picking up the pieces - every last fragment. When, at last, she was finished, she turned in a full circle before climbing into her bed, the clammy sheets still damp with the sweat of her dead husband.

Grace, startled by the commotion, had peered down from her vantage point, but she had made not a sound. She had not been afraid, only mystified by her mother's crazed behavior. In the days that followed, Olivia was distant, and yet she was close by. She purchased new dishes, polished and cleaned, and kept an eagle eye on Grace, who it was obvious, was heartbroken too. The two went for silent walks and had quiet meals together; conversation was sparse, but through it all, they managed to create for themselves what became a new normal - an existence without Gilbert. The only thing that remained the same in their home was Vivaldi, the sounds of his violin seeming to career off the walls from morning until night. And in that, Grace found comfort. Life would never be the same, but it was as it should be for Mother and daughter were inexorably connected by love. Perhaps it was for that reason that neither Olivia nor Grace ever mentioned Olivia's miserable, broken-hearted tirade again. If the truth were told, however, neither forgot about it either.

⌘　⌘　⌘

"Grace, you haven't touched a bite of your dinner." Mildred had scooted up to Grace's table in the dining hall.

"Oh, Miss Millie, I've been so distracted. My mother visits at the most confounding times."

"Grace?" Mildred was concerned.

"It's okay, Miss Millie. I'll eat my dinner, cold though it must be. And don't worry. I haven't gone bonkers. It's just that my mother was such a presence in real life; she was so formidable that when I think about her it's as if she's here in the flesh. My recollections of her are that real. It's really quite extraordinary. Lordy, Miss Millie, what's an old woman to do when memories come creeping in like they're thieves in the dark? Ignore them?"

Millie chuckled. "I don't have a clue what to tell you, Grace. It is a definite conundrum, I suppose."

"Indeed, it is," Grace replied, shaking her head as if to dispel her thoughts while absently poking at the mound of cold, mashed potatoes and gravy congealing on her plate.

"Well, finish quickly, Grace. Our little group of residents should head back upstairs together. Don't you think?" Mildred glanced around the room. "Oh dear, that Louie. He's holding court again."

"He certainly is, Miss Millie. That, on the heels of nearly giving poor Maude a heart attack earlier today." Grace took a few bites. She frowned. "Maude didn't miss a thing with this dinner. If she were here, she'd be throwing her usual conniption fit. You can bet your bottom dollar about that. I can imagine her ranting right now - 'For God's sake, what kind of an entrée is this disgusting mess?'" Grace paused. "Is she doing better?"

"I hope so. We let her rest rather than come down to dinner tonight. I'll make sure she's settled in for the night before I go home. My sister, Caroline, is probably wondering what's become of me."

With her mind focused on her sister, Mildred was unaware, at that moment, of what had transpired upstairs. Who ever could have imagined?

Chapter Twenty-Six

MILDRED

Mildred's wait at the elevator for the residents that resided on the fourth floor wing - *her residents, her darlings* - took much longer than she had anticipated, but she knew to be patient. Every one of them moved slowly in practically every aspect of their lives, from walking to chewing, from talking to simply standing up to go somewhere. Bath times and toilet visits often stretched into many minutes. Schedules for doctors' appointments, therapy sessions, meals, or visits from family members (if an elder was so fortunate) frequently became extended affairs. And other issues slowed them down: poor hearing, failing eyesight, incontinence, instability, forgetfulness, and even social and emotional regression. It sometimes felt to Mildred, as if fate was playing a cruel joke on the seniors in her care. *Why is this thing called life being dragged out for so long?* She silently scolded herself when such thoughts flashed into her mind, however. *How callous of me.* She was far from unfeeling, but she always had been a go-getter, a get-things-done-with-expedience kind of woman. Patience, early on, in the elder community had been a challenge. But in time, she learned, and even chuckled when she remembered how she had behaved in her first months at *The Gardens.* Her tolerance for the slothful movements of the residents had made her anxious. *Come on, people, let's go. Get a move on.* She had caught herself, more than once, tapping her foot impatiently or sighing in exasperation, but as she became more experienced, more accepting, and more understanding, her attitude changed. Her awareness of her residents' needs, as well as a clear perception of right and wrong, allowed her to grow into a most beloved caretaker. Besides, she was acutely cognizant of the fact that her birthdays had come and gone as well. *You're no spring chicken yourself, Mildred. Old age is right around the corner. Better be ready to embrace it.*

So, she waited . . . and waited. *These dear old folks have a right to carry on for as long as they can.* That thought led directly into another. *They do, because some people don't have such an opportunity.* Her nephew, Adam, came to mind although she had no visual of him. She had not seen him since he was a young boy, a very troubled young boy, who grew up to make all the wrong choices, it seemed. *Adam. Thirty-seven. Dead. And Caroline?* Mildred recognized instantly that her sister was a shell of a woman now that her son had succumbed to drug addiction. How would she manage her life now that her man-child could no longer drag her along? Caroline had been Adam's puppet, and surely had been manipulated until she finally was dropped, alone, in broken pieces. Mildred felt her throat tighten as she thought of Caroline, now, still safely sleeping, she hoped, at home. *Home. I need to get there. Caroline must be wondering where I am.* A tiny flurry of impatience caused Mildred to take a few steps forward into the dining room. She motioned to Grace and then to Louie, who reluctantly sauntered over to her, leaving four adoring women behind. Grace fetched Lilly, and then touched Ralph on the arm.

"Come on. Miss Millie is waiting. We need to go now."

"Thank you, Grace," Mildred acknowledged when the foursome was beside her. Then to the others, she shared, "We need to get you all settled upstairs. And then, I need to hurry home. My sister surprised me, arriving last night for a visit. Now, won't that be nice?"

Mildred's comment dropped like a lead balloon. Not one of the four responded in any way - not a gesture, not a facial expression, not a word.

Chapter Twenty-Seven

MAUDE

Maude listened for any hint of movement nearby or outside in the hallway, but she heard nothing. She was certain she had heard Millie's voice some distance away, near the elevator, perhaps, only minutes before, but now the fourth-floor wing was as silent as a tomb. *Perfect. Finally they've all gone away and left me alone. I can pack up and go.* She opened her eyes and stared into the dimly lit space before her. *At least someone left a light on, but where is it coming from, and what, in heaven's name, is that?* Maude started. "Judge, is that you?" she squeaked.

She pulled her plush, pink blanket more closely around her shoulders with one hand but extended the other in front of her, reaching, reaching. "How did you get in here?" she whispered. Her long, boney fingers grabbed at the air an arm's length from her face, as the phantom in her sights retreated to a far corner of the room.

"It's you, isn't it?" She was sure; her Judge had come back for her, finally, and just in time. She wouldn't have to travel alone after all. *To hell with that silly, Grace woman. I don't need her after all, do I? I sure as hell don't, not with Judge back with me. Why, look at that, Maude, he's come back just like that, out of the blue, to be with you . . . with you.* Maude's imaginings caused her to blush with unexpected pleasure. *We must go, and quickly too before someone finds us together.*

Maude stood up slowly. Her head pounded and she wobbled unsteadily, but she did not look away from the specter in the corner. *Have to keep my eye on you, Judge. Otherwise, you'll run out on me again, just like you've done a million times. Not this time, you heartless bastard.* She glared at him. His eyes were red-rimmed and weepy and though he stood erect, his broad shoulders thrown back, she could see right through him, literally. A large, gaping, blood-crusted hole in his chest exposed a cracked pane in her apartment window directly behind him. Beyond the glass the sky was gray, dusky, any sun obscured by dark clouds. It had begun to rain.

"It must be time," she murmured to her dead Judge. "We'll have to hurry once we're on the road though, so we don't get wet. It's raining now. Can you hear the patter? But don't worry. I'll be set to go in a jiffy. I won't be taking much with me - nothing much to carry. You'll see. Are you listening, Judge? Damn it, Judge Are you ready?"

⌘ ⌘ ⌘

Maude's drenched and rumpled body was found, by chance, four blocks from *The Gardens*. A young soldier and his German shepherd stumbled upon her as they ran home after their evening jaunt around the neighborhood. She was lying prone, and barely visible, beneath a water-sodden pine tree. Wrapped in a soaking wet, fur coat, she wore a knitted, cloche hat, and clutched a leather handbag filled, it later was revealed, with crumpled, dollar bills, a few coins, a used-up lipstick, and a lace handkerchief. That was all. The man who discovered her had thought, at first, that the body was a corpse, but he instinctively reached for her pulse, and finding a very weak one, called 911 on his cell phone. The police, having been notified earlier that an elderly woman had disappeared that evening from a nearby senior, residential community, were upon the site in only minutes. Paramedics in the ambulance that had followed them whisked the clammy, unconscious Maude back to *The Gardens* and to the anxious, medical staff waiting for her return.

"The guy who found Ms. Litzenberg is a hero, I can tell you," the physician's assistant told a pale, stony-faced Henry Litzenberg who stood waiting alone in the hallway outside the examination room. "An hour more and your mother, as elderly as she is, could have perished from exposure, out in a storm like this. She's very lucky, and I might add, so are you."

"Yeah," Henry managed. *Lucky? I'm not so sure about that. Life without Mother sure would be less complicated. Christ, she's becoming a constant burden. I should be home with Laura and the kids right now . . . not here dealing with this mess.* The accuracy of his thoughts engendered a sliver of guilt that Henry managed to quash in an instant. He jammed his hands in his pockets and stood in awkward silence until he was allowed in, at last, for a look, and perhaps a word, with his mother.

She lay in the bed amid a mass of tubes and humming, monitoring equipment. Her dark hair stuck out in tufts beneath a gauze beanie that had been pulled down on her head like a helmet. The fabric almost touched Maude's arched, thick, black brows that, for Henry, always had been emblematic of her haughty, hateful nature. In his youth, she simply had needed to raise one eyebrow a millimeter for him to know he was in trouble. Now, however, at least for the moment, she appeared quite benign. She had been covered with several, hospital-green blankets, all stretched across her body and tucked securely beneath the mattress. Although Maude was not a diminutive woman, she looked tiny and frail - a porcelain doll ready to crack in pieces if shifted the wrong way. Henry shuffled his feet nervously, his thoughts overwhelming him. *Is she ready to die? Was that her plan? Did she want to end it all tonight, alone, outside in the rain? Is that what she wanted? Was suicide her intention?* Henry swallowed hard. He had to assume the answer was *no* but watching her now, in her current condition, he was far from certain. The significance of Maude's clandestine escape from *The Gardens* only hours before made it clear that she did not want to be there, not that she hadn't already made that fact apparent to Henry and to any other poor soul who had ventured near her since her intake there. Her fury at having been brought to this *place* to live *forever* had whipped up a maelstrom of hostility no one had been able to avoid. Henry had lost count of the myriad ways she had said, in essence, "What have you done to me, Henry, you cutthroat? You know, the last thing I want is to live in this awful place."

But did she actually want to live at all? Henry could only speculate. *What's going to happen when she awakes? She may be livid to find herself alive, still breathing in and out, in and out, as she has for a lifetime; she may resent having to carry on at all.* Clearly, his poor mother had not been pleased about life's most recent, confounding detour, the one that had placed her right smack dab in the center of *The Gardens*. He knew it. He had engineered it. But he also knew Maude's power and her dogged determination. She had fought back, against him, against the system in the only way she knew how. She was old, confused, and angry as hell, but that had not stopped her. She had devised her own plan to change the dynamics of her life and she had acted on it. *I can't believe she was that desperate. And I sure as hell don't understand the tipping point. For Christ's sake, she almost lost it all.*

Henry was staring at her, lost in thought, when she began to stir. She opened her eyes, raised one eyebrow, and spat out, in perfect Maude-like fashion, "What in the devil are you doing here, Henry? And for heaven's sake, where have you hidden my Judge?"

Chapter Twenty-Eight

HENRY

It had taken Henry, an orderly, and the physician's assistant, all working in tandem to calm Maude Litzenberg's hysteria when she understood that her husband, Judge, was not at the residence with her.

"I can't see Judge anywhere," she had cried, tossing her head from side to side on the pillow. "How could he disappear just like that? And without a word."

"Judge is gone, Mother. He's been gone for years. Can't you remember?" Henry was careful, attempting to reason, not wanting to frighten her with details of the man's ghastly murder years before.

"Don't lie to me, Henry," Maude yelled. "Judge most definitely was here, in my apartment tonight with me - the two of us. He must have known I needed him so he came to be with me." She stopped, calmed. "Bless his heart. I talked to him, Henry, at length." Her eyes were teary. And then she paused once more. Looking around the room as if searching, searching, her body tensed; her expression grew stern, anxious. And in that moment, in a more plaintive voice, she whined, "Is he cheating again? Is it Grace? Has he taken up with that woman now, for heaven's sake? Is that where he's gone?"

Henry held his breath. *I'll be damned. Though she can't recall much of anything else, she remembers Judge's unfaithfulness. But, then, how could she, or anyone else for that matter, forget that - the philandering fool?*

Maude grew quiet again and then, without warning, launched into a tirade of profanity that shocked even Henry. *Where in the hell did she learn these words?* "You fucking son of a bitch, Judge. You did it again, didn't you, you damned, deceitful bastard. Show up, act syrupy sweet, and then disappear probably with some hussy with an enormous, damned bosom. You've always admired *that*. I've never been enough for you, have I, you jack ass?"

And then she turned on Henry. "And you, you little ass wipe. You're nothing but a damned punk for leaving me in this shit hole. You can go to hell, too, you filthy piece of dung."

A sedative did the job. When at last, Maude's eyes were glassy and her lids closed, her mouth was mercifully silent. Henry sank down in a chair next to his mother's bed and put his head in his hands. He had known for months that his mother had been growing more and more confused - losing her purse, her keys, the way to the kitchen; forgetting words, doctor's appointments, the day of the week, her granddaughter's name; neglecting to pay bills, to bathe, to eat, to urinate in time - all, all of these lapses had occurred. For several years after Judge's murder, Maude had managed on her own. She had found joy in her garden, her reading, and some friends, but as the years passed, she became more reclusive, settling for short walks and simple meals alone, watching decade-old movies on television for hours on end, or pounding out old songs on a piano dreadfully out of tune. For many months, Maude's had been in a slow, downward spiral, nothing unusual, no cause for concern, but when her hygiene and memory noticeably failed, Henry had taken measures to move her to *The Gardens.* He had done so to be kind, to assure her safety, to show her she was loved. *And in two, fucking days, everything has backfired. She's completely lost it. How did it come to this . . . to this . . . so fast?* He wanted to throw up.

⌘　⌘　⌘

At home, long after he had left his sedated mother in the care of *The Gardens'* staff, Henry sank into a thick, leather recliner and pulled an ancient, plaid blanket up to his neck. He had flicked on the electric fireplace, and the fake logs glowed with tepid heat, but the would-be setting of warmth and comfort mocked him. He was far from relaxed. In fact, he had not felt this edgy since the stressful, first days when he had huddled under scratchy, army-issue blankets at the military school his parents had forced him to attend decades ago. *What a paradox. When I was a kid, Mother had me shipped off to military school . . . to get me out of the way. And now that she's old, I've paid old Maude back. I have, haven't I? I've imposed an ultimatum for her to live out her days in a retirement home she hates. No wonder she's so angry and confused. I guess I would be too.* A twinge of guilt twisted his gut. *But it's in her best interest to be there.*

Henry shivered, deep to his core, as an uneasy feeling of impending and deepening troubles squeezed down on his shoulders like a vice. The ride home from *The Gardens* had been hairy, the wind howling and the rain battering the front windshield of his car. The wipers had not been able to keep up with the torrent, leaving Henry fearful he would lose control. He had not been able to see five feet in front of the car, but he had made it, driving, fingers gripping the steering wheel, up to a house that was pitch-dark save for one, lone, flickering porch light that Laura had left on, probably as a afterthought. At least it was something.

He had hoped she'd be waiting for him, perhaps interested in hearing about, and certainly weighing in on, her mother-in-law's latest fiasco. That had not been the case, however. When Henry finally had slipped into their darkened bedroom, he could hear Laura's familiar, low, ragged snore. She had given up on him. Though he had longed to climb into bed beside her for comfort, for warmth, he did not, stepping, instead, out of his damp clothes and into a pair of comfy, Nike sweats and his worn pair of Uggs. He moved down the stairs of their home like a thief, feeling his way into the family room where he was now, musing about the past and speculating about what, the hell, was going to happen next.

He had poured himself a hefty glass of bourbon and water and sipped it as if were nature's finest nectar. *God this shit tastes good.* For all his adult years, Henry had enjoyed his booze. He drank too much of it, he knew, but his increase in consumption had started only after the gruesome murder of his father right in front of him, not to mention, within the horrified sight of Laura and his mother. He allowed himself the comfort of alcohol, he reasoned, to deaden the pain and to suppress the memory, although in actuality, it did neither. Ironically, more often than not, a bout of moderate drinking intensified not only his recollection of the horrific homicide, but also the personal, emotional baggage that had become an integral part of it. *I didn't do enough to stop the carnage. I betrayed my father and failed everyone - Mother, Laura, myself.* The awful mantra became Henry's burden and it never had diminished even though intellectually he understood that his father's true character was clearly more likely the culprit for his untimely slaying.

His father had been a son of a bitch to both Henry and Maude. Although he had provided for them financially, he had toyed with their psyches and scarred them so emotionally, it had paralyzed Maude and caused Henry to flee. Distance from family had become Henry's salvation. Fortunately, for the most part, David Litzenberg left his son alone once he was in college. Only in one arena was that not the case. Judge Litzenberg had been arrogant enough to be absolutely confident that Henry would follow in his professional footsteps. Any consideration of his son not attending law school had been out of the question.

"Certainly the boy won't reach my heights as a distinguished judge, Maude, but he'll be a decent lawyer. I'll see to it." Henry had overheard the comment early on, and it had stuck with him, a broken record - the scratch indelible and deep. Henry understood. He had been a part of David Litzenberg's plan. The old man would not have accepted anything less than to boast that Henry was dutifully following in his footsteps. "Though he'll never fully fill them," the judge had chuckled to a colleague. "How in God's Earth could he compete with a giant?"

As luck would have it, I didn't have to compete, did I, Judge, you dead son of a bitch? Henry allowed the thought to circle into his thinking and then slide away. *You're long gone, Judge. It's your poor, demented wife who's now dominating my world. What the hell am I supposed to do with her now?*

⌘　⌘　⌘

With his cocktail finished, the glass tossed on the floor beside his chair, Henry slept. His was a deep, confusing, bizarre dream: *He was soring like an eagle over a deep, barren canyon before disappearing behind a cliff where he morphed into a coyote and emerged from a wide, deep, otherwise-deserted burrow in the search of prey. Scenting the air, the animal knew it must find quarry of some kind - a rabbit, a lone fawn, a rodent, or even carrion left abandoned, free for the taking. Running at full speed, the coyote, confident and sure, suddenly stumbled, and it fell into a wide cavern that led to the sea. It was swallowed by wild and unforgiving surf that tossed the animal into the depths. It did not drown, however. Instead, it surged upward out of the water, a dolphin now, sleek, gray, and intent on finding a school of small fish, a squid, an octopus, a turtle, anything to feast on, something to fulfill. It dove deep where the water grew dark and then, like a torpedo, it rose out of the waves and careened sideways onto a rock and sandy beach. Henry knew it was he in the sand, his body naked and sunburned. And he was alone, a solitary figure who did not know his way home. He was absolutely bewildered as to which way to go.*

⌘ ⌘ ⌘

When he opened his eyes, the sun had risen and, through the wide window in the family room, it blasted him full in the face. "Shit, that was weird," he said, aloud.

"What was weird, you sleepyhead? You've been out for hours." Laura stood beside him, her golden hair sparkling in the sunlight. She looked beautiful - stunning, though stern.

"Christ what a dream. Don't know what in the hell to make of it." Henry stared at his wife, her presence most assuring. That was until she spoke once more time.

"Well, you'd better figure it out quick, because someone from *The Gardens* just called. Maude is asking for you."

Chapter Twenty-Nine

GRACE

Mildred ushered Grace, Lilly, Ralph, and Louie into the elevator for the quick ride up to the fourth floor, although Louie, who, incidentally, appeared quite satiated by the attention he had received in the dining hall from a few, adoring, aged females, had been a bit reluctant. *Thank goodness everyone behaved in the elevator.* It had been strangely quiet, actually. Louie had kept his hands appropriately to himself, Ralph had simply dipped his chin downward as if still in prayer, Lilly focused on the bank of numbers positioned adjacent to the silver, elevator door, and Grace stood demurely in the corner, seemingly in a world all her own. Every single one of the old people appeared tired which was not unusual after dinner. A bit of camaraderie with other residents followed by a meal and sweet dessert often did the trick. So, zombie-like, the foursome shuffled down the hall, and into their rooms with hardly a word. *They'll settle in. And I'll be back in the morning for another round.* Mildred had lingered at Grace's doorway for a moment, but did not follow her inside. "Goodnight, Grace. Sweet dreams."

"Are you leaving now, Miss Millie?"

"I am. Remember, I told you my sister, Caroline, was in town. She's waiting at home for me." Mildred shifted her feet nervously. "I'm afraid she might be a little anxious that I'm not there yet."

"Oh, yes, of course, dear. I can imagine she'll have so much to tell you . . . catching up after all this time." Grace smiled at Mildred and clutched her hands together as if holding onto an auspicious kernel of hope for her friend. "Well, go along now. I'm settled in," she asserted.

"Goodnight, Grace," Mildred said again. "I'll check on Maude first, but then I simply must hurry home."

"'Night, Miss Millie." Mildred heard Grace mutter her name as she walked away.

Mildred scurried down the hall, called out a hasty "Goodnight," to the night staff, and stepped into the waiting elevator for the ride to the ground floor. The sudden drop caught her off guard, and she grabbed the handrail to steady herself. *Caroline will be waiting. I hope she's all right.* But first, I simply must look in on Maude.

Though administrative officials at the facility had apprised Mildred of information regarding Maude Litzenberg's clandestine *journey* out of the residence in late afternoon or early that evening, they had presumed, as well as, fortunately, her subsequent rescue and placement in *The Gardens* infirmary, Mildred had not let on to Grace or the others. Having done so would have caused needless upset and worry. It had been difficult to hold the information secret for she had been plagued with guilt for perhaps being the one who had not watched closely enough, although

Maude's safety did not rest solely on her shoulders. Others were culpable too. Still, Mildred felt responsible even though she had been busy caring for her other wards. Self-reproach niggled at her. And that was the reason why, after leaving Grace, Mildred felt compelled to check in on Maude. Once at the infirmary, Mildred gently pushed open the door of Maude's room and peered inside. The ailing, old woman was resting exactly as the medical staff had left her. Her eyes, blessedly, were closed. *She'll sleep through the night.* Mildred's thoughts were begging. *Please, for goodness sake, Maude, for once, you simply must sleep through the night.*

Mildred turned abruptly then and dashed out the back door of the infirmary into a cold evening. A chilly, unexpected fog, she discovered, circled around her; it was an eerie, unwelcome companion home.

⌘　⌘　⌘

In her room, Grace prepared for bed, although, as usual, she would not climb between the warm, flannel sheets just yet. Instead, comfortably attired in a long, cotton nightgown and wrapped in a knobby, chenille robe, she settled back into Frank's chair, feeling his arms caressing her one more time. It was her ritual to be there, as the carousel of memories circled around teasing her warmly while exasperating her with the veracity that her life with Frank had not been perfect, though nearly so. Despite their deep love, they had wrestled in the throes of life's twists and turns.

Frank, ever the gentleman, often had surprised Grace with gifts when she least expected them. They never were extravagant, but served to cement their commitment and love. He brought flowers, of course - bunches of daisies wrapped in newspaper, lavender, violas, or peonies tied up with string, and once each year on Valentine's Day, a hand-delivered dozen, red roses, placing them in her arms with a flourish and a smooch on the cheek. He gave her candies, sweet pastries; warm gnocchi, Chianti, Anisette, and knickknacks galore - the porcelain kitty cat, the small crystal candlestick, a blown glass giraffe, and a tiny stuffed bear. And he gave her books - lot and lots of books - found God only knew where: old bookstores, street venders, libraries, or flea markets. The stories ran the gamut from romance to science fiction. Grace read them all, absorbing, from cover to cover, the sights and sounds of adventures that were not her own. The books kept her grounded when the stuff of life intervened.

Not least of these moments was when Grace learned she would never conceive. She and Frank had hoped for a pregnancy for the first five years of their marriage, but, in the end, it became clear that they would not become parents. And she was devastated. "My fault," she had insisted through buckets of tears.

Frank denied her ownership of any such burden. "Mine, too," he said, "Ours. We own it together. It was not meant to be."

And in time, they accepted, building a life alone and together. The years zipped by with minor illnesses, cuts, and scrapes, with silly arguments that ended in hugs, and with the loss of the odd friendship or loving pet along the way. Significant to both was witnessing the end of life for each of their mothers, but they did not mourn. Frank and Grace knew both women had lived full lives worthy of celebration, worthy of remembrance, worthy of recognition for jobs well done. Grace was convinced that her mother remained with her even after her ashes were tossed into gray and frigid waves that lapped the shore of the San Francisco Bay.

"You're still here, aren't you, Mama?" she said out loud. "You are my comfort, you and Frank, who's still by my side. See, Mama? Frank's with me too."

Grace looked sadly into the empty room. "I miss you both so much . . . so much it hurts." The sigh she issued was long, forlorn. *It's all right, Grace. It's because of the love. That's all it is. It's because of the love. Why does the hurt need to go away? It's the love, the love that counts.*

And she slept. She had pulled her mother's afghan over her lap. Her fingers were laced through the woven loops of yarn and she held on tightly, as if for dear life.

Chapter Thirty

MILDRED

The house was dark and the front door open, only inches, but ajar, unlocked. Midnight, Mildred's house cat, had slinked through the opening and stood on the porch as if guarding the place. His paws were locked firm, his claws digging into a thick, hemp doormat; his back curved upward in a perfect arch, while his black tail swished, and his eyes, like green globes, reflected light from a distant street lamp. It was strangely quiet even though Mildred's cottage was not more than two blocks from busy Broadway. She had walked home from *The Gardens* more briskly than usual, partly because the evening had cooled dramatically beneath a low mantle of fog, but more to the point, because she was anxious to reach her sister, Caroline whom, she assumed, finally had awakened and was waiting impatiently for her return. A quick perusal of the residence, however, indicated that that was not the case. Mildred shivered, both from the cold and from an uncanny sense of doom. Her collective, unpredictable, unsettling interactions with others, from Caroline to a whole host of characters at *The Gardens* for the past thirty-six hours left her with room for no other expectation. *Something bad is going to happen . . . or maybe it already has.*

She scooted Midnight back into the house, flicked on the lights, and pulled the door closed behind her. The living room was empty. The only indications that Caroline had been there was a knotted blanket on the floor, another strewn over the back of the couch, and a damp pillow with a deep indentation in the shape of a skull. *Caroline must have been asleep there for hours. But where is she now?* The room smelled of cigarettes, of body odor, and of something burnt. Mildred stepped into the kitchen where she discovered chunks of blackened toast scattered on the countertop. *At least she tried to eat something, but what a mess.*

"Caroline?" Mildred called her sister's name out loud, a dissonant question that had no answer . . . *of course not. She's run off again. I was expecting her to stay . . . this time . . . with Adam gone. Dead. Only thirty-seven. How sad is that? But where is she? I thought she wanted my help. Didn't she say so?*

For the second time in as many days, Mildred was flummoxed. Should she notify the police? No. Why would she do that? Caroline was a grown woman. She didn't live with Mildred. She had only stopped by to deliver depressing news, to dump the details of her crappy life out on someone else. Or maybe she merely had come by seeking a refuge to rest . . . perhaps to reconnect. *Reconnect? No. If Caroline had wanted that she would have stayed. And I had such expectations. For a few hours, I did. How stupid of me. Get real, Mildred. It's not surprising she's gone. It sure as hell isn't the first time.*

Mildred had lost count of her sister, Caroline's, disappearances. The first time, she had been eleven. *What is it about eleven?* Mildred suddenly remembered Grace's tale about her uncle's death at age eleven, of her ruined eleventh birthday when her mother finally had spoken of it, of the uncle Grace never had known existed at all. And with the news had come a warning: *Don't be foolhardy like Carmine. Be responsible. Stay aware. Don't be like Carmine.*

The irony that Grace's Uncle Carmine and her own sister, Caroline, were, as youngsters, likely similar in nature was not lost on Mildred. The two children, one a boy, the other a girl, born a long generation apart, both harbored irrepressible spirits - that, and vacuous abilities to reason, when a bit of serious cognition surely may have reversed their dismal orbits. As fate would have it, however, such thoughtless impetuosity led to Carmine's unfortunate, deadly, childhood accident, and, as for Caroline, her life-long inability to stop for one moment to consider the consequences of actions that led to years of missteps, the first being when she, too, was only eleven. Mildred never had forgotten the incident.

⌘ ⌘ ⌘

`"Caroline. Where are you?" Mildred called her sister's name over and over. "I know you're in here. Where are you hiding?"

There was no answer. Silence. Their father was at work, their mother buried three years prior; the two sisters, for all intents and purposes, had only each other. When not at school, it was not uncommon for them to spend long hours existing in the tiny apartment, although they were not always together. Mildred assumed her responsibilities - cleaning, cooking, or studying - and Caroline succumbed to her moodiness, often holing up in her bedroom listening to songs on a crackly, old radio, daydreaming, or falling into restless sleep. Caroline was a presence though; she was always around, so why was she not responding?

"Caroline? Answer me."

In the three years since their mother's passing, Caroline had changed from a quiet, rather withdrawn and frightened child to a temperamental, sulky pre-teen, her angry eyes and pouting lips the norm. And though Mildred took notice, she could do nothing. After all, she was only a young girl herself, only days into her fourteenth year. Besides, she had responsibilities - for the apartment, for her father, and, yes, for Caroline, whose budding insolence grated Mildred's tolerance. It wasn't easy. And on this day, Mildred's patience was tested as never before. The apartment was empty, but one window had been raised only inches. It opened onto the fire escape. *Surely she's not out there. She's afraid of heights.* Mildred was wrong . . . as she would be many more times in the years to come as Caroline spawned her reckless habits, the behavior that led eventually to Adam being born to the unprepared, naïve, and unattached adolescent.

On this day, however, Mildred had had, for the first time, to take stock in what was to become her sister's new, unsettling conduct. She pushed up the stubborn window slowly. Years of layered paint molded into the jambs made the task more difficult, but at last it was open, at least wide enough for her to peek out. She saw nothing, but above the drone of a few vehicles passing by below, she heard voices, one the low, hoarse voice of a boy and the other Caroline's, this time in the form of a rare giggle. *Oh, damn. What's going on?* Though she was reticent to do so, Margaret climbed over the sill and onto the metal fire escape. Through the slatted platform on which she stood quivering, she could see several parked cars, pedestrians striding down the sidewalks, and two, feral cats on the platform below. They stared up with wide, green eyes and hissed. Their pointy ears were flattened back, listening and signaling, with feline clarity, their annoyance and distrust. Mildred understood, at her core, that her presence was not welcome. Nonetheless, she did not retreat. Instead, she pressed her body as close to the brick wall as she could and inched her way to the staircase that led to the platform above. Four platforms later, she was one staircase from the roof of the building. Caroline's titters continued; the boy's tone was low, controlled, his words undecipherable. As Mildred stepped onto the first rung of the last ladder, her stomach pitched. She felt as if she might faint, or fall, or vomit all over herself. Her hands perspired. Her grip on the handrail had become noticeably less secure. She was panicked by the height, but she was much more afraid of what she would find above. It took a moment, but she gathered her wits and climbed the last steps, to the rooftop. Her worst imaginings were revealed in plain sight. Caroline lay naked from the waist down, the boy too. Two kids, eleven, and slightly older, were exploring each other with unabashed fervor. Mildred was aghast.

"Caroline! What in the hell are you doing? And who are you? Get away from her. Now!"

The young boy grabbed his shoes and trousers and sprinted to the far side of the roof where he disappeared somehow down a distant hole in the roof. And Caroline froze.

"Oh, little sister, what have you done?"

"Nothing. I didn't do anything wrong." Caroline's giggle had vanished, the pout back in place.

"Pull on you pants. Let's go. Now."

Caroline glanced toward the place where the boy had vanished. Her eyes revealed emotions Mildred could not read. *Is she sad, embarrassed, angry? Does she feel anything at all?*

Mildred discerned it probably was the latter, for Caroline mindlessly dressed and then crawled on her hands and knees to the edge of the roof; she threw one leg over onto the first rung of the stairway and then stopped, clinging onto the hot, metal handrail as if it did not burn at all. Her body had tensed.

"Move on down, Caroline, so I can get off this roof too."

It took a full minute for Caroline to move, on her butt, down one rung of the stairway, leaving just enough room for Mildred to crawl over the ledge and sit beside her. When they were together side by side, Caroline's body began to tremble. Though Mildred tried to comfort her sister by patting her knee and arm, Caroline twisted away, clinging instead to the handrail so tightly her fingers splotched in shades of purple and white.

"We need to go down the stairs now. Come on," Mildred encouraged.

Caroline was silent.

"Come on now. We need to be in the apartment, not out here."

It took a full hour before Caroline loosened her grip and indicated that she was ready. Though Mildred was uncomfortable herself, she did what she had to do. She clutched Caroline's arm and guided her step by step down four flights of stairs to the open window of their apartment. When they both were safely inside, Caroline looked at Mildred with blatant disdain. "You've ruined everything," she said, her voice flat.

"I did not. I did not. Caroline, I rescued you. I saved you from a big mistake," Mildred countered plaintively. Color rose to her cheeks as she spoke. *What is wrong with her? Can't she understand?*

"Don't ever come after me again. Not anywhere. Not ever." Caroline rushed into her room and slammed the door. From outside, Mildred could hear her fury. Inside, Caroline threw books, shoes, anything she could grab against the walls, against the closed bedroom door. There were no other noises - not a voice, not a cry. And when finally Caroline's tirade was over, silence hung like a heavy curtain of dense fog. Mildred had no idea in which direction to turn. And, if she could have confessed the truth, neither did confused, gullible, little Caroline Watson.

Though neither sister would ever forget the confrontation, neither spoke of the incident again.

⌘　⌘　⌘

I remember. "Don't ever come after me again. Not anywhere. Not ever." Those were her exact words. Mildred surveyed her living room, the place in disarray exactly as her sister's life was. The house could be straightened up, put back into order. That would be easy. Her sister was another issue, indeed, but Mildred would do as she had been asked so many years before after the foray on the rooftop. In the short amount of time it had taken for that distant memory to be pulled from a cluttered file of many more, she was clear. Mildred would not go after her sister. She would honor the command. Caroline was on her own.

Only a nagging moment of guilt tugged at Mildred's conscience and then it was over. The pattern of her sister's life was set, a tightly wound whirlwind, from which she had never been able to escape. Mildred had watched from a distance, appalled by the potential for destruction and awed by the all-encompassing force that had pulled Caroline in and held her, the fingers of fate not letting go.

Mildred assumed the storm would move on with Caroline's life swirling even further out of control. She stood absolutely still for a moment, steadying herself, needing to right her own path. *You have to let go. Let her go.* A lump rose to Mildred's throat as she swooped up the crumpled blankets, folded them into neat squares, and said out loud to no one, "I'm done."

Burning, teary eyes, and a quavering feeling inside were indications, however, that perhaps again, one more time, she was wrong.

Chapter Thirty-One

MAUDE

Maude did not wake up slowly from her sedated state as one might have anticipated . . . no, not Maude. As was her norm, she defied the expected. Any other person likely would have awakened groggy, weary, and perhaps a bit disoriented. A nurse or attendant, in most cases, would have spoken softly, encouraging the patient to adjust to his or her surroundings and to understand perhaps why sedation had been necessary in the first place. The interaction generally would have been a slow, kind, deliberate process to assist the individual coming out of a deep sleep. That simple course of action would have been typical. For the medical staff on duty at *The Gardens*, and for Maude Litzenberg, however, this was not the case . . . not even close.

On the morning after her near-escape from *The Gardens*, Maude opened her eyes wide, looked wildly around her, and then sat straight up as if ready to take to the streets in order to hail the next Greyhound out of town. She did not appear groggy and tired. Instead, bursting with an irritation-fueled energy that bubbled up from deep inside, she called out, "Hey. Hey, what the hell's going on? I'm lost here. Damn it, where am I? Why on Earth am I stuck in this stinking, piss-soaked bed all alone? Where's my Judge? And where in the hell is Henry . . . that good for nothing lout? Get him in here. Now. Does nobody work in this awful, damned hellhole?"

For minutes, she had been slamming her tight fists against the metal railings of her bed - *bam, bam, bam* - as hard as she could while, at the same time, letting loose a rather incredibly lewd assortment of profanities no one would expect to be uttered by an otherwise proper, decorous, female octogenarian. As a result of her tantrum, she had awakened half a dozen other elderly patients recuperating from malaises of their own . . . all the while sitting on a urine-sodden pad that had been placed beneath her the night before as a precaution; for the fact was, that when she had been delivered, by ambulance back to *The Gardens*, besides being bruised, dehydrated, and near-hypothermic, her clothing had been saturated with her own excrement and piss. Maude's vile conduct and rudeness already had been established as her normal behavior; the incontinence, however, was new. It would be added to the list of reasons, among so many others, as to why Maude Litzenberg's residency at *The Gardens* could not possibly be cut short. She was there to stay until the bitter end.

⌘　⌘　⌘

Still a bit bleary-eyed, and continuing to ponder his deeply puzzling dream, Henry strode into the vestibule of an extension to *The Gardens* that had been designated as an infirmary. Years before, someone in authority had decided a clinic and small hospital of sorts would be appealing to would-be residents - medical assistance available right on site. *What could be better?* Somewhere the distant CEO of *The Gardens,* and a chain of other almost identical, retirement facilities, continued in all likelihood to tout his brilliance. Henry was not so sure. The facility that had been added on to the main building, and that jutted out to one side like a broken appendage did not appear to be functioning as planned. Not one employee was in sight. *Is anyone working in this place?* He wavered slightly and touched the countertop of the reception desk to steady his aching body. He felt as though he'd slept in a suitcase. *What the hell's going on? Where is everyone?*

The receptionist clearly was absent. He glanced up at the façade above the wide, reception desk. A fading painting of various, resting birds and other tree-adoring critters scattered along a lengthy tangle of leafy branches dominated the wall; below were the words, *Respite Rooms,* the designation swirled into the scene in ornate calligraphy. He stared until his eyes blurred. *Weird.*

Henry was oblivious to a gaunt, gray-faced nurse who finally approached the desk. When she was almost upon him, she cleared her throat noisily; Henry flinched as if he'd been shot but it was she who appeared to grimace in pain. She gawked at Henry and sighed. Exhaustion was etched into every wrinkle of her face. He recalled having seen the woman briefly the night before. She had hovered on the periphery of Maude's ranting, but had not entered her room; instead she had stepped back into the shadows. *No wonder she looks tired. Probably had to deal with Maude, and God only knows how many other feeble, fucked up folks all night long. Tough job.*

"Mr. Litzenberg?"

He nodded.

"Your mother's awake." She paused, unsmiling. "Be prepared, Mr. Litzenberg. We've picked up this morning where we left off last night. Here, sign in. I'll take you to her."

Henry followed the nurse a short distance down the hallway to his mother's room. The poor woman's gait was awkward, labored, her entire body tilting to one side. *Christ, she looks ready for residency in a retirement home herself.* At the doorway she paused, looked uneasily at Henry, and stepped aside. He hesitated stealing a few seconds of final peace before entering the room and facing the onslaught he knew was coming. His apprehension regarding his mother was well established; he had borne the emotion his entire life. When he moved forward at last, however, he was met with a verbal assault that staggered him. Maude's words, spat out from deep in her throat, were so abusive that he instantly moved two steps backwards ramming his shoulder into the doorjamb as he did.

"Damn it, Henry, you rotten, good-for-nothing lout. Why have you had me locked in this hellhole with absolute idiots, who don't have the sense to know up from down and clearly don't give a shit about me? Why? And besides that, they've taken Judge, for heaven's sake. Where the hell have they absconded with Judge? You tell me that, damn it, Henry."

The ashen-faced nurse's assessment as to what to expect had been spot on. Maude and her son, Henry, were back to square one.

It took a moment for Henry to find his voice, and when he spoke, he croaked a hoarse, flat response, "Good morning, Mother."

"Don't start, Henry. Don't dare start with that condescending bullshit."

"I said, 'Good Morning', Mother. That's all."

"It's in your voice, Mr. Lawyer. It's the attitude, Henry . . . always the attitude. Katherine would never address me so coldly."

"Katherine? Who's Katherine?"

"Your sister, of course, Henry. For Pete's sake, have you forgotten your very own sibling?"

Henry stomach tightened. He glanced toward the doorway where *gray face* had reappeared. Her sneakered feet were planted firmly but she appeared quite unnervingly unsteady. Henry was afraid she might fall forward flat on the floor. *Maybe it's fatigue.* She toyed with a stethoscope stuffed into the lower, front pocket of her scrubs, but said nothing even though Henry's eyes, she knew, were beseeching her to speak up. *Tell Maude she's crazy. I have no sister.* Finally he mouthed a comment to the nurse, "I have no sister."

She nodded and stepped farther into the room as Maude snapped again, "There you go, damn it, Henry, talking behind my back. I saw you moving that maw of yours. I'm not blind, you know. For heaven's sake, you look like an expiring fish out of water mouthing words like that."

Henry inched closer to his mother's bedside unsure how to handle this new wrinkle in Maude's failing grasp on reality. *Okay. Okay. What do I say? Do I agree with her? I shouldn't argue with her, should I? You don't do that with demented people. Do you? This person, this Katherine, is not real though. Where in the hell did she come up with Katherine? And Judge? She thinks he's still alive and hanging around in here too. Holy shit.*

"Mother, how are you feeling?"

"I feel awful."

"I'm sorry to hear that. Do you have pain somewhere?" Henry hoped a normal dialogue might quell his mother's delusional state.

"Oh, for God's sake, no. No pain, just heartache. I'm worried about Judge. Do you know where he's gone? And Katherine . . . will she be here soon? She told me she was coming, and, bless her heart, she never lets me down. Your sister's not at all like you, Henry, not one iota like you . . . you, with all your plotting and conniving."

Henry's hands tightened around the railing of Maude's bed. *So this is it. This is how it's going to end for my crazy mother.* He felt a modicum of guilt and a sudden sadness for the parent he had detested most of his life. *It doesn't seem fair, but she's gone already, lost in some fantasy of her own creation. Is it self-preservation? Does it ease the heartache to conjure a make-believe world?* Henry assumed it must be true. Besides, hadn't his mother always tended to live in a daydream? Her home, her *Tara* had been a perfect example - a garish, Southern mansion, complete with a gigantic, imported weeping willow. The grandiose dwelling was an out-of-place monstrosity plopped amid countless, contemporary residences that melded seamlessly into the Northern California coastal hills.

He had made infrequent visits to Maude's home especially after his father's murder there. It was as though the place had been forever stained with violence, and with the deception that preceded it. And Laura had been adamant. "The kids and I are not about to step foot in that fucking house, Henry. Never."

In recent months, however, he, alone, had been to the house more often, out of necessity - Maude's health, both mental and physical, had begun a noticeable decline. As her only child, he had accepted responsibility. And, now, as he stood beside his mother's bedside, recalling the past, considering the future, he felt strangely apprehensive, even fearful. *Am I losing it myself?* He had moved his mother from *Tara* only a few days prior, yet, in this very moment in time, it seemed as if he had not stepped foot in the place for years. He tensed. Time suddenly had warped in his world as well. He looked at the woman, his awful, hateful mother, his only parent, and sucked in a deep breath. *Does Mother have any concept of what's real any more? How did this decline advance so quickly? And how in the fuck is her story going to play out?*

His reverie was cut short. "Henry, answer me," Maude shouted.

"I . . . I don't know," he stammered. "Maybe if you close your eyes . . ."

"Oh, for Pete's sake. Don't tell me to close my eyes. Damn you, Henry. You'd like that, wouldn't you? How damned free you'd be if I closed my eyes and never opened them again. You'd be free of me and up to your ears in my money. You have planned it all out, haven't you, Mr. Attorney?"

"Now, Mother."

Maude's head sank back onto the pillow for a moment as if she had resigned to her son's request but instantly she reared up again, ripping at the injection port in her arm and pulling so hard that the entire IV pole crashed to the floor right in front of the nurse. The plastic IV bag quavered for a moment before bursting and spilling saline solution into a widening puddle at her feet. *Gray face* reacted instantly. Placing both hands firmly on Maude's shoulders, she gently, but decisively, pushed the old woman back against the pillows and secured her hands to the bed railings with restraint straps. The aging nurse moved so deftly, Henry was astonished. Though Maude responded with a yelp, with her upper torso and hands secured, she could hardly move. She tried kicking her legs beneath the blanket and twisting from side to side a bit, but quickly tired. And, at last, she gave in closing her eyes to the reality she could not bear to see.

Chapter Thirty-Two

HENRY

With his mother secure at *The Gardens*, Henry drove home once more. He had spoken with the medical staff, assuring them that Maude's imaginary daughter, Katherine, was just that, a figment of her imagination, and that Judge David Litzenberg, *Judge*, her husband, had been dead for years. The latter, of course, was a matter of public record, but Maude's conjuring of a would-be daughter spoke volumes as to her mental decline.

"It's not uncommon for the elderly, particularly those in the throes of dementia, to invoke the imaginary into their worlds. Perhaps this Katherine is the daughter Mrs. Litzenberg always wanted to have. She may simply be bringing long-denied wishes into the fore. And, who knows, by tomorrow she may not remember mentioning a daughter at all," a nurse practitioner had advised. "Go home, Mr.

Litzenberg. Get some rest yourself. We'll make sure your mother is safe."

Yeah, like last night? Henry had choked back the words he had wanted to say. "Thanks," he had muttered instead. "You know how to reach me."

⌘ ⌘ ⌘

At home, Henry walked straight through the house, past his children who were oblivious to his presence anyway, their eyes riveted on the cell phones that never were far from their hands. He glanced at them sadly, their preoccupation adding yet another layer of despondency to Henry's dark mood. He hadn't had a decent conversation with either child for months. *And whose fault is that, Henry?* He admonished himself because he felt compelled to do so. He was failing everybody - Maude, Laura, his children, himself.

On the backside of the house, he walked slowly along the concrete path that circumvented the well-manicured lawn to the glass-topped patio table. He stared through the opaque glass at the tumbled slate patio that Laura had insisted upon having professionally installed adjacent to the kidney-shaped swimming pool. "You're not touching that damned project, Henry. We're having it done right."

Though he might have liked to try his hand at such an undertaking, he had agreed. Home projects had never been his forte. It would have turned into a disaster, just like everything else. He slumped down into a sling back patio chair and closed his eyes. Though he had a tendency to brood at times about his overly demanding job or about the outcome of a difficult case, Henry was not generally sad or depressed. Life was too busy for that. But on this day, he was down, his energy depleted. In the darkness behind his closed eyelids he began to envision a young woman, a female named Katherine, his mother's unfulfilled desire. *How would she have looked? Dark eyes, sharp featured like Mother?* He felt an odd pang of jealousy. *How can you resent someone who never existed?* But he did. Katherine, fantasy though she was, had been wanted; he had not. He had been raised either by nannies or gruff and demanding instructors at military school before he was on his own. His parents had acknowledged his existence primarily from a distance. And affection had been absent altogether. Non-existent. That was until Laura, beautiful, unpredictable, foul-mouthed Laura.

⌘ ⌘ ⌘

"What in the hell are you doing out here, Henry? I thought you were at *The Gardens* tending to Maude." Laura had slipped up beside him unnoticed. He flinched when he heard her voice. "Are you okay?"

"Yeah, yeah. Just needed time to absorb the latest," he said. "Wanted some space, so I came out here."

"What's going on?"

"Mother's bonkers. She still thinks Judge was with her at *The Gardens* all night and that the medical staff has hidden him away somewhere. She's livid . . . cussing up a storm."

"Well, hell, Henry, I told you her cheese was slipping off her cracker."

"Yeah, but there's more. This morning she was talking about her daughter - Katherine - the wonderful, caring, attentive daughter who, incidentally, is nothing like me. I, in Mother's words, am a goddamned, conniving lout."

"Oh, for God's sake." Laura began to laugh.

Henry glared at her, taken aback by the response.

"What the hell, Laura. Is that funny?" Henry's whole body tensed. *Damn, Laura, that's a pretty screwed up reaction.*

"Well, yeah, it kind of is. Where do old people come up with these things? Is it regression? It must be because it reminds me of little kids and their imaginary friends."

"I don't think Mother's current condition is anything to laugh about, Laura. It was actually pretty startling to listen to her talk about a daughter she never had. And besides when, in your mind, did dementia become a laughing matter?"

Laura took a step back and glared at her husband. "Look, Henry, don't go putting your shit on me. I have every right to respond the way I want. If you're going to get all weepy-eyed over your mother, who didn't give a rat's ass about you her whole life, well, you can wallow in your stupid, fucking distress."

Henry had no words. *Who are you?* Locked within his silence was a powerful, muted scream that had nowhere to go.

"Talk to me when you get your shit together," she murmured, her voice just above a whisper. And she was gone.

He watched his wife stride away from him, her long, blond hair suddenly lifted and tangled by a sharp, cool gust of wind. Her carriage was erect, rigid; her gait controlled and determined; her hands clenched into tight fists.

Is she right? Is she? Fuck, maybe she is.

Henry eyes followed Laura until she disappeared into the house. He had never felt so alone in his life.

Chapter Thirty-Three

GRACE

Grace had slept soundly and awoke refreshed. She had dreamed of sailing on a sleek, teak-decked yacht with Frank and a few, long-forgotten friends on San Francisco Bay. The cruise past Angel Island had been a smooth, sunny one, but once though Raccoon Straits, past the hills of Tiburon, the waters had become choppy, each undulating swell tipped with a fringy whitecap. The wind had intensified as well, gnarly gusts pounding the mainsail and jib with every tack. By the time the *Gracie Rose* had reached the shadow of the Golden Gate Bridge, Frank comprehended instinctively that it was time to beat it back to the harbor. The sailing conditions had altered dramatically in only minutes, with powerful currents silently establishing an awesome control. Frank's expertise as the captain of his splendid, sailing vessel, however, decreed him boss. He would conquer the elements as he had so many times before.

In the distant, western sky, thick fog barreled its way toward Alcatraz, while long fingers of the heavy, gray mist slid eerily over the Marin County hills into Sausalito. It was cold. And the crew onboard had grown anxious. By the time Frank deftly guided *Gracie Rose* into her slip at the Berkeley Yacht Harbor miles across the Bay, she and her passengers were soaked. But it had been an adventure. After tidying up the yacht and spraying her down with fresh water, Frank cracked open two bottles of champagne and toasted the good life. Every person on board raised a glass upward in acclaim for Frank's proficient, sailing skills. And their relief was palpable. Besides feeling rejuvenated, each one understood the significance of being anchored safely, and near solid ground.

⌘   ⌘   ⌘

Grace smiled, relishing the dream, for Frank had been so real, so alive, so responsive, taking care of everyone onboard his beautiful *Gracie Rose.* She sighed. *Thank you, Frank, for paying me a visit.* She was still deep in thought, envisioning the attractive face of her late husband, when Mildred appeared, poking her head inside the room for a quick assessment.

"Good morning, Grace."

"Oh, good morning, Miss Millie." She smiled sweetly at her caretaker.

"You sure do seem chipper this morning, Grace," Mildred replied.

"Oh, I feel like a million dollars, Miss Millie. I had the most delightful dream last night. Frank and I went sailing on the Bay with a slew of folks I couldn't name if you paid me . . . but it was a lovely cruise, though a bit unnerving toward the end when the wind played havoc with our beautiful yacht. Thank goodness Frank is such a wonderful sailor."

The present tense *is* took Mildred aback for a moment but she simply had no energy for judgment.

"Did I ever tell you that Frank and I loved sailing together?"

Whew, she's back in the past. Good. "No, you didn't," Mildred answered. "That must have been quite an exciting activity."

"Oh, it was, Miss Millie. We had many exhilarating times sailing around San Francisco Bay and even venturing out into the Pacific Ocean beyond the Farallon Islands. Frank purchased a most exquisite, forty-foot yacht you see . . . all white with a stunning teak deck. And he named her guess what?"

"What, Grace?"

"Well, you almost have it," she chuckled. "He named her *Gracie Rose*, after me. *Gracie* for Grace, of course, and *Rose* because, Frank said, it was the flower of love. Now isn't that something? Frank could be so romantic; that is when he wasn't behaving like a cranky, old bastard." She cackled so hard she began to snort. "Good grief, Miss Millie. What's gotten into me?"

"Well, I don't know, but it's nice to see you happy."

"It's a new day. Guess that's something to rejoice . . ." Grace stopped mid-sentence. "Oh my goodness, Miss Millie, I've been so taken with myself I forgot to ask you about your sister. Caroline, isn't it? Did you have a lovely reunion last evening?"

Mildred looked down, avoiding Grace's eyes.

"Miss Millie?"

"Oh Grace, Caroline already had left the house when I arrived home last night. The cottage was empty, except for my cat; Midnight always stays indoors, but was out on the front porch, completely bewildered. And Caroline had left the place a mess. No note. The front door left ajar. Her belongings, what little she had, all gone."

"Oh dear, Miss Millie. What are you going to do?"

"What can I do, Grace? She's a grown woman. And believe me, she has a mind of her own. She'll either reappear one of these days or be gone forever, but I worry. She's grieving about the loss of her son who passed away recently, a tragic drug overdose, not that you need to know all that drama."

"Oh my goodness, I am sorry, Miss Millie."

"Don't fret for one second about my sister, Grace. It is what it is. I actually had to give myself a good talking to last night because my initial reaction was to try to locate Caroline at any cost. And then I realized her fate is out of my hands. If she returns, I'll welcome her, of course; if not . . . " Her sentence trailed off before she spoke again, changing the subject altogether. "Actually, Caroline is not the only person who's been on my mind. I can tell you now, Grace, after the fact, that we had a near calamity around here yesterday."

"What do you mean?"

"Maude." Mildred rolled her eyes.

"Now what?" Grace asked.

"She ran away from *The Gardens* in the late afternoon, out into that horrible rain storm, all alone. By luck, a runner found her and called 911. She had fallen apparently; she was unconscious and soaking wet. From what I was told this morning, had she not been stumbled upon randomly, she could possibly have succumbed to the elements."

"Oh my, how terrible." Grace paused. "You know, Miss Millie, I haven't completely lost my mind. After my chat yesterday with Maude, I was afraid she might pull a stunt like that."

"She was fast asleep after you left her, Grace, clearly exhausted by all of her chatter. I remember checking on her, but she must have awakened and made her escape before any of the staff noticed, me included. Of course, the authorities were notified immediately, and well, the rest is history."

That was true, only to a point. Mildred had been immediately concerned when she heard of Maude's escapade. *I hope there are no accusations of neglect from the family.* She understood that, in the aftermath, any legal repercussions from Maude's family could spell disaster for the owners of *The Gardens* and potentially for herself and some other employees as well. Justification played in her head. *But Maude has been growing more confused every day. The family knows that. These things can happen. Old folks wander off.* Mildred's concerns were silent, but troubling musings.

"Is she in her apartment now?" Grace asked.

"Oh, no. She's in the infirmary recuperating. When I looked in on her last night, before going home, I was told her son had been by. I expect that interaction was quite the scene."

Grace shook her head, imagining Maude and Henry completely at odds. "Oh dear. Those two."

"I'm sorry, Grace. I shouldn't be burdening you with all this talk. It's really not professional," Mildred apologized.

"It's all right, Miss Millie. We're friends, you and I, aren't we?"

"We definitely are, honey."

"I don't know what I would have done without you when Frank passed away so unexpectedly. Remember? Oh, my heavens, what a state I was in. And you stayed with me all night."

"Yes, I did. I did, indeed."

"Did I ever thank you for that?" Grace asked.

"Of course, many times, in many ways."

Grace smirked. "Are you patronizing me, Millie?"

"Grace Ainsworth! How dare you," Mildred teasingly countered.

In the moments of silence that followed, the two looked at each other with warm affection. Finally Grace spoke again, "I guess it's time for me to pay it forward."

"What do you mean?"

"Paying it forward. Isn't that an interesting term, Miss Millie - paying it forward? Do you know where I first read about it?"

"You're going to tell me, aren't you?"

Grace grinned. "Of course, I am. The phrase is from an old, old book, older even than I am, Miss Millie, if you can believe that." She chuckled. "Lily Hardy Hammond wrote it in 1916. *In The Garden of Delight* it's called - a lovely, little book. And she mentions paying it forward. You see she had the notion that if people are the beneficiaries of good deeds, they should do something good for someone else, not necessarily for the person who was kind to them in the first place. So because of you, I'm going to pay your compassion forward. Don't you think that's a splendid idea?"

"Well, of course, it's is. It's a fine plan. But who is the person, and what are you going to do?"

"Maude. I'm going to do something kind for her, the way you did for me. Lord knows she must need it based on her latest escapade. I want to pay your thoughtfulness to me forward to her. You *obviously* don't need to hear, again, how much I appreciate you." Grace stopped and smiled slyly. "So, I'm going to do something for Maude instead. Understandably the old gal must be in quite a tizzy. And for goodness sake, it'll get me off my butt so I won't spend all day staring out the window and churning up memories of Frank and my mother, God bless them anyway."

"Oh, Grace, are you sure about that? Maude might be an awfully big undertaking. In fact, I know she will be."

"Maybe you're right, but Maude's at a low point. Plainly. You know, Miss Millie, yesterday afternoon when she insisted that I go to her room for a chat, she talked my ear off. And she tried to convince me to run away with her then; she didn't want to go alone. She wanted me to escape with her - two peas in a pod - Bonnie and Clyde, Thelma and Louise. Maude has some crazy ideas, and oh Lordy, Miss Millie, she doesn't seem to have a friend in the world."

"I'm sure she feels she has nobody, Grace, and it's probably true. She doesn't make befriending her easy. And, not that I want to put a wet blanket on your lovely idea, but as you know, she is quite the champion when it comes to feeling sorry for herself."

"She's old."

Surprised at the blunt comment, Mildred replied, "She's younger than you are, Grace."

"In years, maybe, but not in spirit. In spirit, I have the upper hand. And, damn it, Miss Millie, the old girl needs someone besides that insipid son of hers, to give a hoot. It's apparent, isn't it? Maybe, just maybe, she escaped to get some attention."

"That is a thought, Grace."

"It is . . . and a good one. Attention should not be underrated, Miss Millie. God knows we old folks all appreciate when someone takes time to notice us. That's why we all appreciate you, Miss Millie. You, most certainly, are the best caretaker ever."

Mildred smiled at Grace and shook her head in agreement, but said not a word. Instead she pondered the potential for a most questionable bonding - sweet, lovely Grace Ainsworth and cranky, old Maude. *Oh, for the love of Grace, what an undertaking. I'm wondering already how her scheme will play out. It could be a thorny affair to say the least, but I'll be standing by, if for no other reason, than to pick up the pieces.*

Chapter Thirty-Four

MILDRED

Her shift ended and Mildred walked home in the dusk as she had done a thousand times before. She had managed her duties all day with deft competence, seeing that her wards were comfortable, with their hygienic, dietary, medical, and social needs met all day; that in itself was a feat for, other than being elderly, they were as different as day and night. As she trudged down the sidewalk, she envisioned each one: pensive, sweet-faced Grace, chattering about Frank, Olivia, and days gone by; preoccupied Lilly, a tiny, mute mouse, busily tallying, fingers flying, fixated within a silent world of her own; Ralph, the proper, decorous man of God, always impeccably attired, prepared at a moment's notice for Divinity's final call; and affable Louie, flagrantly inappropriate, but loveable all the same, attested to by a clutch of admiring ladies often scurrying to his side.

Mildred smiled when she thought of Louie, but the fact of the matter was, that she had grown to adore them all. The thought of losing any one of her charges caused her throat to tighten.

And then she thought of Maude. Tense and angry Maude had arrived in a flurry of consternation, and, of course, immediately had become the proverbial fly in the ointment, complicating matters at every turn. Maude, still recuperating in the infirmary from her rash and careless escape from *The Gardens*, had been absent from Mildred's wing that day, and in all honesty, Mildred had been relieved. She had enough worry tormenting her as she speculated about Caroline's whereabouts. *I wonder where my crazy sister is and what she's doing. Is she wandering around alone?* And then Mildred chided herself. *You need to let this be, Mildred. Caroline is a grown woman. She can fend for herself. Besides, she's hardly communicated for years.*

"Damn you, Caroline. Nothing's changed. You only come around when you need something." Mildred muttered the words out loud before sucking in a bitter breath; at the same time, she cringed, ashamed for having voiced them at all. *But it's true. And I don't think I have enough energy to fix anything. My paltry family has departed, one by pathetic one, and I have nothing left to hold onto except my own, stubborn will to carry on.*

⌘　⌘　⌘

She arrived at her doorstep before she knew it. The porch lay in dark shadows, but, undaunted, she unlocked the door, turned on an interior light, and stepped inside. Midnight, perched on the couch, stretched his front legs and stared at Mildred with wide, green eyes that suddenly closed before opening once more. He then stood, arched his back, hissed once, and then, in fickle cat-like fashion, meowed.

"Sorry, kitty. That was a rude awakening, wasn't it?" She scooped up the cat and cuddled him against her chest; he instantly began purring and nuzzled his head beneath her chin.

"Bet you're hungry."

She carried Midnight into the kitchen, plunking him down next to his water bowl and a half-filled dish of crunchy kibble. "I know what you want - kitty tuna, right?"

She fed the cat and watched for a moment as he snarfled the smelly fish as if he were starving. "Good grief, Midnight," she declared. "You sound like a little pig."

She reached down, ran her hand down the length of his soft, furry back, and then turned toward the sink. After washing her hands, she yanked open the refrigerator door, pulled out the remainder of a left over casserole, and shoved it into the microwave. Weekday dinners were always like this - quick, simple affairs - just enough to alleviate her hunger and easy to prepare after a long workday. After eating, she poured a glass of her favorite Merlot, turned on the television, and sank down onto the couch. Once she had watched the news, she would read. A number of books, each with bookmarks in various places, were stacked on the end table. She would choose one to suit her mood, reading it until she was too sleepy to hold her eyes open. Mildred always read five or six books concurrently. Since living alone years before, following the death of her father, and, subsequently, on the heels of that loss, after Caroline and little Adam had taken to the streets to exist on their own, she read. At first she had gone to the public library to check out books, often taking home at least six at a time. She spent her time off from work perusing the narrow aisles of the library, scanning titles, and touching the volumes' spines as if that simple action would give her some indication as to the contents inside. In time, she began a book collection of her own, purchasing volumes at yard sales, flea markets, library sales, or at times, checking out one of two, local bookstores that piled tables high with dog-eared paperbacks or fading hardbacks that had gone unnoticed on store bookshelves for too long. She snatched up those bargains whenever she could. Reading, for Mildred, rapidly became a diversion from reality; paradoxically, however, it was a truth-bearer as well, assuring her that she did not hold her assumptions, judgments, beliefs, and emotions in a vacuum. Others, fictional or otherwise, throughout time, had shared her identical feelings, had had similar experiences, and disclosed hopes and dreams that mirrored her own. And so she read; the simple act of following words on a page was as essential to her well being as breathing in and out. It allowed her to live.

And this night, she reached for a well-worn copy of *Angle of Repose* by Wallace Stegner. She was on her fourth reading of the novel, one that had educated her and that, at times, had been discomforting in the face of its honesty, but more importantly, *Angle of Repose* had amazed her because of the depth of its characters, all perfectly flawed, each one searching for his or her own, elusive truths. The main character, a historian, chronicled the tale of the other characters, cast as his grandparents, with such candor, that Mildred had to wonder: *What in the hell were those folks thinking?* But that's why she loved the story so. *Personal choices run the gamut, don't they? And who is to judge who's right or wrong?* The book triggered her thinking and it left her questioning, not only about her own life, but also about the fictitious lives of Stegner's characters. *What, deep inside, made them tick?* She also was drawn to the notion that the narrator in the novel cared so much about his history and about the lives of his elders that he insisted on the telling, and not in vague, lackluster terms, but in vivid detail. Even though he was a retired historian, the old man narrating in the novel was an enigma in Mildred's view. *Does anyone like that even exist today? What kind of person cares about ordinary, old people any more? And, to boot, who would insist on recounting the life story of a dying, old fart or someone long gone?* Mildred found herself ruminating on the uniqueness of the literary gem in her hand. *The passing down of personal histories, at least for the average Joe, is a foreign concept these days, I guess. I'm willing to bet very few people care a rat's ass about a ninety-year-old person's past. Give a listen? Hell, no. And isn't that a shame?*

Perhaps it was the novel, or simply the fact that she worked day in and day out with old folks, but after her last reading, she had been left to wonder about aging, about living and dying, and about the importance of a life well lived, or perhaps poorly lived, with more questions than answers left in the wake of her pondering. *Who, when one begins this life, has any real idea of how it will go; what twists and turns will alter the way, and how, how in the hell, does one prepare for their own story's end?* She reread the words that recounted her musings for she had scrawled them in pencil on the bookmark that currently held her place. As she read them once more her heart quivered and her eyes blurred with tears . . . and, in that strange, quiet moment, she had absolutely no inkling why.

⌘ ⌘ ⌘

The wine had warmed her, her thoughts had chilled her, and the words on the page were distorted because of her tears. "I'm a hot mess," she said to Midnight who had curled into a fat ball next to her feet. "And I don't even know why." *Is it because I'm alone? No, I love my autonomy. Is it because Caroline has disappeared? No, I half expected that. I don't have a clue where this blue funk came from. Damn. I can't even read.* She closed her eyes, nestled deeper into the cushions of the couch, and pulled an old afghan tighter around her. Instantly she was asleep.

She was a child again, eight years old, running carefree through a field of colorful wildflowers. They were the hues of youth - pink, lavender, blue, yellow, and pure white. The sky was a brilliant azure, not a cloud to be seen, and the wind - it lapped at her face and tousled her long, dark locks. She heard laughter behind her, and a voice, "Wait for me, Millie. Wait for me." And in the distance she saw her sister. She was younger, almost six, her cheeks rosy, her wild, curly, blond hair, tamed into thick braids that fell almost to her waist. "What are we going to do with this bird's nest of yours?" Millie had heard her mother complain each time she had tried to pull a comb though Caroline's hair. But she would not cut it. No. To do such a thing would have been an absolute sin.

Millie slowed enough for Caroline to catch her; they grasped hands, and twirled and twirled, falling at last into a heap of giggles. "I love you, sissy," Mildred cooed.

"Oh yes, me too. Me too." Caroline beamed at her sister as if she were a princess, all her own.

And then they were off again, charging back toward home, hand in hand, away from the countryside and their moments of bliss. As they approached the shadowy streets of the city, they slowed, plodding like little soldiers to their parents' dingy apartment three stories up a dark, dank stairway. They had nearly reached the top step when Caroline tripped over a parcel that carelessly had been tossed there. Mildred reached for the rolled up bundle, drew it closer, and began to cry out, but even a muffled yelp would not form. Yet she held on and tore at the dirty, rumpled blanket until she could make out more clearly what was hidden inside. Her little girl body began to shiver for in her arms was a minuscule newborn . . . a bloody, shrunken, would-be baby - blue, icy, and dead.

Startled and afraid, Caroline shrank backwards into the shadows, slid to the floor, and began to whimper, but then she let loose. Her sobs were unrelenting, echoing into the tight corridor, the eerie reverberations finding no place to fall. When Mildred no longer could hold back herself, she began to scream for her mother, "Mama,

Mama. Come here. Come here. You have to come look. Before it's too late, you have to come see."

But no mother answered little Millie's call . . . and no one came. No one.

The two, young girls were alone. The only sounds were Caroline's cries, and Mildred's heartbeat, that she could feel pulsating inside her chest, the thumping sound as strident and alarming as a siren in the night.

Mildred awoke in a clammy sweat; her arms were tight about her, her mouth filled with phlegm, and her eyes still sticky with tears. And in the distance, not too far away, she heard the screeching roar of a fire engine and the wail of the alarm, shrieking non-stop into the cold, night air.

Chapter Thirty-Five

MAUDE

The sound was deafening and jarred Maude out of a deep sleep, one that had her running like Dorothy in *The Wizard of Oz* down a yellow, brick road into a strange, strange land that bore no resemblance to anything she knew. She had been lost in her dream, and panicked, afraid she would trip again. *These damned red shoes. Get them off. Get them off of me.* She had become paralyzed in her sleep, unable to move one more inch . . . and the noise, roaring inside her head, and maybe outside too, would not stop. She squirmed from side to side, finally sliding back into consciousness, but she could not sit up. *It's those damned restraints.* And she remembered. *They've got me tied up here . . . it's because I've been bad.*

"Help," she finally yelled, the tone a brittle croak. "Somebody, stop the noise. This racket is killing me."

And suddenly someone was there, an apparition in white, head to toe, the face masked, the hands gloved, the actions deft, determined. She felt movement, not her, but her bed, turning, circling, and then slamming into the doorjamb, before becoming stuck.

"Damn it! I need some help here." The cry was feminine, alien, insistent, and though muffled by the facemask, loud enough. A second, stark white phantom appeared, grabbed the railing of Maude's bed, and tugged back and forth urgently. A deeply masculine voice grunted with the effort . . . but success. The bed mercifully was unwedged from an unknown, precarious hold and began rolling, rolling, faster and faster down a dark, smoky hallway. Maude's head lolled from side to side and she opened her eyes but she could make out only a hazy gray, and the back of the white-gowned figure that guided her bed forward. She heard the man's breathing, harried bursts beneath the mask, but whomever it was continued on, undeterred from the serious, previously unforeseen, mission at hand.

At the end of the corridor, Maude's bed was shoved through wide, double doors into the cool night. She sucked in the acrid air, and immediately began to cough. Smoke was everywhere - she could see that - swirling in angry, amorphous circles pushed haphazardly by a cold, relentless breeze. Through the haze, red and yellow flashing lights lightened the sky, but beyond that, Maude had no sense of where she was . . . or why . . . and she was cold, icy to the core.

She heard many voices in the distance, the intonations loud and frantic, but closer, the tones were softer, seemingly more rational, calmer, and perhaps receptive. "I'm freezing," she managed. At that very moment, her restraints were loosened and she was lifted like a broken doll upward before being plopped on a gurney that slid wobbly on rails into a waiting ambulance. "I'm freezing," she muttered again, and this time was rewarded with two warm blankets that covered her from her neck to her toes. She lay back, soundlessly, unable to conjure a reason to protest.

"There's been a fire," someone close by told her. "We are relocating you to the community hospital. Just a precaution."

She was silent. *Oh dear, I bet Judge is gone, and Katherine too, burned into oblivion, as if they were never here in the first place.* She began to cry, the tears stinging her cold cheeks as if to rebuke her for thinking and caring at all.

"Don't worry, honey. I'm sure a family member will be waiting to comfort you when you arrive," she was assured.

But the promise did not reassure at all. On the contrary, she had only one thought. *Henry . . . and that God awful, Laura. They're the only ones, for Pete's sake. As if those bums give a rat's ass what happens to me. It's just my rotten luck that someone dragged me out of that building before I burned too. I'd be better off dead. And, oh dear, poor Judge.*

Chapter Thirty-Six

HENRY

Henry arrived home after squandering a Sunday, late into the afternoon, at his office, first in an effort to avoid visiting his mother at *The Gardens*, and second, to escape his wife, Laura's judgmental eyes. He was met there with silence. His children, as was the norm, were riveted to their precious, social media sources. Their cell phones and tablets, to Henry's way of thinking, had become annoying, permanent appendages likely to be attached to their hands for the long haul. Both adolescent heads, one golden blonde, the other a dark blackish-brunette, were bent downward, silent, unmoving. With their faces obscured, shoulders hunched forward, and their backs curved into wide, concave *C*s, they looked like two, slight, fixated monkeys. He half expected them, at any moment, to break away from their preoccupation and begin grunting, babbling, and smacking their puckered lips. It was a ludicrous thought, he knew, but his very own kids had become so estranged to him, he had almost forgotten the sounds of their voices. *How pitiful is that?* But it was so, and he was stricken by the stinging reality that his children, like he, himself had, were growing up without an ounce of meaningful, parental interaction, at least not from him. Laura was different, he supposed, not often directly involved, but always present at a distance, the perfect helicopter parent simply making sure . . . sure that her precious darlings were not criticized, denied, or ignored.

"I'm making certain both of them get through this precarious time in their lives unscathed," Laura had snapped when Henry had questioned her obsessive hovering. "Growing up and attending school was a shitty experience for me, Henry, and I'd imagine for you too, only in much different ways . . . so get over yourself. Don't carp on me . . . and don't ever fucking expect me to do as I'm told, especially if you're the one dishing out some sort of ridiculous ultimatum. Besides, what would you know? You're not around half the time anyway, for God's sake."

"Yes, mam," he had responded with irritated, mock agreement but in his gut, he knew she was right. The accuracy of her rant smarted like a slap in the face. She was the one taking responsibility for seeing the kids through. *Adolescence. What a horrible time. Who in God's Earth would want to relive those teenage years? I sure as hell wouldn't. But look where we are now. Middle age. Is that so great either? I'm nothing but a bank account. And Laura and I hardly even touch, so where do we go from here? Christ, to the next phase? Look at Maude. Mother's ridiculous, fucking life has gone to hell in a hand basket faster than a heartbeat. A long life . . . I'm not so damned sure.*

⌘　⌘　⌘

Laura had left a covered dish of spaghetti warming in the oven. Henry gulped two short glasses of whiskey before pouring a glass of Cabernet and sitting alone at the kitchen table to eat. The meal tasted good to him, much better than he had expected, and he realized he was starving. He had not eaten all day. He slumped over the table with an elbow planted by the side of his plate, and began shoveling the moist, spicy, sauce-covered pasta into his mouth, slurping like a little kid. *Damn, Laura. You are a pain in the ass sometimes, but this is good.*

When he had finished, he plopped the dirty dish in the sink, grabbed a second, wine glass and the nearly full bottle of Cabernet Sauvignon, and walked down the hall to the bedroom. Laura was in bed, leaning back comfortably against two, large pillows; she had a book in one hand and the television remote control in the other.

"Multi-tasking again?" Henry grinned, although guardedly, unsure of his wife's possible reaction. "Thanks for dinner. Here," he said, handing her the empty wine glass. "Want to toast to my self control?"

She looked at him warily, "What are you talking about?" she asked as he filled her glass.

"I avoided *The Gardens* the entire afternoon and evening. Went to the office instead. I had started driving toward *The Gardens* to see my mother like I thought I should, but then, I said to myself, 'Fuck it.' Figured old Maude didn't need, or want, to see my face again, after this morning, any more than I wanted to see hers."

"Hell, yes. I'll drink to that. Good for you. You can only do so much for your unrelenting mother without paying the price. You understand as well as I do. So, hell, yes, let's drink to my dear Henry's latent restraint. I do hate to break it to you though, honey - dealing with Maude is not over yet." She took a long sip of the wine. "But, yeah, here's to today, and to a decision well-made."

Henry pulled off his shoes and sat on the bed fully clothed. He refilled his wine glass, and topped hers before setting the bottle on the end table. Falling back against the padded headboard, he sighed. He was exhausted but had little awareness as to why. Virtually nothing of substance had been accomplished all day - nothing other than to worry about his mother, about his marriage, about his children, about a few, cranky clients, about himself. *Worry. What a fucking waste of energy that is. It does nothing but weigh me down.*

"Hey, what's on the news?" he asked suddenly in an attempt to get out of his overburdened head.

"Don't know. I was watching the end of *The Wizard of Oz* on that channel that plays old re-runs. Damn, I bet I've seen that movie a zillion times. Never get tired of it . . . but it's over now. Channel seven for news?"

"Yeah, that's good."

Laura changed the channel to the news station just as a bright, red *Breaking News* announcement flashed onto the screen. Immediately the image switched to a live, night scene, brightened only by carefully positioned, portable spotlights up close and flashing emergency lights in the distance. Standing some distance away from a five-story building, in part perfectly intact, in part smoldering, and in part still besieged with stubborn flames, was a male reporter, his fat fist tight around a microphone. His voice, though strong, was edged with anxiety. "We are on the scene of a fire at a local, well-regarded, retirement community, *The Gardens*, here in the heart of the city where less than an hour ago, fire alarms were sounded and staff inside launched into action evacuating residents. Firefighters and paramedics also have arrived on scene to take command of the incident and make sure the building is cleared safely. As you can see behind me, numerous ambulances and other emergency vehicles are in place ready to load the elderly and infirm. Some of the residents, we were told by a staff member, already have been evacuated to one of two hospitals - City Memorial and County General, both in close proximity to this facility. We are unsure, at this time, how the fire started and are further uncertain, at this point in time, whether all residents have vacated the building. As is protocol however, fire officials will have triaged the incident removing the most vulnerable residents first. As of this moment, we know of no injuries or fatalities. Those of us reporting on this story are being held away from the building at a secure distance and have not yet been able to interview at any length either fire officials or executive personnel from *The Gardens* itself. We will remain on scene, however, and get back to you as soon as possible with an update. For now, back to you, Scott, at the station."

For the length of the report, neither Henry nor Laura had spoken, but the moment it was over, Henry did, "Well shit, that's fucked up. What the hell's going to happen next, I wonder?"

In a rare gesture of recent affection, Laura reached over to Henry and gently rubbed his arm. "It'll be okay. Surely the staff had the wherewithal to evacuate the infirmary first. I'm sure Maude is well on her way to one of the hospitals. Someone will call. We'll call."

As if on cue, *Taps* rang out on Henry's cell phone. He jumped as if he'd seen a ghost.

Damn, am I on edge or what?

In only minutes after disconnecting from the caller, Henry, though slightly inebriated, was on his way to City Memorial Hospital, amazingly with his wife, Laura, at his side. "You're not driving," she had told him. "You've been drinking."

"So have you."

"One glass of wine. You've had, how many? I'll drive. We don't need another disaster tonight."

Chapter Thirty-Seven

GRACE

Grace drifted off to sleep in *Frank's arms* shortly after Mildred had left her for the evening. After pulling her mother, Olivia's afghan up to her chin, she settled back into Frank's chair for a short snooze. She had not wanted to fall asleep right away, or so soundly, for she had plans to make. *I feel I've been charged, for some strange reason, to pay the kindness Miss Millie's provided me when Frank died forward, and pretty quick too. God only knows why, but I think I must befriend that crabby woman, Maude, who seems hell bent on doing herself in. I have no clue how to do it - it won't be easy - but I'm going to reach out to poor Maude if it's the last thing I do . . . but not now. I'm so sleepy.*

Grace's planning stopped there. Her intentions had been sincere, but the day had been long. She was tired. Though Frank's face had been crystal clear in her mind's eye when her lids closed, it was Olivia, with the stealth of a stray cat that padded into Grace's weary mind.

⌘ ⌘ ⌘

Mother and daughter were at home on a Sunday evening having spent the day both together and apart - together on their weekly walk to Midway Park; together wading barefoot like toddlers at the edge of the mucky, duck pond there; together throwing pennies, burdened with hope, into a cracked and tarnished fountain that had seen better days; together digging into boxes of sticky Cracker Jacks, noisily munching the caramel-sweetened popcorn and peanuts all the way home; and together essentially because, at this time in their lives, each other was all either one had. Yet, although they had been side by side all day, much of the time they had been silent and awkwardly detached. Words had become sparse since Grace's father, Gilbert, had died. Olivia had drawn inward . . . and Grace had grown cautious, simply observing. Her mother was her entire world, beautiful, loving, and as unpredictable as a winter wind. But Grace had adapted to her mother's changeable moods, to her impulsive choices, and to her abrupt about-faces that made Grace's whole body tense with anxiety, at least for a time. Olivia Graci Brown was a rare combination of strength and fragility, a paradox of her own making. Grace was in awe of her. Nonetheless, regardless of the tension, love bound them. And Olivia clung to that for dear life. Little Grace was her everything. She had had two sudden, heart-wrenching losses in her life: her little brother, Carmine, and Gilbert, and though the deaths had been very different, they were the same. Loss was loss. As a result, the fissures in Olivia's heart were deep, her wounds forever weeping. On the heels of her husband's passing, then, with Grace her only focus, Olivia's notion about how to face an unpredictable life narrowed; her mantra solidified into one, single word - beware.

"You simply never know what's going to happen in this life," she told her daughter. "Beware, Gracie Brown. Stay on your toes."

Grace took the warning to heart, which, on the one hand was good - she was a careful, pensive child; but on the other hand, as she grew into adolescence, young Grace was guarded to a fault. That was the case, of course, until Percy Rawling blindsided her, thwarting her affection, snatching her virginity, and leaving her so disillusioned and sad, it took years to recover. In the aftermath of the mistaken tryst, her reserve reestablished itself and caution became the lens through which she viewed life. She wished for nothing and looked forward to nothing in fear that betrayal and disappointment might thrash her one more time. All of that was true, every bit, until Frank. Frank. Frank caught her by surprise, taught her to trust, and most importantly, consented to her love. That, of course, all happened in the distant future.

On this dreamy night, she was a little girl, alone with her mother, savoring the day, and relishing the evening.

Olivia's Sunday night dinners never disappointed - thin slices of breaded veal, cheese ravioli - homemade, of course - bruschetta, vinaigrette salad, and spumoni for dessert. Mother and daughter even shared an ounce of Chianti, or perhaps a tiny bit more if Olivia gave in. It was Grace's favorite time with her mother. After the meal, while the resonances of Vivaldi filled every room in the house, Olivia and Grace lit candles, placing them on a small table by the front window where they would burn themselves out overnight. The burning of candles was a ritual Olivia had insisted upon holding every Sunday. She lit six votive candles - one for each of her parents, Sophia and Giovanni, one for Carmine and Gilbert, of course, and two more, set away from the others for they were for the living, for Olivia, herself, and for Grace. As each of the wicks of the first four ignited into a tiny flare Olivia bowed her head and mumbled a prayer of remembrance, but with the last two it was different. Instead of bowing, she raised her head and said out loud, "The light from these candles carries my hopes and my resolve for meaningful lives, full lives, for lives lived carefully, and lives lived well." The words never changed. And on each Sunday night, in front of the makeshift alter, Olivia and Grace knelt respectfully. Grace did not always pray; she wasn't really sure how, but it didn't matter. The little custom made her mother happy, at least for a while; that's what mattered.

Grace was ushered to bed shortly after Vivaldi had been silenced; the house was quiet for the first time all day. Grace was asleep instantly, but Olivia roamed the house in the dark, the only light emanating from the burning candles that she had stared at until her eyes blurred. "They'll burn themselves out," she assured herself. "They always do." And with those words, she wandered down the hallway to bed.

It did not take long. Grace woke up first, wrestling her blankets to the floor, nearly tripping over them as she spun sideways to reach the door. Already the hallway was filled with smoke - a gray haze that stung her eyes and made her cough. "Mama," she yelled. "Mama. We're on fire. We're on fire."

Her mother's bedroom was far down the hall, the door closed, and locked. When Grace reached it, she twisted the doorknob and shook it hard. It would not give. She glanced quickly down the darkened hallway; in the distance, she saw flames, not red, but white, burnt orange, blue . . . and billowing above them, the smoke, a swirl of grays with a lighter, white vapor crawling like a specter along the floor toward her. The sounds, however, were what frightened her the most. A cacophony of pops, hisses, and a crackle or two had broken the silent night. Above it all was a loud crack and, then, a crash. The window. The window in front of Olivia's precious alter surely was gone.

Hysterical, Grace began banging on her mother's bedroom door. "Mama. Mama. Fire. We have fire. Let me in. We have fire." And in that instant, she heard her mother scream.

"Grace! Gracie."

Not understanding the danger, Olivia swung open her bedroom door. A loud whoosh that followed virtually sucked Grace into the space in front of her. An empty room with fresh oxygen to spare was like a feast to flames that tore down the hallway. Olivia screamed once more, "Mother of God, help us!"

She grabbed Grace to her, swirled around in one, tight circle and then ran toward a window that was partially opened. She hefted her daughter to the top of the window-sill and dropped her four feet to the ground below. She jumped too, landing beside Grace in the middle of a hydrangea bush, wet and scratchy . . . but not on fire. The two, mother and daughter, clung to each other like frightened monkeys only long enough to realize they needed to run. And they did, directly into the arms of a firefighter who escorted them to safety a short distance away. He draped blankets over their shoulders and stayed right beside them as they watched in horror as their home collapsed, burnt timbers falling like injured soldiers into the ash.

⌘ ⌘ ⌘

Grace had dreamed about the terrifying fire many times, the nuances of what occurred so long ago varying little. When she was younger, each time she woke up, the event that had been a living nightmare lingered, every detail vivid. And her body reacted - racing heart, dry mouth, a sweaty brow, and chills . . . all at once. In time, however, though the vision itself was as distinct as ever while she slept, both the dream and her reaction to it, faded more quickly when she awoke. That had continued to be the case, always, until now. This night something was different. Her heart had begun hammering in her chest. *What's happening?*

She heard sounds - muffled voices and a pounding, repetitive pounding; it was the exact, exasperating banging that had pulled her away from her dream. It did not let up. She jerked forward and stared through the dimly lit room at the door to her apartment. *Miss Millie must have closed it. But who is outside?* Someone was there, knocking, knocking. She scooted out of Frank's chair and shuffled forward.

"Okay. Hold your horses. I'm on my way," she called, her voice cutting out on the word *way*.

"Grace, Grace, open up." The tone was deep. A man. Familiar.

She pulled the door open only an inch and looked directly into the face of Louie Lawrence. "Let us in. Let us in," he ordered.

"What on Earth?" *What is Louie, that crazy pervert, doing here?*

"Fire, Grace. *The Gardens* is on fire. Let us in."

Her body tensed instantly. She smelled smoke - her memory had never allowed her to forget the acrid smell - but the hallway appeared clear of it. "What on Earth?" she said again. "Us? Who?" Though her heart continued to race, she stood numb, unmoving for a moment more. At last she stepped back, opened the door, and peered into the hallway. And there they were, her fourth-floor, wing mates - Louie, Ralph, and Lilly.

Ralph Fisher spoke next; his voice, in complete opposition to the panic she had detected in Louie's, was level, calm, resigned. "Your apartment is farther away from the central part of the building than ours. Fire must be at the far end of the residence but we can smell smoke. Can't you? And hear the sirens? Louie checked for a way out. The doors to the stairs are locked, elevator is sealed shut, and the night staff is gone, probably locked out automatically when they went to investigate. Who knows? It's just us, Grace - Louie, Lilly, and me. You must let us in while we wait for help." Behind him, little Lilly Littleton stood, clinging to his jacket with one hand, fingers on the other flailing at the air. Her whole body was quivering.

It took a few seconds for Grace to realize the urgency and genuineness of her friends' pleas, but the moment she did, she stepped farther back, opened the door fully, and replied, "Yes, yes, come in. All of you."

The three shuffled into her apartment, backing as far from the now-closed door as they could. Lilly's eyes, wide with fright, began to tear. Grace was about to go comfort her when the room went black. Electricity had been cut. She did not move.

"What should we do?" Grace muttered rather inanely into the pitch black. Clearly neither she, nor the old folks beside her had a clue. They were all eighty and ninety-year-olds, sequestered in the fourth-floor corner of a building on fire, without any idea whether anyone even knew or cared.

"We wait," Ralph declared with atypical, matter-of-fact authority. "No other choice."

Outside, sirens sounded, the wails excruciatingly loud before growing less strident as vehicles drove away from *The Gardens* with luckier residents in tow to secure locations. Grace grew panicky. *Some one has to find us.*

Minutes passed. Grace could hear Ralph's voice, a sing-song murmur in the dark. *Praying. He's praying. Certainly, he is, what else would Ralph do?*

Louie had moved to the window, pulled back the drapes, and stood, nose to the glass pane. It had been a shrewd choice on his part, really, because flaring lights of emergency vehicles sent flashes of red and yellow into the room. It was all the light they had. Finally he spoke. "Surely someone is accounting for all the residents, wouldn't you think?"

"Yes, of course. You're right, Louie. And Miss Millie must know what's happening. She won't let us down," Grace agreed.

At that very second, they heard a loud crash and several more, followed by footsteps, loud, stomping outside in the hallway. "Is anyone here?" someone bellowed. "Anyone here?" Noisy rustling brushed the door.

"We're here!" Louie screamed, the shriek so forceful, Ralph gasped in shock. "In here. In here!" Louie yelled again.

Lilly began to cry, her weeping tinny and shrill. It was the only sound Grace had ever heard the old woman make, but it was enough. The door to Grace's apartment was thrown open.

Two firefighters in full gear, with flashlights in hand, marched into the room. "We've got you. We've got you," one of them hollered twice.

Grace took in a deep breath. Despite her proclivity to maintain her reserve, she could not hold back. Her sobs began in earnest. Yet she felt right at home when the hulking figure in front of her reached out. He pulled her to him. "It'll be okay, now. Don't worry. We've got you." And she knew he did. She would be safe . . . they all would.

Grace understood at a most profound level. She had been in the arms of a hero before.

Chapter Thirty-Eight

MILDRED

It was late, but not that late, only ten o'clock. Mildred sat up, reached over to pet Midnight who was purring by her toes, and glanced around the living room as if hoping she had missed something - that perhaps Caroline had left a hint as to where she was going, where she had gone, but the room was silent save for the cat's purring and the usual, ambient noises that hummed in the background nonstop. The kitchen and living area were in perfect order as Mildred compulsively had insisted once she had realized that Caroline had walked out again without so much as a note of thanks or an explanation as to why. That fact, in itself, had irked Mildred to the core, so it had been important that her sister's mess be cleaned up before she sat down to read as she always did at night. Without her tidy house restored, she never could have settled. *My Gosh, how can two siblings be so different? Here I am, Ms. Responsibility, the neat freak, and the caretaker . . . while Caroline, for Christ's sake, is as unpredictable as a winter storm.*

"Stop it, Mildred," she mumbled aloud. "Stop thinking about her."

She reached for the television remote and pressed the switch to turn it on just as several more sirens screamed in the distance. *I've never heard so many sirens. I wonder what's going on?* In seconds, she knew. She was staring at *The Gardens*, her workplace, in partial ruins. The portion that housed the infirmary clearly had been destroyed. The roof appeared to have partly collapsed, the windows had been blackened or were missing altogether, and a smoldering plume of smoke swirled with the whim of a fickle wind. The central part of the building was intact, however, as was the four-story wing where the elderly residents were housed. *Thank goodness.* Standing in front of the large building, was a reporter, microphone in hand. Though he was speaking, his mouth moving, his face animated, Mildred blocked out the sound. *How can I possibly listen? I have to get there.* She jumped from the couch and stumbled forward, a wave of dizziness causing her to feel instantly nauseous. She staggered to her bedroom where she managed to pull on an old pair of jeans and a heavy sweatshirt before grabbing her bag, keys, and the mandatory lanyard she was required to wear around her neck at work; attached to it was a plastic pouch with her photo and pertinent identification. She scuttled to the front door. *Shoes. Shoes. You can't run out there barefoot, for heaven's sake, Mildred.* She slipped into a pair of tennis shoes, awkwardly tying the laces with shaking fingers that were not cooperating. At last, when she was ready, she opened the front door; a cold wind immediately slapped at her cheeks. It was dark, the fog having darkened the night, but in the distance like an errant sunrise, the sky glowed in hues of gold and yellow beneath a mantle of haze. And she smelled smoke, the pungent odor of myriad items - plastic, wood, chemicals, scorched paint - all combining into a heavy stench that almost instantly irritated her nostrils and coated her throat. Although her senses were bombarded, she did not hesitate. She began running.

⌘ ⌘ ⌘

Little Lilly Littleton saw Mildred first but she did nothing but point and then shake her finger as if silently giving the caretaker a piece of her mind. *Why did you leave us, Miss Millie? We were so afraid. We might have died without you. I couldn't bear that, you know. Miss Millie?* Lilly knew exactly what she would have said had the words formed for her, but Lilly had not spoken for years, not for years. The only sounds she created were for her alone - shadowy echoes and distant resonances swirling, swirling, and trapped in her mind by a voice that no longer would verbalize at all.

"What are you doing, Lilly?" Ralph asked, confused by her agitated gestures, but his eyes followed in the direction of her pointing. "It's Miss Millie. She's here. Miss Millie!" he called out with rare, uncharacteristic fervor.

And they were upon her - the four, frightened, old figures, who were all wrapped in silver, Mylar, space blankets had been standing with unsteady patience beside a fire engine. Upon seeing Mildred, however, they shuffled forward clutching the thermal blankets with tight fists, and oohing their relief to have *their* Miss Millie back to tend them again.

"Oh for heaven's sake. Lilly, Grace, Ralph, Louie, I have never been so happy to see you. I just found out minutes ago what happened here. Are you all right? You are, aren't you? Of course, look at you, all wrapped up like silver angels." Mildred was babbling. She knew it, but talking calmed her. "Have these nice firefighters been taking care of you? They have, haven't they? But, oh my goodness, you need to be out of the cold. They need to be out of this icy wind, don't they, sir?" she asked of a tall man who was bundled from head to toe in protective, fire gear. His face, dirtied by ash, was serious, but his eyes, the color of cobalt, were kind.

He pushed his helmet up off of his forehead and looked down at Mildred. "An ambulance is en route, mam."

"Oh, thank goodness. These four are my regular wards, fourth-floor, residents' wing. I look after them every day." She tilted the lanyard up toward the man's face. "See. I work here."

"Yes, mam. I can see you are worried, but our preliminary assessment has assured us these folks, who incidentally were the last residents to be escorted from the building, are stable and okay to transport. They'll be going to City Memorial Hospital to be checked out more thoroughly by the medical staff there."

"Will you go with us, Miss Millie?" Grace asked, her voice trembling.

She's cold and still frightened. Bless her heart. "I'm not sure I'll be allowed, honey," Mildred answered, "but I'll ask. We'll see."

She herded the foursome closer to the fire truck. "Stay close, now. I think I see the ambulance on its way." And she was right. Within a minute a red and white medical, transport vehicle pulled to a stop beside them. One at a time Lilly, Grace, Ralph, and Louie were helped into the ambulance, each seated side by side on a bench that had been folded down from the inside, back panel of the vehicle. They were secured with shoulder harnesses and lap belts, given a sip of warm tea, and assured by two efficient, medical attendants that they were in good hands. Not one of the four said a word. Instead, they glanced at one another before simply looking down at their laps as if in resignation for whatever was in store for them next. As for Mildred, she was told rather bluntly she could not ride in the ambulance with them.

"Sorry, mam. You're not a resident of this facility. You aren't allowed in. You'll have to find your own ride to the hospital. Might want to call a cab if you don't have a car of your own. Or maybe a bus will be by, although it's late."

Mildred watched sadly from outside but called out, "I'll see all of you soon. I'll make my own way to the hospital. Don't fret. I'll be there before you know it."

Someone grabbed her shoulder and pulled her back as the emergency medical technicians secured themselves inside as well. The double, back doors were slammed shut by the ambulance driver who quickly scurried away, hopped in the cab, and started the engine. The van sped away leaving Mildred behind shrouded in an invisible brume of toxic, exhaust fumes.

The last thing she had seen before she had been tugged backwards, however, was Louie turning in her direction, clearly gnawing on his tongue that bulged in his cheek, and winking. *Louie, you old fart. Save it for the hospital staff. Those people don't have the slightest idea what they're in for with old Louie coming their way.* She stifled a chuckle.

And that was it - Grace, Lilly, Ralph, and Louie were gone. Mildred stepped father back toward the sidewalk and stood shivering as the wind whipped at her hair and chapped her face; she felt utterly alone and more than a bit uncertain about where to turn next. Without further consideration, though, as if pulled along by instinct, she began walking in the direction of City Memorial Hospital, at least three miles away. She had no car, buses, she assumed, were no longer running for the night, and a cab was out of the question - too expensive. *I'll warm up if I walk fast.* She tucked her arms across her stomach and shoved each hand into the opposite sleeve of her sweatshirt in order to limit exposure to bare skin. She turned once more to gaze at *The*

Gardens, now no longer burning, but cast in an eerie golden glow from flickering street lamps and the gyrating flashes from the light bars of emergency vehicles that were positioned in place for the long haul. *What dedicated souls those firefighters are. Bet they'll be working all night - and me too, maybe, if I can make it to the hospital, sooner than later. I hope I can get there quickly.* She turned abruptly and began walking again, her strides quick and wide. She had lowered her head to avoid direct blows from the abrasive wind and marched forward with determined purpose.

⌘   ⌘   ⌘

Mildred did not see him, a hulking figure hovering motionless in a dark doorway that she strode past one half mile later. She was lost in thought. *Those poor, old, frightened people. I really must hurry. They'll be confused. Well, Louie won't, and Ralph has his faith, but Grace and Lilly . . . they'll need my comforting. Oh dear, and Maude. Surely she was rescued from the infirmary right away. I wonder where she is, and has her son been notified? I'll find out. I'll phone him. Oh mercy, Grace will be so distressed about Maude because she has her plans to pay it forward - kindness, that is. So sweet, but dear me, I'm not sure Maude would understand kindness or compassion if it slugged her in the face. Now, that's an awful thing for me to think. Well, if anyone can break through to Maude, it's Grace. Grace Ainsworth - what a gem.* Mildred's thoughts flitted like motes of dust, not one capable of being latched onto as they darted through her mind in random discord. *And Caroline. Where is she? Did I lock my front door? Midnight will hate being alone all night. Is Caroline safe somewhere? Where did she go? Why did she not leave a note? I must hurry. My job. Will I have a job now? Will The Gardens continue operating? And what about everyone's belongings? Oh dear, it is so cold. I can't think straight.*

And then she could not think at all. In one second all cerebral notions vanished. A thick arm, stinking of sweat and whiskey, had wrapped around her neck and she was being yanked sideways into a black alley. She struggled to fight back but her hands that had been stuffed into her sweatshirt sleeves were suddenly immobile. The monster that had her held her arms tight, crushing them against her diaphragm. She could not breathe. She began kicking, forward and to the side, over and over, but to no avail. Her whole body, stricken with fear failed her. Her screams, muffled by a hand that pressed hard against her mouth, were useless. She grew conscious only of her heart thumping inside her chest and of the release of urine, her own, the warm liquid saturating her jeans from her crotch to her knees. She was thrown backwards, her head landing hard against cement where she lay stunned and barely conscious; yet she heard sounds - the crash of a trash can, the squeal of a rodent, the howl of a stray cat, the ripping of her clothes, and his labored breathing . . . the obnoxious smell of his rancid breath smothering her. And somewhere in the far distance, she heard the lonely sound of the blues, someone's saxophone weeping into the shadows of the night. Oh how she wished she could have reached it.

Mildred became cognizant of her surroundings again sometime before dawn. The sky had lightened, but daylight was hours away. She managed to sit up. She was naked from the waist down, her jeans and panties in a twisted bunch beside her. With nothing but sheer grit to sustain her, she tugged on her clothing and stood up. She had found her tennis shoes ten feet away and had crawled on her hands and knees to retrieve them before standing. Every inch of her body ached; she knew she was bruised, especially on her arms, her neck, and along her inner thighs where her assailant had pounded against her until he was done. She hurt to the touch, but the pain was so much deeper. In all of her life, and she was closing in on sixty, she had never had sexual intercourse with any man. *I was waiting for the one, the right one. Oh, God, why this? Someone tell me why, why, in the hell, this?* The loss was crushing. Hot tears burned her cheeks. She knew in her heart, from this moment on, she would never be the same. Never.

Though she was numb with shock and stricken with sadness, she moved out of the alley and onto the sidewalk. Her sobs, relentless but strangely silent, fueled her anger, but, at the same time, powered her forward. Her feet moved step after step after step in the direction of City Memorial where her caretaking would resume. *Grace and Lilly need me.* But that was not all. This time, perhaps for the first time ever, she would tend to Mildred Watson as well. She had needs, too.

⌘　⌘　⌘

Two heavy, glass doors slid open as Mildred approached the emergency room of City Memorial Hospital nearly an hour and a half later. The dark still lingered outside, but inside, the place was alive with light and industry. She stepped forward, uncertain, her mind muddled, her clothing disheveled, her body aching. *I must look like a homeless bum.* But around her neck, the lanyard, though bent and dirtied, proved her identity and her position as an employee at *The Gardens.* Fortuitously, unlike most of her clothing, the *monster* had not ripped it away. Just inside the entry, she stopped before moving toward a reception desk. Her gait was so wobbly she was not sure she would make it, but she set her sights and soon was gripping the edge of the desk, beseeching with only her eyes, the help she needed.

"Oh," a woman uttered, before jumping to her feet. "You need help. Chet," she ordered a man behind her, "get a wheel chair."

The next hours were a blur of questions and explanations, prodding and pampering, evaluations and treatment. Mildred had been moved to a private cubicle where a female, emergency room doctor and a very competent physician's assistant conducted a long and invasive set of procedures that, they assured her, were essential in insuring the validity of Mildred's rape at the hands of an unknown assailant. Such documentation, she was told, was vital and indispensible for law enforcement. The examination was horrible. After shedding her clothing onto a sterile paper of some sort, Mildred stood shaking. She was swabbed and poked, plucked, scraped, and photographed - every inch of her. The process, though essential for the police report, felt as if it were the second assault of that long and ghastly night.

At the outset, Mildred had tensed with fear. "Don't touch me. Don't touch me," she had wanted to scream, but she did not, because the women with her were kind - efficient, determined, compassionate, and kind. She understood. They were mirror images of the caretaker she was, of the human being she always had sought to be.

I will survive. The thought sustained her.

When the rape kit had been completed, it held her clothing in sealed bags, semen, saliva, fingernail scrapings, head and pubic hair, urine, and her own blood that had seeped from a ravished hymen, Her vagina, rectum, mouth, ears, neck, hands, arms, breasts, torso, buttocks, and legs had been swabbed. Not one inch of her had been ignored. And she had been photographed from every angle. She had felt humiliated . . . fully, completely mortified.

When it was over, she was more exhausted than she had ever been . . . and she cried, this time a mournful wail that filled the little room with sorrow so deep one could have waded in it.

Chapter Thirty-Nine

MAUDE

Dawn did not lighten anyone's spirits. The sun, concealed by a thick layer of fog and dense clouds would have trouble breaking through this day. Maude couldn't have cared less. All she wanted was to get the hell out of *wherever* she was. *My life is a nightmare, an absolute, godforsaken nightmare. I must get away. Why can't I just go down that golden road home? I have my red shoes. My Tara is waiting.* Confusion had snared her once again. She had no idea where she was or how she had gotten there, and although she recalled a night fraught with activity, she had no understanding whatsoever of what had occurred. Her inability to recall any details had set her on her ear. She was angry at herself and everyone around her.

"Damn it, bitch. Get over here," Maude snapped at a short, frumpy nurse's assistant who had stepped into the room only moments before.

"Mam, I'm here to assist you, but do not curse at me," the woman replied. Her face had flushed with irritation, but her voice was calm. "What can I help you with?"

"I want out of this damned hellhole. They've got me all tied up here."

It was so. She had been restrained once more. From the moment Maude had entered City Memorial Hospital, her behavior had been beyond difficult. In the ambulance, she had been subdued - cold, silent, and disoriented. Once inside the building, however, all hell broke loose. It was as though the toasty confines of the hospital fired up the demons within her. She had spit at an attending nurse, had attempted to kick a kind orderly in his crotch, had urinated and defecated all over herself and her gurney, and had set a bevy of nurses' assistants running in her direction to silence her screams. She had hollered obscenities for half an hour before she had fallen asleep, exhausted. Only a mild sedative had been necessary; in less than a minute, to the relief of hospital staff, Maude appeared dead to the world. Even when her son, Henry, and his wife had slipped into her room for a look, around midnight, she had not roused.

"Thank God, she's asleep," Henry had murmured to Laura who stood beside him looking at her mother-in-law as if she were a stranger.

"She doesn't even look like herself," Laura commented, cocking her head in amazement. "When she's sleeping, her whole face softens. Isn't that interesting?" She paused. "It's the eyes. They're closed . . . and we're safe."

"What are you talking about, Laura? For Christ's sake." Henry looked as his wife as if she were loony.

"Her fucking eyes, Henry. When they're open, all dark and menacing, she can cut a person down with one damned look sideways. You know exactly what I mean. She's stared at me enough times to make me feel like I'm nothing but a piece of dog shit. And you've been there, too. I've seen you wince and recoil when she's at her witchy worst." She stopped again. "It's never been a pretty sight, Henry, watching you cower like an injured puppy when she's dishing out her nasty, bitter venom on you like she does."

"Oh for God's sake, Laura. I do not at this time in particular, need a psychological evaluation from you. Hell, let's just get out of here and go home. Call ourselves lucky that she wasn't wide-eyed and raving at everything in sight like she usually is."

"Now, that's my guy. Searching for a positive in the midst of this goddamned mess. Yeah, let's go home, because, you know what? It may not be solely ours for long. If *The Gardens* is uninhabitable for a few days, guess where old Maude probably is going to be when she leaves this hospital? You've got it. Camped out, in all her glory, in our guest bedroom. Won't that be a joy?"

Henry glared crossly at his wife, making her pay for being right. "Holy shit," he said. "That scenario has *bad dream* written all over it."

"Sure as hell does. Come on."

The two slipped out of the room and walked hand in hand like newly primed lovers, down the hallway toward the exit. Their enigmatic relationship had evolved over the years but as fiery as it could be, it was theirs, and each, in their own way, relished the exclusivity of it. Neither could imagine life without the other.

Life without Maude, however . . . well, that was another thing altogether.

Chapter Forty

HENRY

Five hours of sleep had not been enough. Henry and Laura had arrived home from the hospital and had fallen into bed, partially clothed; it had been nearly two o'clock. Now, however, though barely functional, Henry realized, with harsh clarity, that he had to retrace his route back to City Memorial where his mother, Maude, surely was awake and likely fuming that he had not appeared before her already so that she could abuse him in some other new way.

Damn I could go back to bed and sleep for a week. The exhaustion was due to sleep deprivation, of course, but also was caused by layers of stress that had made Henry's shoulders tighten and his neck ache for days.

"Better get on with it," he heard. Laura clearly was awake, but her eyes were closed, dark smears of mascara streaked beneath them.

"I know. I know," he murmured. "Want to join me? I'm sure you do."

His sarcasm sparked her ire. "Hell no. You're on your own, honey. We dodged a bullet last night, but, sorry to tell you, Henry, you're going to face the firing squad all alone this morning."

"Yeah, right . . . quaint analogy, Laura. If I don't come home, rest well in knowing you predicted my complete obliteration at the hands of old Maude," he replied, giving credence to her trite equivalence. "Ding, Dong, the witch's son is dead."

She scooted up in bed then and grinned. "You've got this, Henry. Strap on your balls and go deal with her."

"Thanks for your encouragement, dear," he sneered and then he chuckled. "Jesus, Maude is miles away but might as well be smack dab in the middle of our bedroom. Now that's fucking power if I've ever heard of it."

Laura's face grew serious. "You're right. Scary, huh?"

"Creepy, is what it is," he responded before adding, "Go on back to sleep. I'll be home before you know it. Be ready to dig out the shrapnel."

⌘　⌘　⌘

Henry had been correct. His mother was in a fit of rage when he entered her hospital room mid-morning.

"Where have you been, you lout?" she started in on him. "I'm surprised you showed up at all."

"Hello, Mother," he replied, not willing to buy in to her antagonism.

"Hello, Mother. That's all you have to say? I've been dragged to this new place, without my permission, might I add, restrained to the bed like a prisoner, and you, it's obvious, don't care one, darn iota," Maude's dark eyes were exactly as Laura had described them - vicious, cutting. Her mouth had twisted into an ugly snarl.

Henry took a step backwards - the *injured puppy*. Isn't that what Laura had called him? He gained his composure. "Laura and I were here last night, Mother. You were fast asleep and we were advised to let you rest. You went through quite an ordeal before we got here."

"Whatever are you talking about, Henry?"

"You don't remember, do you?"

"Remember what, for heaven's sake. What's to remember?"

"A fire started at *The Gardens* last night, somewhere near the infirmary. You and the other patients were apparently rescued just in time," he explained. "I was notified late last night that you, along with several others, had been taken here. Do you know where you are, Mother?"

She glared at him, though her head had titled; she was puzzled by his words.

"You're at City Memorial Hospital. You were brought here by ambulance," he told her.

"I'm at City Memorial - that awful, sub-standard hospital? I'm there? How in the hell ..."

Stopping in mid-sentence, suddenly she began to recall. Voices were yelling. Still tied to her bed, she had been spun around in circles and shoved down a long corridor and out into the cold, frosty air. She had been freezing to death. The memories came in quick, disjointed flashes - an icy wind, the smell of smoke, blinding lights, cold, more cold, a man's soothing words, movement, a siren, a hand against her cheek, a blanket, warm. She very clearly remembered the blanket. It smelled of rubbing alcohol, and she had considered dying there beneath it. She had not though. Instead, she was here looking dazed at Henry's grim face. Her son had shown up after all.

"You showed up after all," she muttered in a voice so un-natural, Henry quivered.

"Of course, I did," he assured her, but instantly his heart seemed to skip a beat. He sucked in a deep breath, and in that space, he experienced a sorrow he had never felt be-fore. It was chilling. And it alarmed him. *What's happening to her? Is she going to die?*

Chapter Forty-One

GRACE

Along with Lilly, Ralph, and Louie, Grace was situated in a private, curtained-off cubicle, in a four-bed mini-ward at City Memorial Hospital. Each was assigned a patient number, labeled with a plastic, identification wristband, and examined by a young, female doctor who looked, in Grace's opinion, to be about eighteen - tops. Perhaps it was the long, blond hair, gathered into a perky ponytail at the crown of her head. Or, perhaps it was the young woman's large, blue eyes and deep dimples, tiny craters, punched right into the center of each cheek. Whether she smiled or was serious, those dimples dominated the doctor's face. Grace had a preposterous urge to reach out and poke a finger into one of them, but she restrained herself, and instead, blatantly stared; she had never seen such remarkable features on anyone.

"Are you all right?" the doctor asked when Grace did not divert her intent gaze from the woman's face.

"Oh, oh, yes, I am. I'm gawking at you. So sorry," Grace muttered, abashed by her own ghastly manners. "It's simply that you look so young to be a doctor, and so pretty with those charming dimples."

The doctor grinned. "I'm thirty-four, Mrs. . . . " She glanced down at her tablet. "Ainsworth. Grace, is it?"

"Yes. Grace Ainsworth. Eighty-eight and fit as a fiddle, although events tonight were a bit unnerving, I must say. Fire at *The Gardens*. What a shock. Thank goodness for those lovely firefighters who helped us out of the building. Once outside though, while we were waiting to be transported, we were all chilled to the bone in no time."

"I'd say you had a right to have been alarmed and, yes, it is cold out tonight. It's been quite an upheaval for all of you, I can imagine. By the way, I'm Dr. Brown. Cynthia Brown. I'm here to check your vitals - make sure you really are *fit as a fiddle* - before you rest for the night." She offered a genuine smile, patted Grace's arm, and added, "I'm so glad you and your friends are safe and sound here now."

"Yes, for heaven's sake so am I. Thank you. Oh, Dr. Brown . . ." Grace leaned forward, placed a flat palm next to her mouth, and whispered secretively, "Just so you know, Lilly, next bed over, doesn't talk. I thought you should be aware. Sweet, old lady, never says a word. And as for Ralph and Louie across the way, well, Ralph will be no problem, but Louie, best to watch out for that one. You won't want to turn your back. He's a letch."

"Thanks, Grace," Dr. Brown smirked. "I appreciate the heads up." She gently squeezed Grace's arm. "You lie back and get some rest now."

"I will. Thank you, doctor. I sure do wish Miss Millie were here."

"Miss Millie?"

"The caretaker on our wing. Miss Millie usually watches over us like a hawk but she's not here yet." She paused. "But she will be. Miss Millie won't let us down. She was probably held up somehow and had trouble getting to the hospital."

"She's probably on her way now," the doctor assured, though, of course, she had no possible way of knowing. "Good night, Mrs. Ainsworth," she added. "Have a good sleep."

⌘ ⌘ ⌘

The face Grace saw first when she opened her eyes was Mildred's. Her old friend was sitting in a blue, plastic chair next to Grace's bed, her head cocked awkwardly to one side, eyes closed, hands wrapped protectively around her. Her hair had been pulled back in a tight bun, and prominent above her left eye was a dark, purple bruise. Her lower lip, swollen and inflamed, bore a deep cut. *Oh my heavens, what happened to Miss Millie?* Grace's heart thumped erratically and then calmed. *I don't want to wake her.*

She didn't have to for exactly at that moment, Mildred stirred. She issued a low groan before she sat upright and opened her eyes.

"Miss Millie," Grace blurted, "What on Earth happened to you. You've been injured."

Mildred sucked in a deep breath. *I can do this.* "Oh it was the silliest thing, Grace. I tripped on my way over here and really gave myself an awful fall, head first onto the pavement. I was rushing, not paying attention, and down I went." The lie irked her but she had no choice. Not one of the old folks she cared for would ever know the truth about the horrible assault she had endured. Mildred could not have borne the telling and she knew her wards never could have come to grips with the fact that anyone could have attacked *their* Miss Millie. But the lie, such a blatant untruth, loomed like a dark veil that cast a shadow on the trust Mildred had worked so hard to forge with her charges. "Don't you worry one more second about me, Grace. I'll be just fine. I'm tough." She swallowed hard. *Be strong, Mildred. Keep up the pretense. These old folks cannot know.*

"Well, you look a little peaked, Miss Millie."

"Oh, just a little blow to my ego, Grace, falling down like I did. What a klutz. What we have to worry about now is you, Lilly, Ralph, and Louie. I learned from the administrative staff that you and the others must stay here at least one more night so officials can make sure residences at *The Gardens* are safe and secure; then you can go back. How does that sound?"

"I suppose it has to be. How bad was the fire, Miss Millie?"

"Damage was contained to the infirmary, thank goodness, and all the patients who were there were rescued quickly, including your friend, Maude. She's here at City Memorial too, I understand, though I haven't seen her yet."

"Oh dear, she must be in quite state, I'd imagine."

Mildred shook her head. "Yes, likely so."

"Miss Millie?" Grace asked. "Does anyone know how the fire started? It seems so odd, because *The Gardens* is so well maintained."

"I don't think the source has been determined yet. Fire and police officials are investigating, I'm sure. I did hear, and I can't for the life of me remember where, that the blaze possibly started in one of the dumpsters behind the infirmary. Maybe a vandal was up to no good or maybe a homeless person was trying to stay warm, you know, lighting debris in the garbage bin for a little heat. One way or the other, we'll know soon enough, I'm sure. Those investigators definitely know their business."

"I guess so," Grace mused, her eyes examining the ceiling as if trying to capture an image of a modern-day ruffian at the dumpster with matches in hand. When she looked down, she blurted, "Are you staying the day with us, Miss Millie?"

"Actually, no. I need to get home to check on my cat, and my house really. I can't remember if I locked the door when I rushed out last night. Besides, I want to freshen up after my fall last night. You can understand. But I'll be back."

Grace gazed again at Mildred's bruised face. For the first time she noted her eyes, red-rimmed and puffy as if she had been crying. *That must have been quite the tumble.*

"Tell the others, when they wake up, that I was here, will you, Grace? I'll be back this afternoon." Mildred stood and backed out of the room.

Grace watched her go, noticing immediately that she was wearing dark blue, hospital scrubs and a wrinkled, cloth jacket at least two sizes too big. *Now why on Earth would Miss Millie be dressed up in that kind of garb? What in the devil happened to her clothes?*

Chapter Forty-Two

MILDRED

Mildred took a bus home, stepping out at the bus stop only one block from her front door. When she reached it, having hurried there as quickly as she could, she sighed with relief. *Thank goodness. I did lock the damned thing.* Inside, Midnight greeted her with a loud meow. "I know, it's about time," she said aloud to the cat as though it understood her completely. She freshened Midnight's kibble, patted his back, and said, "And now I'm off to take a hot shower."

⌘ ⌘ ⌘

She stripped out of the borrowed, hospital clothing she was wearing, left the garb in a heap on her bathroom floor, and stepped into the shower. The water warmed rapidly. Mildred stood absolutely still letting the near-scalding spray pepper her sore body. The heat did not bother her; instead, she was soothed by it, for she had never in her life wanted more to feel, to feel anything rather than the terror that had consumed her the night before. And, at this moment, she had complete control. The hot water pelted her skin until it reddened and burned before she adjusted the temperature. She washed her hair and lathered her entire body with soap, the fragrance of lavender wafting in the steam. A fleeting vision of her childhood, she and Caroline picking fronds of fresh lavender for their mother, warmed her spirit, but instantly the memory disappeared when she reached down to swab between her legs. She staggered forward, overcome with nausea. Afraid she might faint, she gripped onto a grab bar as a touch of bile crept into her throat. And she sobbed once more, the cries so forceful that spasms wracked her throat; she began to cough over and over until she was bent over, gagging, and dry heaving. She stared at the soapy water trapped in the shower pan until her eyes blurred. *I'm never going to forget, am I? I can't. But I'm afraid, and not of some stranger in the dark; I'm afraid of myself, of losing my self-control, like now, or forever. I can't let that happen.* She tightened her grip on the bar and straightened before spitting angrily into the pooling water at her feet. Anger. It felt right; it was powerful and formidable, a compelling emotion that could not be denied. Yet, it was an imposter. That, Mildred knew, was a tacit truth. For beneath the rage, with perhaps no way to find its way out was anger's certain, inescapable nemesis - grief.

Had she hit rock bottom? Would a lifetime of losses be too much to bear? Would anger consume her? And what about grief? Would it be smothered far underneath? It had happened to others. She thought instantly of Maude. Maude - inexplicable, irrepressible, unrelenting Maude. Clearly she was ensnared in a rage that she refused to release. How could she? Anger was normalcy to her. Her survival depended on it.

All of her anger really is grief though, isn't it? And in that moment, Mildred understood implicitly that she could not allow herself to fall victim to the very same fate. She could not. She could not.

Chapter Forty-Three

MAUDE

Maude could not take her eyes from her son's face. It was as if she had not looked at it in years. *He's not a little boy any more, is he? He's a man. Older now. Serious. Why, he has wrinkles splaying from the corners of his eyes. When did those appear? What happened to that bratty, little toddler who ran through my parties and upset the guests?*

Simultaneously, Henry studied his mother's appearance - the pallid, wrinkled cheeks, the black eyes darting, and her lips pressed into s stiff pucker. *Is she judging me?* His unease grew. *What the hell is she thinking?* "Mother? Are you feeling all right?"

"I'm quite well, Henry." She tilted her head to one side as if contemplating what to say next, but fell silent. Yet she continued to peruse his face. All the while, her hands fluttered like agitated birds on the railings of the bed. *I don't think I know you at all, Henry. Of course, I don't. We sent you away, Judge and I, but can't you see? We had to. You were a distraction. Judge had his practice, and I, I had to keep him from leaving me alone. And he did. Often. It was those women, always a slew of women lurking around, rotten tramps, every, single one. Poor Judge. They waylaid him, and for the life of him, he didn't seem to know how to resist.* She squirmed in the bed, her eyes dancing with rage.

"He was up to no good, you know," she blurted.

"Who?"

"Oh, for God's sake, never mind. You've never listened, Henry."

"I'm not sure I follow, Mother," Henry replied, finding words for his own confusion in regard to Maude's baffling demeanor. *Does she think she's been communicating with me?*

She gave her son a haughty stare before huffing out a deep breath that filled the air around her with a putrid, sulfurous stink. Henry moved back from her bed and feigned a cough in order to cover his nose. *Disgusting. She reeks like she's rotting inside.*

"Mother, have you eaten? Would you like something to eat? Are you hungry?"

"No, of course not, for heaven's sake, Henry. Are you out of your damned mind? How can I eat when they've disappeared? And why in God's Earth do you ask me the same damned question in three different ways. I'm not a witness being cross-examined in a courtroom, you fool."

"I just wanted to know if you were hungry," Henry spat. His exasperation was increasing by the moment. *How does Mother manage an iota of logic, because most of the time she's bat-fuck loony?* "And who are you talking about disappearing, Mother? Everyone was rescued safely from *The Gardens.*"

"Don't fib to me, you scoundrel. Not everyone made it out. Judge and Katherine didn't, I'm convinced. I can't locate them anywhere. They've simply disappeared." She stopped speaking once more and glared at him. Her mouth returned to its tense pucker, pursed lips tightly sealed.

"Mother . . ." he began, but he felt a presence. He looked toward the doorway and issued a sigh of relief. *Saved by the bell.* Standing tentatively at the entrance to Maude's room was that little, old lady, Grace *something*, and a younger woman who looked familiar as well.

"For God's sake," he heard his mother squawk. "How in the hell did you two find me? You're not the ones I've been looking for."

"Hello, Maude," Grace said softly, "Miss Millie and I came for a visit."

"Oh, hell's bells. Whatever for?" Maude faced the two women as a look of incredulity shadowed her features. "I certainly did not ask for the company of you two, for Pete's sake."

"But we're friends, aren't we, Maude? I'm certain you told me we were friends, best girlfriends like Thelma and Louise. Remember? I'm here because I'm your friend, and Miss Millie . . . well, Miss Millie takes care of us all." Grace stood awkwardly for a moment, expecting a response; when Maude offered nothing, she moved forward and added, "And how are you feeling, dear?"

⌘ ⌘ ⌘

Having finally placed Mildred as his mother's caretaker from *The Gardens,* Henry pulled her gently aside and whispered, "She's very confused, disturbingly so." His throat tightened, but he continued. "She believes her dead husband and a daughter, who never existed at all, were here yesterday, and now have disappeared somewhere, perhaps consumed by the fire. Just so you know. I'm at a loss. After her running away and nearly perishing in that awful storm, and then with this horrendous fire, her mind seems completely muddled.

Maybe you can help her find her way back. I know I sure as hell can't. She detests the sight of me."

"Oh, I'm sure that's not the case, but you take a break, Mr. Litzenberg. Grace and I will sit with your mother for a while. I know this is all very exhausting."

"It is new territory, that's for sure," Henry muttered. "I have to admit I'm a little shaken by Mother's current condition."

"Understandable. With elderly folks like your mother, circumstances, mental and physical, can change in a heartbeat. Don't blame yourself though; you're here. That's what matters."

"I suppose," Mildred hear him mumble as he slipped into the hallway. He remained just outside the door watching, his face pale and solemn. Mildred looked away, and in that second, he vanished.

⌘ ⌘ ⌘

Maude was not pleasant. "What in the hell are you doing here, Grace? I didn't ask for you. And you dragged Mildred along. What are you thinking? You know I loathe the woman," Maude announced, seemingly oblivious to the fact that Mildred could hear everything.

"Now, Maude, we've all been a bit upset over what's occurred the last few days. You're not the only one. I asked Miss Millie to come with me to see how you are doing," she explained as Mildred moved in beside her.

"Maude? How are you feeling?" Mildred inquired.

"Better yet, how in the devil are you? You're all cut and bruised. You look like something the cat dragged in, Mildred. Did someone attack you?"

"She had an unfortunate fall," Grace offered, but at the same instant, she heard Mildred suck in a sharp breath.

"Yes," Mildred declared quickly. "So silly of me."

"Well, be careful in this place. One damned fall and the doctors tie you to the bed around here. They've still got me tethered here."

"It's for your safety, Maude," Mildred defended.

"Oh, bull. That's hogwash. If people were safe in this hospital, my Judge and Katherine wouldn't be lost. It's an outrage. Someone has to know where they are, or, at least what's happened to them." Maude's eyes welled with tears. "And nobody will tell me a goddamned thing."

Mildred glanced warily at Grace but said nothing.

"Did you bring your bags, Grace?" Maude asked abruptly. The issue of the missing Judge and Katherine appeared to have been forgotten on the very heels of it being mentioned.

"My bags?"

"Yes, for our trip. Remember? I've been packing all morning. It's so hard to know what to take, though." Maude exhaled a heavy, aggravated sigh.

Mildred reached over and gently touched Grace's hand as Maude continued. "I sure as hell don't want to go down that road alone. What will you be wearing, Grace? Dress warm. Do you have comfortable shoes? I do . . . my red ones. Now don't pack too much, Grace."

"Oh, I certainly won't, dear." Grace was confused by Maude's ramblings, but additionally saddened and afraid. The sudden dramatic shift in Maude's mental state was shocking and starkly revealing. *Is this the end?* "Maude, my dear friend, when will we be leaving?" Grace played along cognizant that her words were phony, an awkward charade of her own making.

"Oh, soon. Soon. People are waiting for me." Maude's eyes shifted from Grace's face to a space in the distance and then back. "I'm so glad we became best friends. That means the world to me, Grace. You're the only one I've ever had . . . the only friend. Did you know that?"

"No, Maude, I didn't, and to learn that is remarkable."

"Well, it took a while to find you."

"I guess it did," Grace chuckled. "We're sure not young whippersnappers any more."

For Mildred, listening to Maude's prattling was disturbing and she felt certain Grace was ill at ease as well. She shifted uncomfortably in her chair and finally spoke. "We need to get back to your room, now, Grace. The others will be wondering what's become of us."

"Yes, we do." Grace immediately struggled to her feet. Simply being with Maude had been exhausting, but she felt strangely satisfied because her goal of being kind, of being a friend, had been carried out. And though she had feigned her understanding of Maude's gibberish, she had not let on. Instead, she had been compassionate. She had been considerate. She had cared. She had paid kindness forward just as she'd planned.

"We'll visit again, Maude," Grace said, patting her gently on the arm.

"Yes, do. You can meet me at my *Tara*. It's lovely there and not too far down the road. It's home, Grace, and you know what everyone says - 'There's no place like home.'" She paused. "Oh dear, look there, I do believe Judge and Katherine have returned. There in the distance." She pointed her bony finger toward the vacant hallway. "They're waiting for me. I must hurry and gather my bags. Good-bye, dears. Good-bye."

As Grace turned to leave, she was overcome with sorrow. She knew with instinctive certainty that there would not be another visit to her friend and that the lie - that she understood Maude's every word - would fester alongside her until the very end.

Chapter Forty-Four

HENRY

Word of his mother's passing, delivered in a succinct, though not uncaring manner came before dawn. Henry's cell phone vibrated on the end table and though *Taps* was barely audible even in the quiet dark, it awakened him. He had not expected to learn of his mother's demise so quickly; she was stubborn. And he recalled his thinking when he had left her hospital room only hours before. *Old Maude is as cranky as ever. She'll be around for months to come. Mother may be confused and angry but she's not hell bent on giving up on this life. No way. Being a royal pain in the ass gives her too much pleasure.* Yes, he had been certain . . . so the news was a shock. Secondary to the death, however, was his response to it. He could not possibly have anticipated his reaction, the antithesis to how he had envisioned it.

⌘ ⌘ ⌘

"Mr. Litzenberg," the voice had said, "This is Dr. Cynthia Brown, City Memorial Hospital. I am so sorry to disturb you in the middle of the night, but it's about your mother."

"Yes?"

"I'm afraid, sir, that your mother has passed. A nurse on rounds found her only minutes ago. I'm so sorry," she stated again.

"I'll be there."

"No hurry, sir, but you will need to identify the body. And, of course an autopsy is required to establish the definitive cause of death. For now, however, please be assured that Mrs. Litzenberg's remains are safe. And, again, you have my deepest condolences."

"Thank you." Henry said not another word. Instead, he bent at the waist and began to sob, deep, moaning cries that awoke Laura who rushed to his side.

"What?" she asked.

"Dead. Maude's dead," he answered. "Just like that."

Laura gasped, gave Henry's arm a quick squeeze, and ran into the bathroom, slamming the door behind her. And though his crying did not abate, he heard his wife, retching over and over, as if expelling a demon from deep inside her. Henry understood. The wretched woman, his own mother, was gone but alive still was hatred and animosity accumulated over time, the bitterness rising like harsh bile to choke and sicken. He ached because of his wife's anguish, and he was angry, for he had been cheated by his self-serving parents of a childhood, of love, of the support that may have led him on another career course. He knew what had been expected of him, however, and though he always had felt he was a speck in his father's shadow, he had strived in some perverse way to be like him - successful, wealthy, admired. But he had managed just so far. Yes, he was a well-to-do attorney, but Judge and Maude had lauded their power over him, putting him over and over in his place. *"Oh Henry, you'll never be the man Judge is."* And though the ladder to reach upward was solidly in place, Henry made little leeway, instead, hanging on desperately to the bottom rungs, flailing with uncertainty until he was bleeding from every pore. Now, in the throes of this loss, Henry felt more impotent, in every sense of the word, than he ever had before. He was trapped in a sham, for despite his innate integrity, he deemed his crushing, unexpected sadness as if it were an imposter. Did he grieve for his mother, his father or himself? *It's for all of us.* He knew it to be true. For the entirety of Henry's lifetime, he and his parents had been a triad of absolute, unadulterated dysfunction. With the sharp angles of the triangle shattered at last, would he be freed?

⌘ ⌘ ⌘

When his sobbing finally subsided, Henry made his way outside to sit beside the pool. For a lifetime, that had been his go-to place where memories and concerns, like carousel creatures, rose and fell, circled, circled, until they stopped. He often was astounded that such reflective rides took him nowhere. His musing on this day seemed a bit different. *How have I ended up here - a half-ass husband and father, and, more to the point, an estate attorney, planning for the end, and all the while pitting siblings against siblings, fathers against sons, mothers against daughters, stirring the pots of greed, manipulation, and contempt? Of course, I chose this path for I understand it so well. It's a reflection of who I am; it's my whole fucking life in a nutshell. Thanks, Mother, thanks, Judge, thank you very fucking much.* He slammed a fist onto the arm of the lawn chair so hard it shuddered with the blow. He tightened his fingers around it and looked up just in time to see Laura inching her way toward him.

"Hey, babe," he murmured as she knelt beside him. "You okay?"

"Yeah, I am. You?"

"Better. Surprised though. Didn't think her dying would hit so hard."

"Me either," she replied. "God, she was so fucking awful to me most of the time, but . . . I don't know . . . she was a living, breathing soul who lived a life. As flawed as she was, and I think it was pretty damned flawed, she probably tried the best she could. You know?"

"I do. What's weird for me right now is the void. Her being gone leaves a big, fat divot in my world and I'm not sure if I can fill it. Is that stupid?"

"No. Our parents do that to us, I guess. No matter how terrible, or how wonderful, or how fucking weird they are, when they go, there's a vacuum. Something's missing."

"Yeah," he mulled. "Wonder if it will be the same for our kids when we kick the bucket some day?"

"Ha. Good question. I can hear them now. 'Glad those flippin' freaks are gone for good.'" She smirked. "Or, hell, maybe they'll actually be sad."

The two fell silent for several moments, each considering the possibilities. Finally Henry spoke, "Look, I have to go to the hospital. You know, to identify the body, sign papers, all that shit."

"I'm going with you."

"You don't have to go, Laura. It's okay. It won't be pleasant."

"I'm going. We've come this far. This is one of those things we do together."

"I love you," he said, the words slipping out unexpectedly and flittering in the air between them.

"Back at you, Henry." She smiled the dazzling smile that had smitten him in the beginning and added, "I could not love anyone more."

And in that rare, tender moment, Henry felt a sense of hope. The void that had stunned him, and the resentment that had resided with him always, were not deniable, but at the sane time a renewed sense of promise buffered the pain. He and Laura would be all right. Not he, not she, but the two of them would make sure of it.

Chapter Forty-Five

GRACE

Grace sat alone in her apartment at *The Gardens* after a two-day stay at City Memorial Hospital. The building smelled faintly of smoke, but it had been inspected, cleaned, and deemed perfectly habitable for the one hundred or so elderly residents who for a couple of days had had their lives tossed upside down. She had plenty to think about as she leaned back in Frank's chair. *Wish you were still here, Frank, so we could talk like we used to. Remember? We could chat for hours, couldn't we? Believe me sweetheart I could give you an earful about now. My heavens, I am astounded, and you would be too, by all the goings-on around here.* Plainly Grace was a bit dazed, but as a matter of fact, she, and a good number of other old folks at *The Gardens* had every right to be with their entire residential community having been turned topsy-turvy without so much as a warning. Grace's head literally swam with visual recall, each memory clipping along so quickly she could not hold on to any image for long.

First and foremost, of course, had been the sudden devastating fire in the infirmary of *The Gardens*. It had frightened the daylights out of everyone, staff included. Furthermore, it had endangered the lives of numerous elders, many of whom were, to some extent, in varying stages of discomfort with aches, pains, chronic ailments, and disabilities. Beyond that, a few residents suffered from incontinence, absentmindedness, irritability, onset dementia, random impropriety, and bouts of gloominess for times gone by, for loved ones lost, and for years that could not be retrieved and lived over, for better or worse. The past, the good, bad, and in-betweens of it, never could be regained, merely recalled and for many of the old folks at *The Gardens* simply remembering became a burden in itself. It was not incomprehensible, then, to recognize that this fire, and the chaos that ensued, rattled many residents to the core. The bedlam undoubtedly conjured events and traumas from yesteryear and planted anxiety and panic directly in the laps of those who were woefully unprepared to handle it. All of that, combined with being exposed to the cold, being shuttled away in the dead of night by screaming ambulances, and being manhandled, although respectfully, by strangers in transit and at the hospital had amped up fear and distress to a whole new level. Grace understood. She had been right in the middle of the ordeal, as panicked as her friends and floor mates, Ralph, Louie, and Lilly.

"But hurray for us. We made it through this mess like real champs," Louie had announced after all four had been examined by compassionate, dimple-faced Dr. Brown and deemed safe and sound without question.

"We certainly did," Ralph had agreed. "We make it through, just like four ancient warriors." He chuckled at his own, lame comment before adding, "But I, personally, thank the good Lord for giving us the strength."

Grace had not added to the conversation; she had been too tired and a bit mesmerized by Lilly who was silent and serene, finger counting the circles and squares embossed on the blanket on her bed. The men were right though; Grace appreciated their bold assertions. *The old guys had to brag a little, and that's fine. Yes, we did okay. None of us is the worse for wear as Olivia used to say. Oh, Mama, I sure wish I could talk to you. This has been an awful ordeal.*

⌘   ⌘   ⌘

Not one of the four, aged evacuees could have predicted the next incredible shock. Immediately after breakfast trays had been removed from the hospital ward, Mildred, in a calm, careful manner, delivered the dreadful news of Maude Litzenberg's sudden death in he middle of the night; it was astonishing because most had thought she was on the road to recovery. Grace, if she had felt a need to admit it, however, really had not been surprised at all. She had detected early on that Maude appeared ready to take leave of this life. She had hated everything about it and likely everyone in it, as well. *And hadn't she been planning a journey for days? She must have had her own, secret suspicion that the end was near. And didn't she let on to me? Even wanted to take me on a trip somewhere with her. Lordy, now, wasn't that a far-fetched notion?*

Equally significant to Grace's private and personal reasoning however, had been the reactions of Ralph, Louie, and Lilly. Predictably, Ralph had leaned back against the pillows on his hospital bed, closed his eyes, and muttered quietly in prayer; Louie, on the other hand, had gasped and cried what appeared to be heartfelt tears. "Oh, my word, what a shame. That Maude was a haughty, damned broad, but she definitely was a looker. I'm sure going to miss seeing her around. I never let on to anybody, but I was going to ask her out on a dinner date some day soon," he had blubbered.

Grace had listened, astonished. *Oh, Lordy, Louie, do you really think such a feat actually could have been accomplished?* Grace had thought Louie's comment sweet though and had offered him a sad, sympathetic smile.

Lilly, however, had astounded them all. She had looked up from her nimble, constantly moving fingers and verbalized out loud, "Poor girl." To that moment, Grace had never heard Lilly utter a word and to her knowledge, she never did again.

⌘ ⌘ ⌘

And finally . . . the issue of Caroline Watson raised its ugly head. Grace would have learned the news anyway, but rather than hear through the rumor mill, Mildred had lingered in Grace's room after the others - Ralph, Louie, and Lilly - had settled into their apartments.

Mildred's face was pale and drawn; the dark bruises above her eye and on her upper cheek remained prominent. Other than Maude, no one else, to Grace's knowledge, had commented on Mildred's obvious injuries, but to Grace, the purple contusions were quite disconcerting. *What really happened to her? I can't believe it was a fall, but I'm hesitant to ask.* On cue, as if she were speaking from some hiding place in the corner of the room, Grace heard her mother, Olivia, warning, "Don't be a nosey parker, Grace. You mind your own business, missy."

Grace looked over her shoulder. *Mama? Olivia? Olivia Graci Brown, are you there?* The questions were but empty wishes. Her mother had been gone for years. A thick lump suddenly climbed into Grace's throat. She thought she might cry. Instead, however, she swallowed hard, took a deep breath, and began blabbering to her beloved caretaker.

"Ah, Miss Millie, what a few days, it's been. I'm thankful to be home safe, but, now that I'm here, I miss my Frank even more . . . and I miss my mother. Did I ever tell you my mother, Olivia, emigrated from Italy when she was a young girl? Did I?"

"I believe you did tell, me Grace," Mildred replied dully.

Grace noted Mildred's somber face, but with rare indifference, continued her chatter. "Her birth name was Graci. And she named me Grace. Wasn't that a lovely thing to do? Have I told you that before too, Miss Millie?"

"You did tell me, Grace. I remember it well."

"Oh dear, I'm repeating myself again, aren't I? Getting old is so annoying. I'm turning into an old dodderer, Miss Millie, and I don't like it one bit."

Mildred did not respond; Instead, she pulled a side chair nearer to Grace and sat down.

"For heaven's sake, Miss Millie. You don't have to stay with me. I'll be all right."

"It's Caroline," Mildred stated bluntly. "Authorities found her backpack behind *The Gardens*, barely visible in a bunch of wild blackberry brambles."

"Oh, Miss Millie. And I've been carrying on and on, all about myself. I'm sorry."

"You have no reason to be sorry, honey, but there's more."

Grace reached out and took Mildred's hand in hers. It was ice cold.

"Tell me."

"The backpack had her identification in it and police thought perhaps it belonged to someone who worked at *The Gardens*. Of course it didn't, but they were able to match the last name to mine. Doubt if there are very many *Watsons* around here. I was able to identify the pack as hers, but, as

I said, there's more. Caroline has been located, and it's not good. I think she could be in real trouble."

⌘ ⌘ ⌘

Grace sat with Mildred for over an hour while haltingly Mildred explained what she knew, and all the while, Grace conjured images of a story, filling in invented details, as if she were directing a picture show.

Caroline stumbled upon the rambling, retirement residence by chance, the bright lights of the front lobby inviting, appealing, for she was so chilled her body had begun to tremble and her fingers were numb. She plodded up the front steps, stood in front of the wide, glass entryway and peered in but the lighted space inside was empty and the door firmly locked. She placed her flat palms against the glass thinking it might warm her but the surface was icy to the touch. She jerked her hands back as if she had been burned and pulled down the sleeves of her woefully thin jacket in order to cover her fingers. Every tingling digit smarted so much she began to whimper like an abandoned infant.

At last she turned from the front of the building, scanned the expansive lawn in front of it, and stepped onto the wet, spongy grass. It took no time for her tennis shoes to become soaked but she trudged along, every step an effort. A short distance away she spotted a parking lot, scantly occupied by vehicles, but offering light from streetlights surrounding it. The lot led to the back of the building where the glare of light was greatly reduced and Caroline knew she could hide in the shadows. Several dumpsters were lined up in a row and all nearly filled to capacity. They might offer warmth. At least, Caroline recognized, she could find shelter there. It took effort, but by inserting her toes into the shallow grooves that lined the sides of the dumpster, and reaching high to grab hold of the top edge, she pulled herself up and flopped over into a load of shredded paper, cardboard, and filthy linens. The bin smelled of burnt tacos, urine, and rubbing alcohol, the combination enough to make her gag, but she was out of the cold wind. She could cope with the odor and she could sleep; maybe, she would sleep. She felt around for flat pieces of cardboard, placed one between her back and the cold metal side of the bin, and settled against it. She was so tired she ached . . . every inch of her. She closed her eyes, willing herself to drift off but blessed sleep evaded her, and for good reason. Her confines were all too familiar. She and her son, Adam, over the years, had sought refuse in similar places, meeting along the way, countless vermin, human and animal alike, as they sought to survive

Memories bombarded her and she began to cry, the silent tears rolling down her cheeks and into her mouth. She could taste the salt. It was strangely comforting, for at least she was alive. She knew to be quiet though, in this place, for to be found was danger-ous. All kinds of crazy misfits, she knew from experience, roamed the night. At that uncanny second, she heard noises - footsteps, a loud thump, and a hoarse cough - all before a large figure heaved itself over the side of the dumpster almost landing on top of her.

"What the hell?" She could not help herself from calling out.

"Shit! What the fuck? What the hell are you doing here? This is my spot." The voice was that of a man's, a deep bass.

"I'm trying to get warm."

"Well, hell, you can't stay here. This is my place, and tonight I'm lighting this puppy up."

"What?"

"I'm lighting a fucking fire."

"Why?"

"'Cause it's cold, and 'cause I can, that's why. Now get out of here before you go up in smoke like the rest of the crap in here."

Caroline was so frightened, her body had warmed, but she knew she was safer in the cold. As quickly as she could, she dragged her upper torso to the edge of the dumpster and threw one leg over before jumping onto the pavement. "Wait, my backpack," she called.

"Here's your backpack, bitch," the man bellowed as he threw it at her. "Take a hike. Now."

And she scuttled away. She ran and ran until she began wheezing uncontrollably. She had no idea where she was and had nothing of her own except for the clothes she was wearing. She had dropped her pack somewhere along the way. Exhausted, she slowed down to a sluggish walk; each deliberate step took her farther into a city she did not know. At last she reached a park, lit only by decorative, street lamps that gave off a meager glow. She walked until her feet were leaden, finally flopping down on a park bench in the dark. She drifted off then, dreaming nightmarish visions of bloody babies, hypodermic needles, broken bottles, discarded handguns, bloated bodies, and despondent masses hovering under tarps in the rain. And competing with the vile and searing images were ear-piercing sirens, one after the other, every, single one unrelentingly blaring deep inside her head. There was no escaping them. Without even knowing, she had begun to shiver almost convulsively. Alone on the park bench, she fell finally into unconsciousness. By auspicious chance, however, the last thing she envisioned was Adam, her beautiful boy, forever handsome and finally free.

⌘ ⌘ ⌘

"A Good Samaritan found her early in the morning. Paramedics took her to County General Hospital where she was tended to, I suppose, like any indigent person would be. I was able to identify her by photographs officers supplied, but I haven't seen her. Not sure if I can. She apparently has pneumonia, is bewildered, and doesn't know her name, but she's alive and being held under surveillance, because if you can believe this, Grace, apparently, officials think she may have had something to do with the fire." Mildred stopped then, gave Grace a puzzled look, before adding, "You know, Grace, it's a terrible thing to think or say but Caroline's future seems so grim, it might be better if she doesn't survive."

"Oh, Miss Millie," Grace sighed. She could not articulate another appropriate word.

⌘ ⌘ ⌘

Caroline did survive. Under doctors' care, the pneumonia disappeared in two weeks time, and with the physical healing, her memory returned. Though authorities grilled her ruthlessly, she stuck to her story about what had occurred on the night the infirmary at *The Gardens* was gutted, and Mildred reported exactly what she had learned to Grace when they had another moment alone.

"She told them she had been lost and freezing cold when she ran across a building that was brightly lit up but unfortunately locked tight. That would have been *The Gardens*, of course. According to Caroline, the doors in back were locked, too. She admitted that she had planned to climb inside a dumpster for shelter, if you can believe that. My sister hunkered down in a dumpster - the idea of such a thing makes me sick. But her story gets weirder. She told the police that the minute she reached the bin, it burst into flames, an explosion right in front of her, so she ran, somewhere along the way, losing her only possession - that nasty backpack. She ended up in a park - Evergreen Central, I'd imagine. She was unbearably cold, she told the police, but she remembered one thing in particular - hearing sirens. And, of course, that was accurate; there were lots of them that night, the fire engines and ambulances all flocking to *The Gardens* to put out the fire and to collect all of you . . . thank goodness.

Grace listened, rapt, finding remarkable similarities in the scant details as to what actually had occurred according to Mildred's retelling of Caroline's story compared to what Grace had imagined could have happened. "She must have been so frightened," Grace forlornly noted.

"I'm sure she was. You know, Grace, her story was pretty flimsy, but what saved her is what investigators discovered; I don't want to upset you with gruesome news, but they uncovered a charred body buried beneath a heap of smoldering cardboard and wet linens. I think my sister was let go as a result of that discovery - that, and the fact she was found in the park, nearly frozen and sick. She couldn't have started a fire if she had wanted to. We're so fortunate the authorities did not press charges."

"Yes, indeed, you are. Were you finally able to see her?"

"Yes, twice. She was very evasive both times. The last time was this morning. Grace, she looked awful - thin and pale, but at least she was clean, not reeking of stale cigarettes and human grime. I handed over the dirty backpack the police had given me and tried to hug her, but she recoiled like a frightened pup. I could do nothing but step back. I have to admit her reaction to me was shocking."

"Oh dear, Miss Millie, surely it was, but you and your sister have lived apart for years, haven't you? Maybe she felt estranged even in your presence. Guilt perhaps? Were you close when you were children?" Grace asked.

"We were, but times were hard. We lost our mother, and much later our father, and, during her teens, Caroline turned into the proverbial wild child. Honest to God, neither our father, nor I, could control what she got into from one day to the next. She ended up pregnant. She and her son, who was a handful just like she was, took off to the streets when Caroline wouldn't follow the rules. You're right, I'd not seen Caroline for years until she showed up at my door recently, and now, she's gone again. All she said was, 'I'll be on my way.'"

"Where do you think she'll go?"

"I have no idea. When I asked, she muttered something like 'Down the road.' And that was it. Not one more word. I watched her throw her backpack over her shoulder and turn away from me as if I were a stranger. She never looked back."

"I'm so sorry, Miss Millie. I know her leaving again hurts."

"It does, and it doesn't. Caroline and I are so different and I've grown used to being in the dark about her whereabouts."

"Why do you think you grew up to be so dissimilar?" Grace clasped her hands and pulled them to her chin as if she were mulling over the possibilities.

"I don't know. Different choices, I guess. She made her own bed, Grace. Don't we all, in our own ways? I may be wrong, but I believe we've all make choices in life, the good and the bad, that, after all is said and done, plop us down right where we are."

"Destiny, you mean? I suppose so, but people we encounter and experiences we have affect us too, don't you think? I don't believe folks go out of their way to find misfortune, obviously, but we've all had a little bad luck," Grace had responded with an odd smirk. "Lordy, I know I made some silly mistakes when I was young, but, well, I learned and moved on. Not sure it would have been as easy without my mother, Olivia, though. My goodness, she had more notions and platitudes about how to live life than anyone. Besides always telling me to be cautious at all times, and not to be a busy body - a nosy parker, she called it - she spouted one particular, saccharine saying over and over. I can hear her voice now. 'Pay forward the grace you've been given, not the pain you've been dealt.' And, to be honest, Miss Millie, when I recall that old cliché, I think about how fortunate I was to find Frank, my dear Frank. The sweet, old, ornery bastard was the absolute heart of me." She let out a long sigh that was so mournful one could imagine Frank had departed from Grace only moments before.

Mildred looked at Grace, understanding, but comprehending more about herself than the old woman before her. Millie had chosen to play it safe by living a simple lifestyle, securing a satisfying occupation, putting others before her, and always taking every precaution until . . . her face suddenly blanched. She was back in the alleyway, pinned to the ground, panicked, injured, abused. *I made a choice that put me in harm's way. Was the assault my fault then?* She wrapped her arms around her torso protectively. *No. That can't be. I chose none of that.*

"Are you all right, Miss Millie?" Grace intuited the sudden change in Mildred's bearing. *Such despondency.*

Regaining her composure, Mildred straightened. *Don't let on now. Grace can never know.* "Oh, honey, I got lost in thought there for a second. It's nothing."

"Are you sure? You looked a bit wan for a second."

"Actually, and it's the strangest thing, I was thinking about Maude Litzenberg all of a sudden," she said, and although her comment was a singular lie, Maude's wrinkled face appeared instantly in Mildred's mind's eye. "Maude was a difficult soul; we didn't really know her history, not what made her tick, but she is free of her troubles now, isn't she?" Mildred asserted.

"She is that," Grace answered. Her head tilted upward, her eyes perusing the far corners of the room, before she added a simple, candid conjecture, "As far as we can comprehend." The comment rested uneasily in a moment of silence.

Mildred gazed at her friend, her charge, her unlikely confident with such affection her heart quivered. Grace amazed her, for clearly, she still was as astute and insightful as many much younger. *She's made it this far, hasn't she? Eighty-eight and counting, the mind still sharp and sustained by memories flitting like hummingbirds, none landing for long . . . oh, the stories she could tell if only folks would pause and listen. And don't they all - Ralph, Louie, Lilly, and a million more elderly people have yarns to spin and lessons to teach? For the love of Grace, I know that's true, and I promise myself to pay more attention to tales and anecdotes I could not possibly have experienced or even fathomed being integral to some other soul's life. Shouldn't everyone do likewise? I'm convinced if we don't hear the stories and listen to the tales, the treasures will be lost. History will be buried with our elders, forgotten, or never known at all. And for goodness sake, how fair is that to any of us?*

Acknowledgment

An acknowledgment to the original source of the term *Pay It Forward:*

> *I never repaid Great-aunt Letitia's love to her, any more than she repaid her mother's. You don't pay love back; you pay it forward. The great-aunts paid their love-debt, not to their mother, but to me; and I've paid what I owed them to David and Caro; and Caro and David won't pay to me – they can't; they'll pay it to children yet unborn.* (Page 209)

In The Garden Of Delight by Lily Harding Hammond, Publishers Thomas Y. Crowell Company, Copyright 1916

About the Author

Judith DeChesere-Boyle was born in Elizabethtown, Kentucky and with the exception of living for three years both in England and Texas, was raised there. She first attended the University of Kentucky, and then moved to California, graduating from College of Marin with an AA degree in English with a Creative Writing emphasis and San Francisco State University with a BA degree in English. She attended Sonoma State University, earning two teaching credentials and an MA in Education with an English Curriculum emphasis. She taught English at the secondary level for many years, retiring early enough to pursue her love of writing more seriously. She raised two wonderful sons, Alex and Justin, and now lives in Sonoma

County, California with her husband, Rick. Besides writing, she reads avidly, gardens, tends the family's koi pond, and walks her two German Shepherds three miles a day. She is the author of four novels, *Big House Dreams, Nine Bucks and Change, Go With The Flo,* and *Not A Through Street.* She also has written a memoir, including a new Second Edition, entitled *Tumor Me, The Story Of My Firefighter,* a tribute to the memory of her son, Alex.

Learn more at Judith's website: www.jdechesere-boyle.com or visit her Author Page on Amazon.com.